A cold wave washed over her

Belle picked up the foot-high plastic mynah bird. She quickly rifled through her purchases...and found three more. Where had they come from? Then she saw the envelope in her purse—with her name typed on it.

Her hands were icy numb, her fingers clumsy, as she slit open the flap. Drawing out the paper, she took a deliberate breath, and read:

> On the Fourth Day of Christmas, Santa Claus gave to Breeze Four Mantic Birds. It's your curtain call now.
>
> Santa Claus

Reluctantly, Belle picked up one of the birds and turned it over. Nothing. Then she squeezed it...and immediately let go and jumped back, her heart punching into her ribs as a loud, strident voice screeched into the room.

"I'm coming to get you, Breeze. Get you, Breeze. Get you, Breeze...."

Dear Reader,

Ever since I was a little girl, I've loved Christmas Eve. But not for the reasons most kids do—the food, decorations or presents—because frankly my parents didn't have the money for any of those things.

No, what made Christmas special to me was being drawn close to my mother's side in a warm hug as she told me all the wonderful tales of this special season.

I sat enthralled hour after hour, hearing about the sweet babe in a manger and three weary wise men who followed a beautiful star. And a house with stockings hung by a chimney with care and nothing stirring—not even a mouse. And a mischievous Grinch who stole Christmas. And a miserly man who regained Christmas with lessons by angels from Christmas past, present and future. And an enchanted nutcracker and a happy little fir tree selected out of all the other fir trees to be decorated for Christmas. And the gift of the Magi. And the little drummer boy.

And I sat on the edge of my seat. And laughed. And cried. And wished it could be Christmas Eve every night.

And now it is. For my mother gave me a gift more valuable than any money could buy. She gave me the magic of those wonderful stories to hold in my heart forever. And she instilled in me the love of being a storyteller.

This is my wish for you this Christmas: that you be touched with the magic of a Christmas story, and that it, too, lives forever in your heart.

Santa Claus Is Coming

M.J. Rodgers

Harlequin Books

TORONTO • NEW YORK • LONDON
AMSTERDAM • PARIS • SYDNEY • HAMBURG
STOCKHOLM • ATHENS • TOKYO • MILAN
MADRID • WARSAW • BUDAPEST • AUCKLAND

For my mother,
who taught me about the joy of storytelling.
Thanks, Mom.

ISBN 0-373-22254-8

SANTA CLAUS IS COMING

Copyright © 1993 by Mary Johnson.

Printed In U.S.A.

GREATER
LOS ANGELES

Walt Disney
Productions

NBC

Ventura Fwy.

Burbank Studios

Belle's Apt.

Hollywood District

Universal City

Hollywood Blvd.

Hollywood Fwy.

Sunset Blvd.

Santa Monica Blvd.

Gower St.

N

KALA T.V. Station

Wilcox Ave.

Melrose Ave.

Paramount Studios

Beverly Blvd.

CBS

Wilshire Blvd.

CAST OF CHARACTERS

Belle Breeze—Santa was watching her.

Max Wilde—What was his special Christmas present for Belle?

Neal Fort—He was the resident Scrooge.

Paula White—She was certain Belle would get what she deserved this Christmas.

Jim Apple—Would this security guard protect Belle?

Russell Ramish—Like the Grinch, he was determined to ruin Christmas.

Justin Daark—He was always lurking in the shadows.

Sergeant Morse—What side of the law was this officer on?

Luana Halsey—What did she want in her Christmas stocking?

Chapter One

The first "gift" arrived Tuesday, December 13, at the KALA television studio in Hollywood.

Movie critic Belle Breeze stepped through the open archway to her tiny office in back of the newsroom. She shed her peach-colored suit coat, slipped her matching gloves inside the pockets and draped both over the gray metal coat tree just inside the door.

Her spot had gone effortlessly and smoothly tonight. She smiled in remembrance at what a bundle of nerves she'd been after her first televised review for KALA. Had a whole year really whizzed by since then? Amazing. And a reminder—time to call her agent and find out what was delaying her contract renewal.

She headed for the phone, then paused in midstride when she saw the large Christmas present taking over the top of her compact yellow metal desk. Surprise then delight were her first reactions.

She moved closer to get a better look at the package, which was about four feet high and three feet wide. Red holly and silver bells dotted the cheap green paper held together by visible strips of Scotch tape; no bow adorned the top.

Who would leave a present on her desk twelve days before Christmas?

"Good spot tonight, Belle. Well, well, looks like at least somebody got an early start on Christmas. You giving or getting?" Neal Fort, KALA's program director, called from behind Belle.

Belle turned to find him leaning against the open archway to her office. "Oh, hi, Neal. Didn't see you there."

Neal was pudgy, probably in his mid-to-late twenties, barely five-seven, with brown hair slicked back into a ponytail, small intense eyes, a wispy mustache, and a baggy brown suit. His twitching mustache and nervous hands always made Belle think of a furtive, foraging mouse.

He scurried into the office. "That's a bad habit you've got."

"Bad habit?" Belle repeated, distracted by finding her name typed on a plain, business-size white envelope taped to the backside of the curious Christmas present.

"Ignoring me. I'm your boss, after all. Seems to me you've been around Hollywood long enough to know you're supposed to be sucking up to me. Particularly around contract renewal time. What's your problem?"

Belle smiled. The undercurrent of truth in Neal's otherwise joking remarks wasn't strong enough to shake her self-confidence. As they both well knew. "Must be a slow learner. I wonder what this could be?"

Neal hugged a clipboard to the coarsely-woven lapels of his suit coat as he eyed the present with interest. "So, you going to just stand there, or open it so we can both find out what's inside?"

"Now?"

"Why not? You're not one of those people who thinks you have to wait until Christmas Eve or something, are you?"

Belle circled around her desk and flopped with a comfortable squish into her large, overpadded tan leather chair. She loved the chair, had insisted on having it. A tiny office and desk she could endure. But a tall woman needed a tall chair. "I suppose it wouldn't hurt to find out who it's from."

She tore off the envelope, noticing that Neal hadn't taken his eyes from the package. It tickled her to see the same keen, impatient expression on his face that she associated with her numerous nieces and nephews each Christmas Eve.

As she split open the envelope, she sent him an indulgent smile. "Oh, go ahead and open it, Neal. Make your day."

Neal needed no further encouragement. He put the clipboard on the edge of her desk and reached for the package. Belle smiled and dropped her gaze to the single sheet of paper she removed from the envelope. She unfolded it. In the background, she could hear Neal's eager fingers tearing Christmas wrapping as she silently read the typed message in her hands.

On the first day of Christmas, Santa Claus gave to Breeze
A vulture in a palm tree.

I'm reviewing you now,
Santa Claus

Belle's smile faded.

"One of your admirers has a strange sense of humor, Belle."

She looked up. A plastic, hunched-back vulture, clutching a shiny green frond of a plastic palm tree, stared hungrily at her. Drops of blood had been painted around its beak and feathered black chest.

Belle laughed nervously, hoping humor lurked somewhere within this bizarre gift and message. "I doubt this is from an admirer. Here, read this, Neal."

She handed him the paper. Neal's mustache twitched as he silently read the message. "Screwy. Really screwy. Hey, wait a minute. This wording sounds familiar. Isn't it a take-off on the 'Twelve Days of Christmas' song?"

Belle nodded. "Except the 'Twelve Days of Christmas' song starts, 'On the first day of Christmas, my true love gave to me—a partridge in a pear tree.' And the 'first' day of Christmas is actually Christmas Day."

Neal looked back at Belle's desk. "And this one has substituted a vulture in a palm tree and Santa Claus in place of your true love. You have friends who go in for this kind of...uh...humor?"

Belle shook her head. "No friends, certainly. But maybe someone not so friendly. Nasty-looking vulture, isn't it?"

She reached out to the four-foot palm tree and its hunched-over occupant, but then drew her hand back, finding herself curiously disinclined to touch it. Silly. Only plastic. Deliberately, she grabbed the base of the plastic palm, dumping it on its side in order to get a look at the bottom.

Her smooth brow furrowed. "Wacko? Talk about well-named. This sticker says this monstrosity is from some place called Wacko."

"Oh yeah, Wacko," Neal said as he leaned over Belle's shoulder to take a quick look at the sticker. "It's a gift shop down on Melrose Avenue. One of those places that sells Hollywood souvenirs and keepsakes."

Belle righted the palm tree again. "Well this is hardly what I'd call a keepsake. How did it even get to my office?"

Neal's eyes darted to the outside of the envelope. "It couldn't have come through the mail room. Look, no address. Just your name typed on the envelope."

"Are you saying someone just waltzed into the station with it under his arm? I thought we had better security than that!"

Neal frowned as he set the letter down on Belle's desk. "We certainly should, considering what the station pays for it. Speak of the devil, there's the internal security guard for the studio now. Hey, Jim Apple! Come in here a moment, will you?"

A big, bony man, his light blue uniform visible through the upper glass partition of Belle's office, poked his head around the entry arch. "Yes, Mr. Fort. Something I can do for you?"

"Yeah. You see this monstrosity on Ms. Breeze's desk?"

Jim Apple trotted inside the office. Belle guessed the horsey-looking man to be around fifty, and she had the impression that to know his exact age all she'd have to do was lift his lip. He took in the discarded Christmas wrappings on the carpet and then the plastic palm tree with the vulture. "So that's what was inside. I kind of wondered."

Belle rose to her feet. "You mean you saw who set this on my desk, Jim?"

Jim Apple circled the desk to get a better look at the vulture. "Well, I guess you could say so, Ms. Breeze. You see, I put it on your desk. Guard at the entrance to the building gave it to me when I came on duty this afternoon. Said he found it at his desk when he came on duty. Figured one of your admirers left it. Except it don't appear too admiring now that I see what's inside. Who's it from?"

Belle sat down again, frowning. "An anonymous Santa Claus. This letter came with it."

Apple followed Belle's pointing finger and picked up the letter from the desktop.

"Look, Apple," Neal began, his tone browned to a crusty edge. "People in the public eye sometimes become the targets of some pretty strange kooks. You don't just pick up a package left at the front and deliver it. We've got a mail room staff trained to screen for stuff like this."

"Sorry, sir. It didn't occur to me that—"

Neal interrupted him with a wave of his hand. "I know you're new here, so I'm willing to let it go this time, but you must be more careful. This is Hollywood, for Pete's sake!"

Apple straightened, positioning his free hand over the butt of his holstered revolver as though, having been reminded of his surroundings, he understood a quick draw might be necessary at any moment. "It won't happen again, sir."

Neal nodded, looking satisfied that he'd done his duty. Apple's eyes dropped to the altered stanza. A frown creased his bony forehead as he slowly shook his thick, brown mane. "I don't like the sound of this, Ms. Breeze. Mr. Fort is right. Crazy folks sometimes can get a fix on a television personality. Why, there's no telling what one of them might do. No, I don't like the sound of this at all."

Belle felt a new prickle of unease traveling up her spine at the sober note in Apple's voice.

Neal's mustached twitched. "Apple, why don't you do something useful like getting rid of this eyesore for Ms. Breeze."

"What do you want me to do with it, Mr. Fort?"

Neal waved his hand impatiently. "Throw it in the trash bin out back. Burn it. I don't care. Just get it out of here."

Apple shrugged as he leaned across the desk to gather the awkward monstrosity into his arms. But as he lifted it, the vulture came loose from its palm perch and pitched over, its bloodied beak heading directly for Belle's lap.

Belle quickly jumped to her feet, swatting the vulture to the floor. She stared at it lying on the gray carpet, her heart beating wildly in her chest.

Apple leaned down to pick it up. "I'm sorry, Ms. Breeze. It just sort of got away from me."

Neal looked over at her, frowning. "You all right, Belle?"

Belle took a steadying breath. "Yes, of course, Neal. I just…it startled me for a second there." Belle began to feel rather foolish. A plastic vulture couldn't hurt her. Still, as she slowly sank back into her chair, persistent little shivers lapped through the muscles in her back.

"Get it out of here, Apple," Neal directed.

Belle knew she would be glad to see the end of the thing, but her strong streak of practicality nudged her. "Maybe we shouldn't be so quick to destroy it. Maybe the police—"

"The police?" Neal's voice had ascended into squeak range. "Belle, you're not going to tell me you're thinking of calling the police about this?"

Belle straightened, somewhat defensive in the wake of Neal's incredulous tone. "The thought crossed my mind."

"Well, uncross it. The last thing we need is police involvement." He looked out at the several reporters milling around in the large adjacent newsroom and lowered his voice as though he didn't even trust the station's own reporters.

"Belle, newspeople hover around police blotters for the sole purpose of picking up juicy little tidbits to sensationalize. Do you want to give a fruitcake who'd send you something like this media attention?"

"That's not my intent, Neal. But if some fruitcake—"

"You're better off ignoring him," Neal finished for her. "You're a celebrity now, Belle. You've established a solid name for yourself in critics' circles. If one of those supermarket scandal sheets got wind of this sick little stunt, who knows what nonsense they'd blow it into. You don't need their kind of publicity trivializing what you've achieved."

Belle had to admit Neal had a point, although she seriously doubted his motivation for playing down the incident stemmed from a desire to protect her reputation. More likely, Neal didn't want to generate bad publicity for the station.

The security guard paused in the entry arch waiting for her response. She gave him a nod. "Go ahead and destroy it, Jim. Neal's right. The less attention we give it, the better."

Apple nodded and picked up the discarded wrapping on his way out.

Belle felt better now that the tiny surface of her desk had been cleared of its unwelcome occupant. Time to put the unsettling experience behind her and get on with business. She turned back to Neal. "So you liked this evening's spot. Something else you wanted to say?"

"Oh, yeah. I can't believe I almost forgot. I've got some great news. You're going to love it!"

Belle braced herself. Every time Neal told her he had great news or that she was going to love something, the news turned out anything but great and she'd found absolutely nothing about it to love. A wary glint entered her eyes. "What?"

"Well, you know how the theaters are getting flooded with all these new movie releases?"

She nodded. "The typical rush to get films out for the holidays. Makes reviewing them all impossible with just two minutes airtime two nights a week."

"Exactly. So I've talked with Paula and convinced her to expand the movie critic's spot to four minutes, six nights a week, Monday through Saturday, beginning tomorrow and running up to Christmas."

Belle shot forward in her chair. "Paula White has agreed to expanding my spot?"

Neal smiled his mousy little smile. "Now don't sound so surprised. As station manager, Paula was the one who brought you on a year ago, remember? She likes you."

Belle delivered a choked cry that lay somewhere between incredulity and absurdity. "Likes me? Who are you trying to kid? You know Paula's had a vendetta against all critics ever since one tore apart her first sitcom."

"That all happened a long time ago, Belle."

"Might as well have been yesterday as far as Paula is concerned. If it were up to her, the news segment wouldn't include an entertainment critic at all. We both know that if the network hadn't insisted, I would never have been hired or given the two-minute, two-night spot I've got now. And you're telling me all of a sudden she's agreed to four minutes, six nights a week? I don't believe this."

"It's true. Cross my heart."

Belle studied Neal, trying to gauge the degree of sincerity in his expression. She'd lay odds this mouse hid some rotten cheese somewhere. "All right, Neal. What is it?"

He tried to look innocent. "What's what?"

"The catch, Neal. Come on. What's the catch?"

"Catch? There's no catch, Belle. It's just that— Oh, here he comes now."

"He?"

Belle rose from her chair to see Paula White approaching with a tall man by her side.

He was at least six-four, with thick, black hair that waved loosely down his neck, resting on broad, imposing shoulders. A chest of smooth tanned muscles rose defiantly out of a denim vest, open to his lean waist. Bare, brawny arms swayed easily with each long stride. Not an inch of fat showed through his tight-fitting, faded blue jeans. Every woman's head in the newsroom swung as he passed—like needles pointing to a magnetic north.

And no wonder. His larger-than-life presence fairly dwarfed the other men in the room. Belle's eyes drew to his face—strong, prominent forehead, deep-set eyes, square jaw—an ideal match for the build below it.

And boy, did this guy know it, too. Arrogance was evident in every movement of that powerful body as well as in the expression of those eyes, which were black as polished obsidian.

Of course she recognized him. No woman in L.A. could fail to recognize this man. She spun toward Neal. "What's going on? What is *he* doing here?"

"Sh! They'll hear you. Now keep it together, Belle. This deal is too big to blow."

He and Paula White reached the tiny corner office, and Paula stepped inside all smiles. She was a streamlined, attractive, fortyish brunette with dark eyes, short, straight, stylish hair and a passion for lilac fragrances and purple outfits. Today's ensemble was a slit skirt, a V-necked blouse and two-inch heels, relieved only by a silver belt.

She reminded Belle of a Siamese cat, sleek and single-minded. Her long purple fingernails tapped excitedly against one another. "Have you told her, Neal?"

"Not the most important part, Paula. I knew you'd want to do the honors."

Paula's smile swung toward Belle. Paula never smiled at her. Belle automatically stiffened. "Belle Breeze, I'd like to introduce Max Wilde, the former movie critic at Channel Ten."

Belle swallowed as she immediately latched onto the most telling and significant word in Paula's sentence. "Former?"

Paula beamed. "He's come to join us, Belle. From now on Wilde will be doing the counterpoint on all your movie reviews. I can't tell you how much pleasure it gives me to know that I'm setting two critics at each other's throats. Shake hands, you two, and come out fighting!"

Belle gasped. "What?"

She felt Neal grabbing her shoulder and pushing her toward Max Wilde's outstretched hand.

Neal's voice jabbered excitedly in her ear. "We're doing it, Belle. We're putting the top two television critics on the same show. Think of it. The two critics known for their totally opposing stands expressing their opinions face-to-face. What controversy you'll generate! Isn't it a brilliant idea?"

MAX WILDE watched Belle's horrified expression with growing amusement. Obviously the lady considered this idea about as brilliant as the casting director's original selection of Ronald Reagan for the male lead in *Casablanca*.

In truth, the idea of being in an adversarial role with another critic hadn't particularly appealed to Max either. But he'd been feeling flat and restless lately, in need of a change. And when they mentioned the money and who the other critic would be, well . . .

The money clinched it, of course, but her presence definitely sweetened the deal. He'd seen her at a distance several times over the last year when they'd both attended the same screenings.

Beautiful women were the proverbial dime a dozen in Hollywood. But this one stood out primarily because she steadfastly refused to blend in. She had a strong sense of herself that he couldn't help but admire.

The trades dubbed her "Ms. Clean Breeze" because of her frequently expressed dislike of bad language and gore in the movies she reviewed. He'd also heard a lot about the "Arctic Breeze," as countless spurned men from showbiz circles more informally labeled her. And each new story further piqued his interest.

He sent her a brilliant smile as he reached out and captured her unwilling hand.

She was stunning—nearly six feet with thick, honey-colored hair almost to her elbows, a silky peach complexion rare among the leather-skinned dwellers of Southern California, and eyes so intensely blue he was reminded of the calm waters of the Pacific Ocean on an April morning.

Their expression at the moment looked a lot more like a stormy Atlantic in December, however. She snatched back her hand from his as though determined not to become contaminated.

Max experienced an interesting twitch deep in his stomach.

Paula White looked positively entertained at Belle's stormy expressions. "I'll just leave you two alone so you can start drawing each other's blood," she purred before turning. She left a trace of lilac in her wake as she headed out the entry arch, her purple pumps etching the spongy gray carpet.

That left Neal Fort as the primary recipient of Belle's wrath. Max could tell Neal didn't relish the part as the angry lady spun on him. She spat out her next words like machine-gun fire. "How could you do this to me, Neal? You know I do a solo. We have a contract—"

"Exactly right, Belle," Neal interrupted her as he waved the document on his clipboard in front of her face. "We have a contract that ran out today. I have a new one here. In this one your spot has been expanded to six nights—until Christmas—at four times the going rate. Plus, we're picking up your option for next season at a twenty-five percent increase in salary over last season, even when your spot drops back to two nights a week."

That gave her pause. A long pause.

Max watched Neal pressing his advantage. "The debut of the new show is tomorrow night, Belle. Still, you needn't change what you're doing. That's the beauty of it, you see. We're just incorporating Max's review, too."

Max felt the ice in her tone lowering the temperature in the office several degrees. "What do you mean 'incorporating'?"

"I have the schedule here for the next two weeks' reviews. You've seen a couple of these flicks already. Both you and Max will critique that new psychological drama, *Dr. Nelson's Couch,* tomorrow night. After you've finished your point, Max will deliver his review, the counterpoint."

Max watched her eyes flash at the program director. "I haven't discussed my review with anyone—including you, Neal. I haven't even typed it into the computer yet. How do you know what I'll say?"

"Oh, come on, Belle. It doesn't matter what you say. Anyone who's ever seen Max's and your critiques knows you've never agreed on a film."

Her face shot from Neal to Max. Max smiled.

Her returning glower underlined her clear dislike. Definitely not the normal reaction he got from women. The lady lived up to her reputation and then some. He felt his pulse quicken.

She swung back to Neal. "I'm doing the counterpoint."

Neal frowned. "What? Why?"

She jammed her thumb at Max, but refused to look his way, as though she could pretend he didn't exist if she didn't see him. "He's the new kid on the block. Let him go first."

Neal looked upset. "But, Belle, you'll get to set the tone of the critiques that's likely to stick in the viewer's mind."

Max watched her shoulders straighten into a tight line. "I said, I'm doing the counterpoint. Or I'm not doing it at all. That's the deal, Neal. And I want it in writing. You know my agent. Send her the appropriate contract tonight."

The determination in Belle's tone surprised Max. Definitely an opinionated and stubborn woman. She wasn't disappointing him.

When Neal sent a questioning look in Max's direction, Max nodded his assent. If the lady wanted to throw the opening spot in his direction, why should he stand in her way?

Neal turned back to Belle. He looked and sounded put out, but Max suspected that he really was satisfied that the negotiation had gone pretty smoothly. "All right. Tonight. I'll have the new contract sent through your agent. I expect it to be countersigned and back in my hands before we begin shooting tomorrow. Have your agent send it by messenger." And with that Neal turned and scurried off.

Max watched Belle sit down in her chair, carefully avoiding looking in his direction. She frowned as she picked up and folded a piece of paper that had been on the desk, slipped it into an envelope and put it into the center drawer. Then she brought out a pad with some notes and began to read them, jotting down comments here and there.

The tiny office had no other chair. Max sat on the edge of the desk, intent on waiting out her silence. He smiled as her eyes stayed glued to the same paragraph for several minutes. He knew she was aware of him. Very aware of him. She couldn't pretend to ignore him indefinitely.

He caught a glimpse of her notes and the preview on *Dr. Nelson's Couch*. She must have felt his gaze because she made an effort to cover her notations.

He leaned back. Her reaction to the movie would be no surprise. He concentrated on the curve of her forehead, her slightly tilted eyes, no-nonsense nose, determined lips, well-defined chin—and that peachy, smooth skin.

She was a cameraman's dream, all right. And the dream of probably most of the male population tuning in to KALA.

But she was also the unapproachable, untouchable Belle—the Arctic Breeze. Guaranteed to give any man frostbite.

At this moment Max was sincerely glad he was not just any man.

The tone of her voice declared he might as well have been. "The meeting is over, Wilde."

She still refused to look at him, despite her pointed dismissal. She didn't know yet that he wasn't the kind of man who could be dismissed.

He moved closer. "Don't be so inhospitable, Belle. We're working together. Despite what our philosophical differences might be, let's try to be professional about this. I'm really not such a bad guy once you get to know me."

That brought her eyes to his face.

He gave her his most heartwarming smile. At least, it had never failed to warm countless other female hearts.

Blue glaciers swirled in her eyes. "We are not working 'together,' Wilde. And you do not have permission to use my first name. Nor to sit on the edge of my desk. Now, please leave."

He remained where he was and didn't even try to keep the smile off his face. "You might as well face it, Belle. I'm here to stay."

Her voice remained calm and confident. "Not in my office, you're not. I'll call the security guard and have you put out, if I have to."

"Go ahead and call. But you won't be putting me out. According to my contract, this is *our* office now. At least until Thursday, when mine will be ready. In the meantime, it's share and share alike. Cozy, huh?"

Unease shifted in her eyes. "I don't believe it."

He smiled. "Shall I show you the fine print on my contract?"

She started to get up. "I'll get Neal to—"

He motioned her back down. "You're wasting your time. This is Paula's doing. She just couldn't resist forcing two diametrically opposed critics in the same small office together. Even if it is for only a couple of days."

The frustration in her eyes told him she knew Paula well enough to believe it.

He lowered his voice. "Relax. This is a good opportunity for us to get to know each other. Actually, I rather like the cramped quarters." Max deliberately slid closer.

He saw the flash of wariness cross her face. She scooted her chair back. "What is this, Wilde?"

He smiled as he let his eyes travel to her lips and linger there. "This is the start of what is bound to be one sensationally hot collaboration. I'm looking forward to every second both in front of and behind the camera."

He watched as the implication in his words hit her. The next instant she shot to her feet. He marveled at how calm and controlled her voice sounded considering the icy torrent swirling in her eyes.

"Get two things straight right now, Wilde. There'll be nothing behind the camera, and this is not a collaboration. This is war."

He laughed at the absolute sincerity in her tone. She threw her shoulders back, grabbed her notes, locked her computer and pocketed the key. Yanking her shoulder bag off the back of her chair, she stomped over to the coat tree to snatch at her suit coat and shoved her arms into the sleeves with a vengeance.

He called after her. "Retreating in the face of fire?"

She spun back at him before stepping through the entry arch, her long, thick hair whirling around her shoulders like a golden cape. "I never retreat. I attack. You'd best remember that, Wilde."

Deliberately, he looked her up and down and broadened his smile. "What delightful images that provokes. How did you know I love an aggressive woman?"

He watched her sail out on a tidal wave of renewed anger and frustration. He laughed again as he got off the edge of the desk and swung into her chair.

Still warm. From her. Traces of her distinctive perfume—heady flowers, dizzying woods and smoky musk—lingered in the air. He inhaled deeply as he settled back in the roomy chair, rubbing his hands over the smooth leather, finding it a surprisingly good fit.

She would be a good fit, too. Her icy-cold passion was exhilarating. He could feel the faster flow of his blood, the heightened tension in his body, just from having been around her.

He planned to be around her a lot. He didn't need an office here at the studio since he had a computer in his Pasadena town house. But he was glad his agent had insisted an office be a part of the contract. And he was more than glad that Paula had made the sharing of Belle's office for the next few days an issue.

He couldn't remember the last time he'd felt this challenged by a woman. She'd called it war and she'd called it right. A man needed a woman like Belle Breeze to come along every so often to add some spark and spice in his life. Make him remember how stimulating the battle of the sexes could be.

They'd drawn the lines. The war had begun. He smiled to himself as he thought about how sweet it would be to sample all the delectable fruits of his inevitable victory.

SANTA CLAUS WATCHED BELLE leave the KALA studio and walk to her beige Saturn in the parking lot.

Finally the action began. These next twelve days had been a long time in coming. A very long time. But time well used. Getting to know everything about her. Designing the sets. Arranging for all the proper props to go with each of the settings.

Any production demanded painstaking planning. These upcoming scenes of terror had been staged with careful attention to every detail.

The vulture in the palm tree kicked off the first act. Now the others would follow as each scene unfolded.

Until the last scene. Her death scene.

Just killing her would never have been enough. She had to learn about fear first. Santa would teach her, one terrifying lesson after another. And Santa would be around to see her fear, hear it, smell it.

Revel in it.

Then Santa would kill her. At just the right moment. In just the right way. According to the script.

Belle drove her Saturn out of the guarded gate to KALA's parking lot.

The watching face smiled as it sang a favorite song of the holiday season. "Here Comes Santa Claus, Here Comes Santa Claus...."

Chapter Two

"Belle, over here!" Luana Halsey called in her deep voice as she waved a hefty arm from just inside the entrance to Burbank Studios.

Belle weaved her way through a throng of extras to reach her agent. When she had finally sliced through the mass of bodies, she held out her hand and was treated to a hearty handshake that rattled her bones.

Luana wasn't particularly tall, but she was built like a rhino. With bowl-cut salt-and-pepper hair, big baggy pantsuits and no makeup ever, she charged into her many lucrative Hollywood deals, seemingly oblivious to the obsessive pursuit of physical beauty going on all around her.

"Sorry you had to run me down like this, Belle. I had a small emergency with a temperamental actor who threw a fit because his trailer at the shooting site was two inches shorter than his costar's."

Belle couldn't help but smile. "Obviously a major disaster. You straighten everything out?"

"Struck a compromise. He's got a bigger refrigerator and satellite dish for his TV now. Come on, we'll have to walk. Your new contract is in my briefcase, and I'm parked out on the street."

"I didn't think parking was permitted on the street."

Luana had already started off at a characteristically fast clip toward the gate, and Belle scurried to keep up.

She flipped her answer over her shoulder. "Can't park *legally* anywhere in L.A. anymore. Except on the freeway during rush hour, of course. I really shouldn't be talking to you, not after you agreed to a contract yesterday without even calling me."

"Except for burdening me with Max Wilde, the contract's a good one and you know it. Otherwise you wouldn't have told me to meet you here this morning to sign it so you could send it by messenger to the studio before this evening's broadcast."

"And that statement is precisely why you need an agent, Belle. The station's 'burdening' you with Max Wilde, as you so smugly put it, is what makes this otherwise mediocre contract a good deal. Don't you understand what kind of an audience you'll draw with Wilde?"

Belle frowned. "Oh, I understand, all right. 'Wilde, the Wild Man,' the TV fan magazines have dubbed him. And not because of his reviews. Wilde's affairs with countless female celebrities rival those of the heartthrobs on the daily soaps. The fanzines run as many articles about Wilde's love life as they do about the stars' in the movies he reviews!"

"Get that disparaging tone out of your voice, Belle Breeze. You should get such coverage. That kind of attention is what this entertainment industry is all about."

"Well, it's not what I'm about. Do you know he had the nerve to make a pass at me? And right after giving me a speech about professionalism, too. Hypocrite."

Luana's eyebrows lifted. "So, he's looking for a more personal teaming? Let me give this some thought. Viewers do seem to enjoy couples who fight. I wonder if you two becoming an item would help ratings?"

Belle shook her head at her agent's one-track mind. "Stop wondering, Luana. It's not going to happen."

"Oh? So what makes you impervious to the famous Wilde charm?"

"I grew up with four older brothers. I witnessed all their adolescent romantic scheming with countless females. There wasn't a line I hadn't heard by the time I was fifteen. I couldn't have been better prepared for the high school and college Don Juans or for the slick, slimy showbiz types who have tried to put the make on me ever since I arrived in this tinsel town."

"Wilde's not in that category, Belle. From what I understand, he's generally the one receiving the passes—not throwing them."

"I don't care what end he's on. Even apart from his tawdry personal life, the man hasn't the faintest idea of what makes a good movie. With three gory murders and three young actresses stripping to the buff, Wilde will no doubt be calling the movie we review tonight a four-star masterpiece. And I'll have to sit next to him while he does it!"

As they walked past the guard at the gate, Luana raised a brow at Belle. "My, my, you are worked up over this. That's good."

"Good? Luana, why can't you generate a little sympathy for my side?"

"I'm an agent. I don't have time for sympathy. And the only side I'm on is success. Max Wilde is a great reviewer and so are you. The fact that you're going to clash is a plus, not a minus."

They had reached the sidewalk surrounding the studio, and Belle followed Luana's lead when she turned left. Horns blared as cars and buses whizzed by the heavily traveled street, spewing out their choking exhaust. The bright morning sun beat down on Belle's head. She began to feel trickles of perspiration as a result of their hurried pace.

Her physical and emotional discomfort was evident in her next words. "Saying Wilde and I will clash is putting it mildly. Wait until he hears my counterpoint."

"That's the spirit. I've learned that those reviews you're most passionate about generally turn out to be your best. Maybe I'll drop by KALA to hear what you have to say firsthand one night this week. By the way, if you're going back to the office now to write tonight's review, you can carry your contract along and save me a messenger service fee."

"Sorry, I'm headed for my apartment. I'm going to have to dig my old electric typewriter out of the closet and fumble my way on it for the next couple of days."

"That wouldn't be because you and Wilde have to share an office for the next few days, would it?"

"Even one day is too many," Belle confirmed as a tanned couple jogged by in tank tops and shorts. The small radio strapped around the man's waist blared out "White Christmas." Belle squinted up at the garlands of bows and holly draped sadly over the street lamps like the frayed edge of an old cuff.

She dragged the warm, heavy air into her lungs. "This can't possibly be December with Christmas just around the corner, Luana. How do you drum up any holiday spirit?"

"Get thee to the Beverly Center shopping mall. That always does it for me."

Belle sighed. "I should have done my Christmas shopping weeks ago. I haven't bought even one present for any of my family yet. Am I a fool to be missing the sleet and snow and sweet, cold air of Minneapolis?"

"A complete fool. But you won't fully appreciate that until you've been here at least three winters and then try to spend one back in that ice-bound arctic place you call home."

Belle laughed. "You sound like an authority. Are you originally from somewhere else?"

"Everybody in L.A. is originally from somewhere else. Here's the car."

The car was a new gray Volvo with a personalized license plate that read I AGENT. Belle had quickly learned that in L.A. a car was definitely considered an extension of one's personality, and its selection was very serious business. She decided the unpretentious, sturdy, tanklike appearance of this Volvo fit its owner quite well.

I AGENT was parked under a No Parking at Any Time sign and sported a ticket on the windshield that Luana slipped into her purse with the nonchalance of someone who had a secretary to take care of such minor annoyances.

While Luana opened the trunk and reached inside for her briefcase, Belle glanced casually up at the huge billboards marking the famous Warner Bros. wall around the studio. She knew the better the movie's box office, the longer the billboard stayed up.

Belle was just thinking that most of what was there didn't merit even a day's display when she caught sight of something startlingly familiar on the billboard directly in front of Luana's car. She sucked in a breath.

Prominently displayed before her eyes was a picture of a vulture sitting in a palm tree, a perfect replica of yesterday's plastic palm tree and the evil-looking black vulture with the blood-red splotches around its hideous beak.

Belle froze, staring at the black beady eyes of that larger-than-life paper vulture, feeling her feet glued to the pavement, her heart beginning to pound in her chest.

"Belle?" Luana called. Her voice seemed far away. "What's wrong?"

Belle swallowed into a dry throat.

"Belle?"

She took a deep breath, tried to steady herself. "I've seen that before."

Luana gazed up, following Belle's eyes. "How could you? That billboard for *Pound of Flesh* was only put up an hour ago when I parked here. You can't have seen the movie already?"

"No. But that billboard of the vulture in a palm tree is already frighteningly familiar."

Luana peered again at the billboard. "Well, I admit it isn't the most delightful image, but since when did you get so squeamish about a horror movie billboard?"

"Since I received a plastic vulture in a palm tree yesterday at the station as some sort of weird Christmas present.

t looked exactly like that drawing, bloody beak and all. Exactly.''

Belle couldn't shake the shiver making its way up her spine.

"Sounds more like a Halloween present than a Christmas one. Could be some publicity agent's idea of a promotion gimmick. You scheduled to preview this film?''

"Yes. Tonight, after the show.''

"Well then that explains it. Someone associated with the movie sent you the vulture and palm tree as a sort of preview of the coming attractions to pique your interest. Here's the contract and a pen. Sign both copies.''

Belle's eyes were still bolted to the billboard.

"Belle? The contract?''

At her agent's prodding, Belle focused her attention on the papers in Luana's hands. "Sorry. Where do I sign?''

"Here. Now keep your mind on business, Belle. This point-counterpoint setup is a winner. Play it right and the next contract I negotiate for you might be in the *respectable* six figures.''

Despite her agent's admonition and probably good advice, Belle couldn't get her thoughts to cooperate. Vultures in palm trees lurked before her mind's eye. The similarity between her gift of the day before and this movie's billboard was just too close to be chance.

Was Luana right? Was her anonymous Santa Claus a press agent for the film? Well, if he was, he'd soon learn that his kind of preview piqued her anger far more than her interest.

MAX LISTENED TO THE NEWS winding down in the sound stage adjacent to where he sat in the entertainment alcove. The clock on the wall flashed 6:54. The stage manager signaled a thirty-second warning. Two harried-looking and decidedly late TelePrompTer operators rolled their screens forward, securing them beneath his and Belle's cameras.

A frown of unease creased Max's forehead. Seemed the TelePrompTer operators weren't the only ones late tonight. A white purse and pearl-beaded gloves sat on the table in front of Belle's still-empty chair.

Then, just as the stage manager signaled the twenty-second warning, Belle emerged from the darkened wings and slipped into the seat beside his, affixing a miniaturized mike onto her collar.

She flashed his open vest a disapproving once-over that made him smile. Of course she must have known that his rugged, casual look was his trademark and he wouldn't be changing it. Even though he was sitting next to a woman whose own trademark was an elegant suit with gloves to match.

She wore white tonight. She dropped her matching purse to the floor out of sight. Then she picked up the beaded gloves resting on the table and slipped her hands inside. The same kind of delicate pearls that encased the front of her shimmering blouse shimmered on her gloves. Absolutely stunning.

They looked a perfect contrast: Belle covered up, waist to chin, all white, which accentuated her light eyes and hair; Max blatantly exposed, waist to chin, in an open, black suede vest that accentuated his dark tan and coloring.

White and black. Prim and progressive. Perfectly depicting their opposing viewpoints.

Her light scent swirled around him in a seductive cloud as he leaned in closer. "Calling it a bit close, weren't you Belle?"

She flashed her icy blue eyes in his direction. "I call it on time, and it's Ms. Breeze to you, Wilde. Now, if you'll be quiet, I can concentrate on the stage direction."

The stage manager signaled the ten-second warning.

She looked so luscious and so perfectly poised. Max couldn't deny his sudden urge. He leaned over and quickly kissed her on the cheek.

He saw the shock of the kiss hit her square in those lus-ious blue eyes and chuckled as he took the final count-down. If she had had to go first, he guessed she'd probably flutter her words. He turned confidently toward the cam-ra and smiled as the news anchorman gave the lead-in to the entertainment segment.

"Tonight we are beginning a special critics' corner, fea-uring not only our insightful and delightful Belle Breeze, but also the well-known and highly acclaimed Max Wilde, the man all Hollywood watches before they watch any-hing. Welcome, Max."

"Thanks, Frank. Great to be part of the fine staff here at KALA. And I'm particularly glad that I can start off on such a positive note. Coming to theaters everywhere this Wednesday is an outstanding new film called *Dr. Nelson's Couch,* a real thriller about a psychologist who uses his professional expertise to seduce, torment and terrorize the unsuspecting female patients who seek his help.

"Dr. Nelson is determined that his female patients will come to consider him the man of their dreams. Having learned of those dreams through the confidence of the couch, Nelson insinuates himself with ease. His patients soon realize, however, that he is not their dream come true but instead an incredible living nightmare from which they cannot awake.

"Here is a scene from *Dr. Nelson's Couch* in which one of his patients, Janie, who's beginning to suspect what's behind the psychologist's facade, tries to break an appoint-ment with the diabolical Dr. Nelson."

The tape rolled, and Max watched the viewing monitor, appreciating the scene in which Dr. Nelson sadistically blocked Janie's attempted retreat. Eventually he reduced her to tears, and she begged Dr. Nelson to let her attend her ap-pointment as scheduled.

Max continued reading his review from the TV prompter when the control room once again switched to the camera before him and he saw its red light come on.

"*Dr. Nelson's Couch* is a gripping tale that paints an af
fecting picture of how a supposed healer of our society ca
manipulate and victimize those who put their trust in him
and even get his victims to validate their own torment an
beg for more. The psychological tension builds to an un
conventional and unnerving ending.

"I can't remember the last time I've seen such authenti
or believable performances. I rate this movie a four-sta
must see. Don't you agree, Belle?"

Deliberately he turned to Belle with a taunting smile. He'
set the tone all right. Great performances. Riveting stor
line. She didn't have a leg to stand on to justify a low ra
ing. He pictured the egg about to be plastered all over tha
beautiful face.

That beautiful face didn't smile back at him but at he
camera as its tally light came on and his went off. Max go
the faintest twinge when he saw her first few lines on th
TelePrompTer.

"On the contrary, Mr. Wilde. I totally disagree with you
Any real-life, qualified psychologist will tell you that wha
a human being seeks in entertainment reflects who they a
inside. When I go to a movie, I seek uplifting, thrilling sto
ries of intelligence, courage, love, hope and humor, be
cause that is what I want inside of me.

"*Dr. Nelson's Couch* offers no intelligence, courage, love
hope or humor. Dr. Nelson's character is that of a sadisti
madman who mentally and physically assaults the wome
under his care and then slices up those women on screen
one by one, with all the gore of a slaughterhouse. And whe
all the women are dead, we see him in the final scene, un
remorseful, unpunished, calmly interviewing his next vic
tim."

Max sat forward in his chair in shock. She couldn't hav
just said what he thought he heard.

"For those of you in this studio or out there in viewe
land who consider such sleaze entertainment, the last thin
you need is the name of a movie containing more of th

same mind-decaying trash. For your sake and that of the society in which you live, I urge you to go see a real psychologist who can help you out of the emotional gutters and garbage bins this darker side of the motion picture industry is trying to dump your minds in.''

Belle turned to look at Max then, a deadly sparkle in those icy-blue eyes. Max got a sudden uncomfortable premonition that things were about to go from very bad to worse.

''But if, like Mr. Wilde here, you won't seek the professional help you need to rid yourself of the belief that women being emotionally and physically abused on screen is entertainment, then you needn't waste your money in a movie theater. Tragically, you'll find the most authentic performances appearing nightly at the Center for Battered Women in Hollywood.''

Max stared at the woman beside him, actually feeling his mouth drop open.

Belle swung her face back to the camera. ''Ladies and gentlemen, if you check the *TV Guide* tonight, I'm sure you'll find a rerun of *It's a Wonderful Life,* a favorite for this holiday season. Yes, I know you've probably already seen it. But it's hard to get tired of a movie that leaves you with a smile on your face and a hug in your heart—the mental and emotional nourishment we all need to keep us head-and-heart healthy. Back to you, Frank.''

As soon as the red light on the camera went out, Max turned toward Belle with mayhem burgeoning in his chest. ''What in the hell do you think you're doing?''

She flashed him a brilliant smile, her voice dripping with sweet, satisfied sarcasm. ''Counterpoint. Did you like it?''

Several responses came to mind, but before Max could mentally censor the worse of the adjectives, he felt Neal's hand clapping his back. ''Great job, Max, Belle. Now, that's what I call controversy!''

Max shouldered Neal's hand away. Seeing the look on his face, Neal quickly scurried away. Max swung back to Belle.

"You just told thousands of viewers that I liked seeing women battered!"

"No, Wilde. *You* told them you liked to see it. I just mentioned where you could catch those authentic performances that obviously impress you so much. Now, I have a previous engagement, so I know you'll excuse me."

Max grabbed her arm. Her calm control only incited his anger further. "I don't excuse you, Belle. You're staying right here until we have this out. How did you know what I was going to say tonight? Did you get a copy of my review to read from the TelePrompTer editor?"

She had the nerve to smirk. "So what if I did? I didn't have to read it to know what you'd say, Wilde. Your mind is an open page."

"The expression is open book."

"You flatter yourself. I don't think you have enough thoughts to fill even that one page."

Max watched the amusement in her eyes and could see how much she was enjoying herself. At his expense.

He tightened his grip on her arm. "What you just did on camera is inexcusable and totally unprofessional. Even forgetting the way you made me out to be some kind of sadistic monster, how could you reveal the ending of the movie like that, even describe the final scene? Don't you realize you've ruined that film for the people who wanted to see it? Why, you've broken a sacred rule of all critics!"

Belle's eyes flashed, her cheeks flushed, her chin rose defiantly. Max caught his breath at the sudden passion behind her icy shield, radiating out in flashes of amazing strength and depth.

"Sacred rule? Ha! And where it this so-called sacred rule written? I've never read it. And if by revealing that ending I saved even one person from wasting their mind and money on that mental pollution, then I've done a good day's work."

Max stared at her flashing eyes, his gut clenching, not knowing which of the two emotions flowing through him was the stronger—the desire to murder her or make love to her.

He grabbed at her gloved hands, then sucked in a shocked breath as the strength of his conflicting feelings buttressed into a new, overwhelming alarm.

Her hands dripped with blood.

BELLE COULDN'T MISS the web of horror that suddenly netted Max's eyes. She looked down to where he stared at her hands. Her eyes widened as a choked cry escaped from her throat. The cuffs of her white suit coat were wet with crimson stains. A bloody stream turned the tiny pearls of her pure-white beaded gloves pink as it splashed onto the table.

She stared immobile, barely breathing, as Max grabbed her wrists and stripped off the gloves. Quickly, he turned her stiff hands within his, rubbing gently at the liquid red splotches covering her skin with the rough edge of his thumb.

Belle submitted to his touch and scrutiny, too numb to move. She felt no pain. How could she be bleeding?

He exhaled, a sound that echoed with relief. "It's okay, Belle. There are no cuts. As far as I can see your hands are uninjured."

Her stifled breath escaped gratefully from her lungs. She continued to stare at her hands. "It looks just like blood."

She didn't even know she had said anything until the words echoed hollowly in her ears.

Max clasped her hands more firmly. As she looked into his eyes, she saw the worry there. It confused her, until with a surprised jolt she realized his concern was for her.

She began to realize other things, too. Like how closely he stood next to her and how warm and safe her hands felt nestled in his firm and steady grip.

She sucked in an uneasy breath as she fought to reclaim her emotional balance. Slowly she drew her hands away.

Resolutely, Belle's eyes refocused on the stained gloves on the table where Max had discarded them. She picked one up, ran her finger over the pearls and felt a sticky residue. Where her finger had come in contact with the sticky residue, a new slash of red stained her skin.

Max picked up the other glove, ran his fingers over it and looked at the bloodred stains appearing on his fingertips, too. "Where did you get these gloves?" he asked.

"I've had them for months. Worn them several times. I've never noticed this sticky stuff on them before. This is . . . crazy."

"So it seems."

Belle became aware then of the production crew's curious looks straying in their direction, focusing on the gloves. Their pointed interest and the hot lights increased her discomfort.

She leaned down and retrieved her purse from beneath the studio table. Then she took the glove from Max's hand. The tension narrowing her shoulders eased somewhat as a new thought came to mind. "The dry cleaners must have used the wrong mixture of chemicals or something. Yes, that has to be it. Luckily this red dye didn't appear while I was on camera. Thank you for your concern. Excuse me."

Belle turned and quickly exited the stage, lengthening her stride as she reached the hallway leading to the stairs. She normally took them up to the newsroom on the next level because the slow-moving elevators made her impatient.

Tonight she welcomed the climb as a chance to pull herself together. By the time she opened the stairwell door to the newsroom and slipped into her small office at the back, she felt a lot more like herself.

Until she entered her office and approached her desk and saw the long white envelope in its center with her name typed on it.

Belle tensed. Slowly, deliberately, she forced herself to walk to her chair and sit down. She reached for the envelope and slit it open with her fingers. Her hands quivered in apprehension as she unfolded the paper inside and read the verse.

On the second day of Christmas, Santa Claus gave to Breeze
Two bloodied gloves.

> You've blood on your hands,
> Santa Claus

Belle's heart began to beat in sickening jabs against her rib cage.

Max could see the unnatural stiffness in Belle's body as he moved into the office. She didn't even raise her head at his entrance; her eyes were transfixed on what she read. Quickly, he circled to the back of her chair to examine the paper she clutched in her hands.

Surprise and anger washed over him as he read the typed words. "Who's this message from?"

At the demand in his voice, Belle swiveled in her chair and looked up at him. Her pupils had dilated into black pools. Her voice quivered, giving his heart an unexpected jab. "I don't know."

Of its own volition his hand moved to touch her. He gripped her shoulder tighter when he felt her trembling beneath the fabric.

A sarcastic Belle Breeze he'd prepared for. But this shaken woman with the wobbly whisper pulled disturbingly at his normally cool demeanor.

He snatched the typed note out of her hands. Anger stirred inside him. "What's going on here? Where in the hell did this envelope come from?"

"It was lying on the desk when I walked in just now."

Max snorted. "I used the office all afternoon and it wasn't here then. Someone's put it here in the last hour."

"Oh."

"'Two bloodied gloves,' it says. Seems your assumption was incorrect. What just happened on the news set had nothing to do with a dry cleaner's mistake. Whoever typed this note made your gloves turn red on the set just now. You realize that, don't you?"

"Yes."

Max didn't like the continuing faint, subdued quality of her voice. His anger at the perpetrator of this sick little game grew by leaps and bounds. "Why would someone do this to you?"

"I don't know. But this isn't the first message or present I've received. I found another one on my desk yesterday."

"What kind of present?"

"A plastic vulture in a plastic palm tree. Accompanied by a similar message."

She reached into her desk and drew out the envelope he'd seen her place there the day before. "This."

He took the envelope she handed him and withdrew the sheet of paper from inside it. He read it quickly, then slowly and carefully. Finally, he compared it to the second one she had just found on her desk. The paper and typing were identical.

Max's forehead furrowed into a deeper frown. "It's the 'Twelve Days of Christmas' song with the stanzas modified to fit some kind of new message. A vulture in a palm tree instead of a partridge in a pear tree. Two bloodied gloves instead of two turtle doves. Make any sense to you?"

"The vulture and palm tree looked exactly like ones from the billboard of *Pound of Flesh*. I was beginning to think someone from the movie had sent it. But now that this second stanza has arrived and this has happened to my gloves, I don't know what to think."

"What happened to the vulture and the palm tree?"

"I asked Jim Apple, the security guard, to throw them out."

"That wasn't a very bright thing to do."

"I didn't know this wasn't going to be a one-time thing."

"Well, you know it now. Come on." Max leaned down, took her arm and lifted her to her feet.

Her spine straightened in indignation. "What do you think you're doing? I don't need help."

Her sudden show of spirit reassured him. He removed his hand from her arm. "All right. You don't need help. Move it."

"Move it where?"

"To the police, where you should have gone yesterday with that vulture and palm tree. The sooner we place this nasty business into professional hands, the better."

A light frown creased her brow. "*We?* This has nothing to do with you, Wilde. Why are you getting involved?"

"You're wrong, Belle. This has everything to do with me. My deal with KALA hinges on both of us maintaining a hot controversy in the reviews we do. This bizarre business looks like a particularly vicious scare campaign to me. Perhaps someone is trying to convince you to curb your outspoken critiques. If your reviews start getting lukewarm, so do our ratings. I have a job to protect."

He felt her eyes watching him for what seemed like a very long time. The ghost of a smile wavered around her lips. "So you *don't* want me to change the way I do my reviews?"

"Don't push it," he growled as he grabbed her arm again. "Now, come on. There's a sicko out there. And he's zeroing in on you."

Chapter Three

Detective Sergeant Wayne Morse of the Los Angeles County Police Department was barely forty-five, with a bulging tummy and flyaway light red hair surrounding a premature bald spot. He reminded Belle of a complacent orangutan.

His gray metal desk was littered with papers and relieved only by a fuzzy blowup of two women—presumably his wife and daughter—and a six-inch plastic Frosty the Snowman hugging the edge with a lopsided grin made out of puckered red jelly beans.

He stayed seated when they walked up, but he leaned over to shake Max's hand. "Wilde, the Wild Man! Never miss your reviews. On the money every time."

Max accepted Morse's compliment with barely a nod. "This is Belle Breeze. I'm sure you recognize her from KALA. She's being harassed, but I'd best let her tell you about it."

Max held a chair out for Belle in front of Sergeant Morse's desk, then pulled one up beside her for himself. He sat down and draped his arm protectively across the back of her chair.

Belle surprised herself by finding the small gesture comforting.

Max Wilde had provoked a lot of surprises in her this evening. Out of all the people at the studio, she never dreamed he'd be the one she could turn to in a crisis. Not

hat she'd actually turned to him. But he'd been there. On
his own. Which made it even more surprising.

And she didn't for a moment believe that line he gave her
about protecting his job. Both his anger at the person harassing her and his insistence on taking her to the police had
been very supportive emotionally.

Belle wasn't used to getting emotional support from a
man—even the ones who knew what emotional support
meant. When they met a gal who was six feet tall and knew
her own mind, most men just assumed she could fend for
herself.

And certainly Belle knew she could. But this protective
cocoon she felt Max wrapping loosely around her gave her
a totally surprising feminine thrill.

The automatic male once-over that Sergeant Morse gave
Belle was far from thrilling, however. He leaned forward,
took her hand and treated it to a brief, tight shake. "I've
seen your spot, Ms. Breeze."

Belle leaned back as he released her hand and decided his
lack of elaboration meant he probably hated *her* reviews.
Not unexpected after his glowing comments about Wilde's.

"So how can I help you?"

Belle laid the typed messages and the stained gloves on the
desk before him.

Having gotten his attention, she took a deep breath and
explained about the notes and presents she had received over
the last two days from her anonymous Santa Claus. When
she finished, Morse's brow was deeply knitted in a frown.

"You have any idea who sent these things?"

"No."

"And you say this vulture and palm tree looked like the
advertising billboard of *Pound of Flesh?*"

"Exactly."

"Have you seen this movie?"

"The critical screening is scheduled for tonight."

"Can you think of any connection these red gloves may
have with the movie?"

"Hard to say since I haven't seen the film yet. But afte hearing about the first package, my agent suggested the could have been sent as an advance publicity teaser."

Sergeant Morse shook his head. "I rather doubt thes came from a press agent. He'd have to know a stunt like thi would backfire."

"I agree."

"Of course, friends sometimes pull these kinds of pranks Ms. Breeze."

She took a determined breath. "Not my friends."

He frowned and squinted as he pulled out a pad and pei to take notes. After getting her full name, address an number, he began his next questions.

"How old are you?"

"Twenty-eight."

"Ever been married?"

"No."

"Ever dated any married men?"

Belle's chin rose. "Of course not."

"Who are you dating?"

"No one."

"No one?"

The last "no one" had come out of Sergeant Morse mouth in a disbelieving tone, as though the idea of an at tractive woman without a man was a totally alien concep Belle looked him straight in the eye and repeated hersel "No one."

"Any cast-off boyfriends around?"

"No."

"How long have you been in L.A.?"

"A year. My job at the station began just a year ago."

"And where were you prior to then?"

"I lived in Chanhassen, Minnesota. I worked at a televi sion station outside of Minneapolis."

"As a movie critic?"

"Yes. I also had a column in the Sunday entertainment portion of the local newspaper. I moved to L.A. when KALA offered me the job."

"For more money?"

"And exposure. KALA is owned and operated by a national network. The station I worked at outside Minneapolis was small, local to that area."

"Leave any brokenhearted boyfriends back there who might have followed you out here?"

"No. Sergeant, my partings from 'old boyfriends' have always been amicable. Of that I can assure you."

Sergeant Morse put down his pen to stroke his overlarge belly. He chewed on his bottom lip. "That's a shame, Ms. Breeze. If it had been an old boyfriend, we might have had a chance. As it is, well..."

"What are you trying to say, Sergeant?"

"The chances are pretty slim of finding this guy."

Belle hadn't been prepared for this reaction. She took another deep breath, determined not to give up. "Isn't there any way you can check these envelopes and typed messages for fingerprints?"

"I'm afraid it would be a waste of time. From your own description, several people handled both. Any prints the preparer might have left are no doubt smudged beyond recognition."

"What about those red-stained gloves? Can't you find out what made them turn red—while they were on my hands?"

Sergeant Morse leaned forward. His tummy rubbed against the edge of his desk and he picked up the gloves. "I don't have to send them to the lab for that. It's obvious. They've got rendered animal fat smeared all over them with a special dye mixed in that is white when cool and red when warm."

"Animal fat? A special dye?"

"It's an old trick, Ms. Breeze. The warmth from your hand combined with bright stage lights would be enough to

heat the fat and liquefy it. The dye turns red as the anima
fat melts, which is why it looked like dripping blood.''

He dropped the glove back onto the desk with a casual-
ness bordering on boredom. ''Seen it a hundred times when
I was in bunco and investigated the bleeding-statue kind o
religious 'miracle' some of the gullible were tricked into be-
lieving. This kind of thing is drugstore-quality flimflam.''

''Who would know how to do such a thing?''

Sergeant Morse shrugged. ''Anybody who wanted to read
up on it.''

''Anybody?''

''Look, Ms. Breeze, you're a celebrity and an attractive
woman. Millions of people see you on their television a
night in the privacy of their homes. Some of these people ar
disturbed and have difficulty separating what's on TV and
what's real. They fantasize. Begin imagining they actually
have a relationship with you. This person's fantasy may go
on happily for months. Then suddenly you take a vacation
or wear a particular color or do almost anything different o
unexpected and this viewer suddenly gets it in his head tha
you've slighted him. He feels betrayed. He tries to get back
at you, punish you.''

''You really think some disturbed viewer is doing this?''

''Wouldn't surprise me. I get all the TV personalities in
this precinct. It's my desk they end up at when they've re
ceived nasty letters and even telephone calls when some
crazy gets a hold of their unlisted numbers.''

''What can you do for someone in my position?''

''Unfortunately, not a whole lot.''

''But these things have occurred at the station where
work, where there is a guard to check people at the gate
another guard just inside the building and a third assigned
to watch the offices and studios.''

''When someone is motivated, he can find a way to slip
by a few security guards.''

''What about checking to see if anyone at that Wacke
store remembers who bought the palm tree and vulture?''

"I will do that of course, Ms. Breeze. But I very much doubt the inquiry will prove productive. You saw that shop's tag on the plastic palm tree—an item they probably sell dozens of every day. But from the way you described the vulture falling off its perch so easily, I'd lay odds your Santa bought it elsewhere and just glued it on to the plastic palm frond."

Sergeant Morse's logic only heightened the frustration Belle was feeling. "There must be something else?"

Sergeant Morse's hefty shoulders tried unsuccessfully to straighten as he gazed over at the weighty stack of papers already littering his desk. He looked at the new sheet he had begun on Belle and let out a small, weary sigh. "I'll do what I can, Ms. Breeze. Everything I possibly can."

"SERGEANT MORSE SOUNDS like he's probably already swamped with more cases like this than he can handle," Belle said as they approached Max's sparkling black 911 Porsche Speedster in the parking lot of the police station. From the instant Belle had seen the car and its personalized license plate—Wilde 1—she decided it fit its owner altogether too well.

Max forced a calming tone for Belle's sake, despite the fact that the detective's response left him feeling very unsettled. "He did say he'd do what he could."

"And still there seemed to be nothing concrete he could offer. I wonder what I'm supposed to do now?"

Max checked his watch. "You'll do what I'm going to do and head for Burbank Studios. We don't have much time to make the screening of *Pound of Flesh*. We're supposed to be reviewing it for tomorrow's show, remember?"

Belle stopped in her tracks as her eyes flew to her watch. "Look at the time! I didn't realize it was so late. I'll never make it. I've got to stop by my place and change. My suit cuffs—"

"Won't be seen in the darkened screening room, Belle. Come on. I'll get us there in time."

"But if you drive, you'll have to bring me back to Hol-lywood afterward. I don't think—"

"It's not that far out of my way. Think of it as our night's contribution to cutting down on excessive automobile emissions."

He watched her wary look as she evaluated his offer, clearly suspecting his motives. Of course, the only choice she had other than to accept a ride from him was to find a taxi. And waving down a taxi on Wilcox Avenue was well-nigh impossible.

She gave a little sigh of surrender. "Okay, Wilde. I'd ap-preciate the ride."

Max sped along the Hollywood Freeway, glad for the power and maneuverability of his car as he zipped in and out of traffic.

"You keep frowning. Is something bothering you?" Belle asked after several silent miles.

Max wondered if she realized she had just admitted to watching him. As he glanced over at her questioning face, he decided she was probably too preoccupied. Damn. He'd be glad when this anonymous Santa Claus business was be-hind them and they could both concentrate on the much more enjoyable business of the battle of the sexes.

He exhaled an impatient breath. "Yes, something is bothering me. You said the plastic vulture and palm tree looked exactly like the billboard for *Pound of Flesh?*"

"Exactly."

"The studio just released that billboard. How did your anonymous Santa Claus know about it?"

"That's a good question. You have any ideas?"

"Just one. What if your Santa Claus is somehow in-volved in this movie?"

"You think he may not be just a fan who's gone off the deep end?"

"Let's assume for a moment Morse is mistaken. What if someone associated with the movie is sending you these things because he's angry at something you've said about him in one of your past reviews?"

"I don't know, Wilde. I find it hard to believe that someone in the business could be responsible. I think Morse is right when he says there's a disturbed mind at work here."

"Some of the most disturbed minds I know are in this industry."

She chuckled. "You do have a point."

"So let's pursue it. Who do you know in this *Pound of Flesh* production?"

He saw the small shake of her head in his peripheral vision. "The credits were on the review list Neal gave me, but I haven't had a chance to look them over."

"No matter. We'll soon find out. This is our turnoff."

They flew off the Barham Boulevard off ramp and zapped over to Warner Boulevard. The gate guard directed them to the screening room in a back lot.

They made it just on time. The lights had started to flicker in the screening room in warning, and everyone was taking a seat. Max waited until Belle selected a seat and then slipped in next to her.

Her special scent and warmth drifted to him. He found focusing on the movie—something that generally came easy to him—a struggle as his body maintained a far-too-acute awareness of her. With an effort, he directed his attention to the screen.

Horror films weren't Max's favorite, but he generally liked director Russell Ramish's exceptional cinematography and strict adherence to the genre. He easily recognized the director's signature of excellence coming through in this scary thriller.

But enjoying the movie did not let Max forget for one instant that it was the image from this flick that had been used by Belle's anonymous Santa Claus to engender a real-life scare.

When the lights came back on as the credits faded, he turned to Belle. "I didn't see one bloody glove. Did you?"

"No."

"Anything about the picture give you a clue as to why you received the vulture in a palm tree?"

Belle shook her head. "A pet vulture trained to kill and eat its owner's enemies doesn't exactly parallel any of my life experiences."

Max smiled at the look of incredible distaste on her face. "What about the cast and production crew? Any previous bad reviews?"

"None of the actors looked familiar. But last year I reviewed two separate movies—one involving the director and another the writer of this film. Neither was favorable."

"You've given unfavorable reviews to Russell Ramish and Justin Daark? They're the acknowledged best in horror today. Their stuff is great."

"You would say that."

He smiled at the flash of ice in those blue eyes, relieved at this evidence of her full recovery from her scare.

He shook his head in mock resignation. "So, I see it's another battle on the air tomorrow."

She got to her feet. "You really didn't have any doubt, did you?"

He rose with her. "What's your main complaint about the movie? Too scary? Too bloody?"

He rather enjoyed the small satisfied lift to her lips as she failed to rise to his bait. "You'll find out tomorrow night with everybody else, Wilde. Not a second before."

Max circled her arm with his, feeling excited by her warmth and nearness and spark. "Come on. We'll crash the Christmas party for the cast and production crew next door. Ramish and Daark should be there. Give us a chance to talk to them. If one of them is behind this business, maybe we can sniff him out."

"But we weren't invited," Belle protested.

"You think they're going to throw out a critic? Come on. I do this all the time."

She lifted a censorious eyebrow. "Now why doesn't that surprise me?"

She was so lovely, so near. He looked into those clear eyes and lowered his voice as it brushed by her ear. "If surprises are what turn you on, Belle, stick close. I'm full of them."

A new flash of wariness—and he could have sworn excitement—shone in those expressive eyes. She eased her body slightly away from his. "I'm hungry. I really should be getting home and fixing myself some dinner."

He tugged her closer. "If you're really hungry, then we should definitely check out the next room. They lay a generous and tasty table at these bashes. Come on, take a look. What can it hurt?"

She still eyed him warily, but she followed his lead into the next room. He loved the feel of her beside him and the battle call back in her voice.

The room's decorations remained faithful to the foreboding movie theme. Its walls had been painted in dark, murky shades of blue and gray, its lighting dim to nonexistent. Headstones with the names of the cast members devoured by the vulture in the film stood over mock graves throughout the room.

Max's eyes followed the outline of an enormous black palm tree that dwarfed a whole wall; its fronds were arranged in a mockery of a Christmas tree, and the stark presence was relieved only by a single thin strand of pulsating, liquid, bloodred Christmas lights. A live band dressed like undertakers strummed a downbeat tune on their guitars. Drinks from the open bar were being served in black goblets chilled by dry ice, the vapors of which oozed over the sides.

Seemed more like a funeral than a Christmas party.

The buzz of many conversations filled the room. Max watched Belle studying faces in the crowd as they jostled their way through. She stopped at one point and stood on her tiptoes to put her lips next to his ear so she could be heard. "I don't see Ramish, and I don't know what Daark looks like."

Her scent pulsed through him like a heartbeat as her warm breath caressed his ear. A jab of desire punched him below the belt. He clamped down on the chain reaction it threatened, knowing this was hardly the time or place for a follow-through.

He took in a deep, steadying breath and let it out soundlessly before answering. "They're probably squeezed somewhere in this sardine can. Come on. This way to the food."

Max steered Belle through the thick crowd toward the spread—the only halfway cheery sight in the otherwise somber atmosphere, despite the fact that it was laid out on top of a coffin. It began with inch-high hors d'oeuvres, included enormous cracked crab in mounds of ice, baby shrimp poised above red cocktail sauce, black caviar in deep silver bowls, a dozen different types of quiches decorated like Christmas wreaths, and ended with millimeter-thin Swiss chocolates.

Belle and Max each filled a plate with an assortment of the offered selections.

"You're right to try to get something to eat now," a familiar voice said from behind Max. "After this group stops drinking, they get down to serious eating and will be attacking this buffet like Elvis fans after souvenirs."

Max turned to see Luana Halsey and immediately heard the surprise in Belle's voice as she stepped forward. "Luana, I didn't know you'd be here tonight."

Luana shrugged her thick shoulders. "Why should you? I didn't know you'd be here. You normally don't make an appearance at these things. But I represent one of the stars of this fright flick. Besides, I never miss these parties, particularly around Christmas time. Food's too good."

Luana grabbed a jumbo shrimp and popped it into her mouth. Her appreciative munching was audible but she didn't seem to care. "Max, Belle, have you met the screen-writer of *Pound of Flesh?*"

Max actually started as a man slid out from behind Luana's considerable bulk. Justin Daark was a short, twen-tyish, bespectacled, nondescript young man who people seldom noticed because he tended to blend into the back-ground.

"Yes, we've met," Max said as he put out his hand for a quick shake. "Nice to see you again." He could feel the clamminess on Daark's limp palm, despite the fierce air-conditioning of the room.

Daark didn't acknowledge Max's greeting. His light green eyes and all his attention appeared firmly fastened on Belle. Slowly he maneuvered himself next to her.

His voice was high and breathy. "So, this is the Clean Breeze of critical fame. Finally. In the flesh."

He watched Belle slowly take Daark's outstretched hand, as though she had every intention of rushing to the ladies' room afterward for a thorough wash. "Mr. Daark."

Daark's other hand settled on top of Belle's, holding on to it so she couldn't immediately withdraw it. "We should get to know each other. Intimately."

Belle slid her hand free with difficulty but determina-tion. "Mr. Daark, pretense is not my play. I don't like your work and you don't like my reviews of your work. I don't see the need to imply otherwise. Let's just agree that we both are free to express ourselves in the ways in which we've chosen."

Daark laughed. At least, his mouth looked as if he was laughing and his narrow chest heaved as if he was laughing. But no sound came out. He reminded Max of a movie without the sound track.

"You want me to validate your right to criticize me? Now what makes you think I'd ever do that? A deaf and dumb person could recognize a box-office winner better than you. I'm writing movies the public goes to see—in droves."

Belle's calm aloofness did not falter, nor did the inflection in her voice so much as twitch. "Yes, they gather in droves, like lemmings marching their minds off the cliffs of sense into a sea of nonsense. And tragically, you drown them in that nonsense. Now, if you'll excuse me, I see someone I'd like to talk to."

And with that Belle turned and walked away.

Daark said nothing, just stared after Belle. He showed no anger. He showed absolutely nothing.

Max had to remind himself that it was this breathy-voiced, bland little man who concocted tales of such chilling horror. He asked himself if this same man could have concocted the threatening stanzas and sent those chilling presents to Belle?

"Of course, she's entitled to her opinion," Max remarked casually, fishing for a telling response.

Daark turned toward Max, his face expressionless as always, his voice high and breathy. "She's out of step. No other critic in town judges movies by their messages instead of by the merits of their production and the talent involved."

"I agree she has her own way of looking at things."

"She gave away the ending of that movie you reviewed tonight."

"She sure did."

Daark reached for a toothpick, stabbed a piece of shrimp off the buffet, ran it quickly through some cocktail sauce and flipped it into his mouth, swallowing it in one gulp.

His eyes fastened back on Max's face. "You are reacting with considerable restraint after that pointed swipe she took at you on the air."

Max smiled. "You appear to have a great deal of restraint yourself, Daark, considering the swipes she's taken at you."

Daark stabbed another shrimp. "Can you really say Breeze's jibe didn't bother you?"

"Can you really say her jibes haven't bothered you?"

Daark stared at the impaled shrimp thoughtfully. "I say someone's going to have to straighten her out."

Max put down his plate of half-eaten food. "Belle may be unconventional compared with the rest of us critics, but she's got a loyal following of viewers who like the way she rates movies. She's obviously a voice they want to hear."

Daark shoved the shrimp into his mouth and again swallowed it in one gulp. "That's precisely the danger, Wilde. She's swaying people to her way of thinking, imposing a censorship in their minds. You for censorship?"

"Trying to stop Belle would be censorship, Daark. Much better if people hear what she has to say and then be allowed to make their own decision. Don't you think?"

Justin Daark regarded Max from behind his thick glasses for a long moment. Then he turned and quietly slid into the milling crowd. Instantly, he was out of sight.

Max felt very uncomfortable with that parting stare and the content of their conversation. Clearly Daark strongly disliked Belle. But that strange talk about straightening her out—was Daark the kind of man to act on his feelings? How deeply did his hatred go?

"Always hard to tell what's really behind that little man's bland face, isn't it?" Luana Halsey said from beside him, mirroring his thoughts almost exactly.

Max turned to the agent, his focus on the screenwriter making him forget she was even there.

"You know him well, Luana?"

"Does anybody know anybody well in this town?"

"He seems angry at Belle."

"Anybody who has the gall to publicly denounce the cash cows of this industry is bound to make people angry. If they thought they could get away with it, probably half the people in this room would lend a hand in lynching her."

"And Daark would be carrying the rope?"

Luana laughed. "Maybe. That is, if he could wrestle the rope out of Ramish's hands."

"Ramish has been vocal about disliking Belle?"

"Ramish is vocal about everybody he dislikes, and there's a long list. But he's a talented director. Just like Belle's a talented critic. Ramish's talent and vigor draws loyal followers. Just as Belle's outspoken convictions draw a group who find them quite exciting and refreshing. Or maybe you already noticed that?"

Max watched the intensity in the sharp eyes of Belle's agent and wondered if she could tell just how much he had noticed.

Luana smiled slyly as she looked away to make a quick sweep of the room. "I've got flesh to touch. See you around. Oh, and keep your dukes up with Belle. I'd hate to find out you were the kind of guy who'd throw a fight for a pretty face."

And with that, Luana bounded off into the frantic fray with her characteristic speed.

Max watched her disappear, a rueful grin lifting his lips. Luana saw more than he would have liked, but she didn't know him at all if she thought he'd let a pretty face—or even a beautiful face like Belle's—make him hold back a professional punch.

Thoughts of Belle's beautiful face prompted Max to look around for her. He caught sight of Belle on the other side of the room talking with some of the editing crew, special effects artists and the stunt director. She gave them as much time as she did the director, actors and their high-powered agents. Apparently clout didn't mean much in her book.

Unusual attitude for a Hollywood critic, which he rather admired.

That wasn't all he admired. Her hair glowed as it rustled around her shoulders. The light captured the moisture on her lips and made them shine.

Her eyes flashed with spirit as she gestured in animated conversation with a young production crew worker who looked as if he'd just died and gone to heaven. Max smiled to himself. He'd never agree with her viewpoint, but he admired the fact that at least she had a definable viewpoint, full of depth and style.

He made a beeline for her. One proprietary glance at Belle followed by an unsmiling stare at the crewman and the young man disappeared for parts unknown.

"What are you drinking?" Max asked as he took the empty glass from her hand, intending to get her a refill.

"Club soda."

He chuckled. "Imported mineral water is what's chic for the health conscious in Hollywood. You're the only person I know who'd be drinking plain old club soda at a studio Christmas party—and brazen enough to admit it."

The corners of her lips lifted. "Then you should know more people."

He liked that bold look in her eye and her sassy response. She was not the kind of woman who cared for what was "in." She was also not the kind of woman a man could subdue. If she let down her guard with him—*when* she did— it would be a hard-won victory indeed.

Max was just about to get her another drink when there was a sudden commotion from the other side of the room.

"Ho! Ho! Ho!" called a hearty-voiced Santa Claus as he stomped into the room with a bagful of presents slung over his shoulder.

Behind the white beard and matching wig, Max knew instantly that it was the movie's director, Russell Ramish. Out of costume, Ramish was a dark, hairy, bearish kind of man with sagging jowls and a temper that raged at the slightest provocation. He had a reputation around Hollywood more for barroom brawling than giving presents.

He seemed in a good mood for once as he hustled around the room handing out gifts to the movie's staff. When he was finished he sauntered over to Max and Belle.

"So, did you like the movie, Wilde?"

"You know I can't tell you before my review, Ramish."

Ramish turned to Belle, his tone suddenly dropping acid. "Of course, you already judged it before you saw it, didn't you, Breeze?"

Belle's calm expression didn't change. "On the contrary, Mr. Ramish. I always approach a film I'm about to critique with the expectation that I'm going to see the best movie ever made."

Max smiled at the naiveté he found in her words. "Why?"

She turned to face him. "Because I sincerely *want* it to be. I want to be entertained. I want to discover something wonderful. That's what this whole motion picture business is supposed to be about—lifting an audience out of reality and merging them with a joyous fantasy on the screen."

Ramish snorted. "Wake up and smell the alleys, Breeze. People want the nitty-gritty. They crave life's raw realities peeled naked before them on the screen."

"I disagree. Hollywood's never been about reality—or at least it shouldn't be. Why else do you think that during the Great Depression, when most other industries suffered, people flocked to the motion pictures?"

Ramish's hands went to his square hips. "All right, I'll bite. Why do you think?"

"People spent their last dime not on a loaf of bread, but on the hope they'd find an emotional nourishment on the silver screen—a dream of a better life."

Her statement so surprised Max that he asked the next question. "Belle, are you saying you think dreams were more important to those people than food?"

She turned to look at him, her chin held high, her blue eyes crystal clear. "Sometimes I think dreams are all people can cling to when reality gets too raw. Hollywood is the symbol of dreams, of hoping for something better, even if those responsible for the dreams have frequently forgotten they hold the torch of such an important symbol and insist instead on producing nightmares."

She turned and stared straight at Ramish. She couldn't have communicated her message any clearer.

The man's thick, heavy jaws clenched. Several veins in his broad forehead pulsed noticeably. "Who do you think you are, lady?"

In her two-inch heels, Belle was slightly taller than the burly director even if she couldn't begin to compete in breadth. She looked Ramish right in the eye. "I'm a critic."

Ramish's rapidly reddening face sizzled. Max knew one of Ramish's angry looks could toast the weakhearted. Belle Breeze stood her ground and sent back a glacial mask.

The contest didn't last long. Ramish's clublike hands fisted at his sides as he stomped from one boot to the other. He glowered at Belle a moment more before his eyes dropped from her face.

A nasty smile replaced the heat of his earlier look as he took in her less-than-tidy appearance. His eyes once again raised to hers.

"You seem to be missing your gloves tonight, Breeze. And your suit cuffs are a mess. This is so unlike our Ms. Clean Breeze to be so untidy. Now, what could have happened? No, no, don't tell me. Let me guess. Wallowing in some of your latest victim's fresh blood?"

Chapter Four

Belle sucked in her breath as the meaning of Russell Ramish's words and his Santa Claus costume both suddenly hit her like a jab to the jaw. "So it was you!"

Just as she shouted out her accusation, Max stepped in front of Ramish and grabbed the lapel of his Santa Claus suit with a powerful hand. He pulled Ramish's big, burly body toward him like he was no more than a paperweight and held Ramish steady. He stared directly into the director's eyes.

"You'd better explain yourself, Ramish."

An unhealthy flush rushed into Ramish's cheeks to match the startled look that widened his eyes. His voice sounded strangled as he stretched to keep his balance on tiptoe. "What in the hell do you think you're doing, Wilde? You're pulling the hair off my chest. Let me go!"

The whole room grew silent in the wake of Ramish's outburst. Belle could see all faces turned in their direction, eyes bright with interest.

"Somebody get this guy off me," Ramish yelled.

A couple of the crew started forward, but after one glare from Max, both quickly stepped back. The director was on his own.

Belle knew their response was not atypical in Hollywood where people seldom put their neck out for anyone else.

Except she had to admit that at the moment, Max Wilde's neck looked more than stuck out for her.

She watched the cool, controlled anger on Max's face—both fascinated and excited as a distinctly feminine warmth rushed through her.

Max tightened his grip on the producer. "I've got no use for a man who gets his jollies from scaring women, Ramish. You and I are going to take a little ride down to the local police station."

Ramish's Adam's apple jutted out in his throat like a stuck cork. "Scaring women? Police station? What in the hell are you talking about?"

Belle stepped forward. "Let's just say I haven't appreciated your anonymous presents and poetry."

Ramish's eyes darted from Max's face to Belle's and back again. Belle could see the confusion in them vying with the fear. He looked like anything but the mean-tempered, intimidating man of his reputation. His voice rose to almost a squeak. "What presents? What poetry?"

Doubt sliced through Belle as she watched fear cloud the man's eyes. Is that how the writer of those stanzas would look? The person who had picked out the vulture in the palm tree and smeared fat over her gloves? Of course, it could be this director had some acting ability. Or had his comment about her sleeves been just a coincidental jab? Had she jumped to the wrong conclusion?

Those same thoughts appeared to be crossing Max's mind. His hand was still clenched, holding Ramish in place, but his tone thawed from the cold anger it held only a moment before. "Are you trying to tell us that you didn't send Ms. Breeze any crank packages?"

Ramish swallowed nervously. When he finally could speak again, his words trailed out in strangled whispers. "Of course I didn't. Tearing my work apart hardly got her a place on my Christmas list."

"Then what did you mean when you referred to the stains on her sleeves as someone's fresh blood?"

Ramish's tone took the down escalator, becoming more like his normal growly voice. "Mean? I didn't mean anything. It was a joke. Just a joke. Okay, maybe not a very good joke, but you can't blame me. Breeze once said the only people who would watch my stuff are brain dead."

Max's head turned in her direction. His words and look were deadly serious. "You say that?"

"Sounds familiar," she acknowledged.

"You believe him?"

She exhaled a frustrated breath. "I don't know. I don't see how we could prove it one way or the other."

Max nodded. Belle watched him slowly release his grip on the front of Ramish's Santa outfit. As he let Ramish go, the warning tone in his voice was so cold, it even gave Belle a small chill. "If I find out you've lied to me, Ramish, I will not be pleased. I will not be pleased at all."

Ramish turned away from Max's look and words as soon as he was free. He scrambled over to the bar and pushed aside the offered goblet, grabbing for a bottle. The crowd began to mumble and shuffle, disappointment written all over their faces that the real-life scene they'd just witnessed hadn't had more action.

Belle stepped to Max's side. "I'd like to leave now. If you want to stay, I'll understand. Getting a taxi won't be difficult."

His black eyes shone at her. "I'm a man of my word, Belle. I said I'd drive you to your car, and I will."

He took her hand gently, his smile completely disarming her. A jumpy excitement began to pulse inside Belle.

Then suddenly a creepy feeling ran up her spine and she whirled around to see Justin Daark standing there watching her, his light green eyes eerily magnified through his thick glasses. He casually sipped from the black goblet in his hand.

"So someone's been sending you nasty presents?"

Belle decided the moment she met Justin Daark that the man personified the antiheroes of his screenplays. Seeing that he had slithered up behind her, she stifled an involuntary shudder. "Yes. The first was a vulture in a palm tree. Any guess whose idea that might have been?"

Those emotionless eyes stared at her for one long, silent moment, during which time goose bumps erupted on every inch of Belle's arms.

"Sounds as if I should consider suing for plagiarism," Daark said. Then he slowly turned and disappeared into the crowd now converging on the buffet.

The slippery, unnatural presence of the man and this morosely decorated party room suddenly began to close in around Belle. She tried to tell herself she was overreacting.

Max brushed against her, a warm and reassuring contact. He laced her arm within his. "Shall we go?"

She nodded gratefully.

As soon as they were outside, she asked, "Do you think Ramish could really have been behind the stanzas?"

Max's arm tightened slightly around hers. "He could have sent the package yesterday. He might have found a way to get onto the KALA set today to doctor your gloves. Still, if he's the one, maybe our little conversation will deter him from any more songwriting."

"Yes. That was... good of you, Wilde."

"Not a problem."

His casual dismissal of what he had done made his efforts on her behalf all that more important to Belle.

Once they had reached his car in the parking lot, he held the door open for her and she slipped into the passenger seat. Thoughtfully, she watched him circle around the front of the car. He said he was full of surprises and he was right. Damn. No wonder the females flocked to him. He had more than just looks. He was that rare, courteous breed of urbane male who exuded power and polish in equal, effortless measures.

When he slipped into the driver's seat and started the engine, she watched the muscles flexing in his forearm, the large capable hand on the gearshift. She wondered what that hand would feel like on her bare skin. Would it be smooth or rough? Would it stroke slowly or would it be impatient?

"How does Daark strike you?"

His question dropped into her hot daydream with the precision of cold reality.

She looked away from his hand and stared out at the blanket of dark gray smog—the Los Angeles basin's version of evening—and refocused her thoughts with effort. "Like a slippery, slimy eel. And if your next question is 'Do I think he's our culprit?' the answer is yes. As a matter of fact, if my choice was between Ramish and Daark, I'd pick Daark."

"Oh, why?"

"Ramish is more of a straight shooter. If he wanted to make a point, I think he'd do so openly like the barroom brawler he is. Daark, on the other hand, is the furtive type. I doubt he allows anyone to see his true personality. A sick stunt like this might be just the kind of thing to appeal to him."

Max nodded. He was quiet for several minutes. Belle didn't find the quiet uncomfortable as she often did when she was with a man. Perhaps their professional relationship helped to eliminate the necessity for small talk.

Max turned on the car radio. It was set on her favorite station that played a mix of mellow modern. Yes, this man was full of surprises. Selections of soft jazz and gentle rock mixed with the purr of the Porsche's engine, pushing the freeway noise into the background. Belle sank into the soft leather seat and let the music wash her mind clean of angry directors and slimy screenwriters and vengeful vultures.

Max parked his Speedster in the deserted KALA studio parking lot next to her car and circled around to open the door for her. The temperature had dropped to the low sixties, and Belle felt a small chill beneath her light coat as she got out. Her blood sure must have thinned over the last year for her to start feeling chilled in sixty-degree temperatures.

Obviously the cooler night air was not a problem for Max. Even in his skimpy vest that bared those massive muscled arms and chest, she could feel the warmth radiating from him. And a different kind of warmth was beginning to swirl inside her stomach.

As she got out her keys, she felt Max move close behind her, and tendrils of anticipation danced up her back. She stood facing the driver's door to her Saturn with the keys extended into the lock. She should just say good-night. And leave. Quickly. With no look back.

She unlocked the car door and then turned toward him.

"Thank you for what you did tonight, Wilde. And just for... being there."

He raised his hand to her cheek and caressed it with a gentleness that sent unexpected shimmers of sensation clear down to her toes. His deep voice vibrated through her ears, hummed in her blood. "My pleasure, Belle."

His scent, sharply clean and potently male, filled her, and she found herself drinking it in eagerly. He moved closer, his breath a warm puff against her cheek. She felt his chest brush her breasts and sucked in a startled breath. Her palms turned clammy, her pulse pounded, the blood raced into her cheeks.

She knew he was going to kiss her. She knew she should turn from him, drop into the driver's seat, start the engine, drive away.

She knew she should but she didn't.

His fingers lightly traced the hollow beneath her cheek, the edge of her jaw and wound their way to the sensitive skin of her neck. Pleasurable sensations shimmered down her spine, spreading deeply and deliciously through her chest.

His other hand circled around her waist and found the small of her back. His fingers lightly stroked her spine through the fabric of her suit coat, and Belle felt the responding quiver running like a current through her hips. A pleasurable sigh broke through her lips.

She saw the corners of his mouth lift at her involuntary sound. He knew exactly what he was doing to her. Exactly

He leaned closer and just allowed his lips to brush against hers. His brief touch bolted through her, spreading enough heat to melt the polish right off her toenails. Her reaction was pure, undeniable female instinct, as ancient and powerful as time itself. Eagerly, her lips opened beneath his and she pressed her body to him.

New waves of rippling heat rushed through her. His arms crushed her to him; his mouth was instantly firm and demanding.

She thrilled to his demand, felt drowned in the sensations of his warm, exploring tongue as his rock-hard body strained against her. He tasted so good. He felt so good. This man knew how to kiss and then some.

But that was the problem, wasn't it? All the technique practiced on her tonight would no doubt be practiced on someone new tomorrow night.

With more reluctance than she ever imagined she would feel, she knew she'd have to take steps to end this embrace before things got out of her control.

The first step was back, out of his arms. Her body protested far too strongly, reminding her it wasn't a second too soon. The cold door on the Saturn dug into the back of her thigh. She welcomed its firm feel of reality. She trembled but not from the cool night air now whooshing between them.

Max tried to close the distance again. She held him back with a firm grip on his forearms, fighting for the breath she needed to get out her words. "Time to say good-night."

His voice sounded husky with just a hint of surprise. "Good night? No. Not now. I want you, Belle. And you want me."

She knew he wanted her, of course. But when she heard that husky voice say it, her knees began to shake. She swallowed, glad for the hold she had on his sturdy forearms because she was sure it was the only thing keeping her on her feet. "I don't deny I'm physically attracted to you. But that's all it is, Wilde."

That experienced mouth smiled. "Great."

"No, it's not great. Physical attraction isn't enough for me. When I get intimate with a man, it has to be emotional intimacy as well as physical."

He stared at her. She couldn't clearly see his eyes in the dark parking lot, but she felt the intensity of his look. "Physical pleasure is a joyous, uncomplicated fact, Belle. Don't expect it to be wrapped up in some soap opera sentimentality. You'll be missing out on too much life if you do."

"If you mean I'll be missing a lot of one-night stands, you're right, Wilde. When I make love to a man, it's because we are about to share an expression of our deep feelings for each other, nurtured over time."

He laughed. "Your attitude is more like *eighteen*-ninety-three than nineteen-ninety-three. You can't be serious."

His words returned the strength to her knees with a painful jab. She released her hold on his forearms. Of course she knew this was the way he'd respond. She knew the kind of man he was. Why was she surprised? Disappointed?

Because of the way he had stood up for her with Ramish. Because of the way he'd been so supportive in the face of those stanzas. Because for a moment there she hoped...

She gave herself a mental kick. She'd been foolish to hope for anything from him.

She took a deep breath. "I've never been more serious. I don't have casual affairs, Wilde. That is not who I am. Good night."

And with that she turned away, got into her car, started it up and stomped on the accelerator.

BELLE CHARGED PAST Jim Apple into Stage Five with mere minutes to airtime, Wednesday, December 15.

Fortunately, she had her review memorized. She should after staying up all night to perfect it. True, that devastating kiss from Wilde had been the lead-in to her all-night insomnia. But she'd ended up putting the time awake to good use.

She was about to cream him. She couldn't remember having worked so hard on a review before. Or so long. Or enjoying it so much.

She removed her suit coat and draped it over the back of the makeup chair. Neal scurried up almost instantly. "Belle, you're late. Everything okay?"

"Fine. What makes you ask?"

"Some of the technicians were just telling me your gloves turned red after your spot last night?"

"Oh, yes. Nothing to worry about. Just some dye."

"You don't look like you slept too well. I can see an unnatural darkness under your eyes." He turned to the makeup artist. "Make sure you fix that."

Belle lifted her head for damage repair. "So how did the response to last night's spot go?"

A small smile curved his lips. "Switchboard lit up like the proverbial Christmas tree. We got more calls last night than we've had all month on any show. Paula ran a clip from your review as a promo today. Even 'Entertainment Today' called. They're considering doing a piece on you two."

"Looks like we're getting some good publicity."

"It all helps. By the way, what is this I hear about a commotion you and Wilde kicked up last night at a Christmas party out at Burbank Studios?"

Belle shook her head. Good old Hollywood gossip mill was in full grinding production. "Don't have time to discuss it now. Tell you later."

"Well, you better tell me right now where your copy is for tonight."

Belle smiled at him and brought a finger up to tap at her temple. "Right here, Neal. Don't be such a worrywart. At least I'm on the set. Where's Wilde?"

"He's been here all afternoon. And he's reviewing his copy on the TelePrompTer just as a real professional does prior to airtime."

"If Wilde's been here all afternoon, why did he wait to review his copy so close to airtime?"

Neal shifted on his feet, uneasily. "He made a last-minute change or two."

The light came on in Belle's brain. "Oh, I get it. He was waiting to see what my copy would say. No wonder you're upset at my not turning in my copy. You agreed to let him see it!"

Neal at least had the grace to look uncomfortable. His tone sounded defensive. "Well, you had a pretty good shot at him last night after previewing his review on the Tele-PrompTer. Seemed fair that he should get the same chance."

Belle smiled at her cosmetically altered face in the mirror as the makeup artist brushed her hair to a golden sheen. "If there's one thing I've learned from men, it's to forget about playing fair. They never do. Don't expect any more copy from me, Neal. I'm not letting anyone get the jump on me."

"No copy for the TelePrompTer? But how can you—"

"Watch me, Neal. Just watch me," Belle said as she swung off the makeup chair and headed for her seat on the stage set.

Max entered the set at the same time Belle was circling the table and reaching for her chair. How was she going to give a review without having supplied any copy to the Tele-PrompTer, he wondered.

There were no papers in front of her. Damn. She must have memorized what she was going to say. This lady was just full of uncomfortable surprises.

And beautiful outfits. He couldn't help but notice how great she looked in this blue suit that deepened the intensity in her eyes.

He smiled as he mentally visualized her out of it. Ever since he'd kissed and held her the night before, his mind had been overwhelmed with erotic visions of her. He couldn't ever remember a woman taking over his thoughts so thoroughly before.

He'd heard her rules about needing emotional involvement. Not that he took them seriously. Physical pleasure didn't need to be buttressed with foolish promises that hadn't a chance of being kept. He was looking forward to teaching her all about those very enjoyable facts of life.

"Ten seconds," the warning came.

Oh, hell. Might as well make it a tradition. He leaned over and quickly kissed her again on the cheek.

Her eyes widened as she sucked in a startled breath. Max chuckled to himself as he listened to the anchorman's lead-in.

"Once again we are proud to present the movie review section of our program with Belle Breeze and Max Wilde— the yin and yang of critical fame. What do you and Belle have for us tonight, Max?"

SANTA WATCHED and listened as Max Wilde and Belle Breeze squared off again in a heated controversy over *Pound of Flesh*.

As she tore it apart with that razor-sharp mind and tongue of hers, Santa could personally feel all the pain and fury from that earlier time as though it were yesterday.

She would pay for that crime. And how she would pay!

Santa had planted the seed of fear that grew even now beneath that polished facade. With each new gift it would mushroom until everything else was squeezed out.

The review spot ended and the news anchorman did his normal sign-off. Wilde had done a good job of recommending the movie. But she had done a better one of tearing it apart. Of course, having the counterpoint accorded her the real edge. And she obviously loved it.

Well, one day soon, this Santa Claus would be introducing her to another edge.

She wasn't going to love that one at all.

BELLE LOOKED SO delectably pleased with herself after blasting both him and the movie that Max had to work to keep his voice calm as he faced her across the seat.

"Damn it, Belle. You did it again. You described the last scene of that movie and ruined it for everyone who wanted to see it!"

She gave him a composed, blue stare. "I'm glad you're paying such close attention. I've got another bulletin for you. You've got no say in how I review a movie, Wilde, so you might as well put a lid on that excess testosterone."

Max's empty hand clenched. He wanted to wipe that smugness out of her smile—almost as much as he wanted to kiss that smile and give her some firsthand experience of what that excess testosterone could do.

He purposely scooted his chair closer, until they were just inches apart. "That was one too many punches below the belt, Belle. I'm warning you, the gloves are coming off."

Her blue eyes twinkled as her smile widened. "I'm quaking, Wilde."

Damn, she looked so beautiful defying him, taunting him. After successfully jabbing him before millions of viewers, she answered his threat to retaliate with a verbal spit in his eye. This was one hell of an exciting woman.

"So, Max, how are you enjoying this point-counterpoint so far?"

Max turned to see Paula White standing behind him, a self-satisfied smirk on her face. Paula was goading him, he knew. What she didn't know was that he didn't need any goading.

Next to Paula stood Neal and Luana. They all looked far too eager to see a battle.

Max dismissed them with a fleeting nod and turned back to Belle, only to find that she had left her seat on the set in the few seconds his head had been turned. He caught a flash of her blue suit coat as she exited the set.

Damn, but his adversary was one eluding, alluring, frustrating package. Still he'd best her—on every level she challenged him. That was adding up to quite a few levels.

"You see the promos today?" Neal asked from behind him.

Max turned his attention to the program director. "You mean the one where my jaw drops when she reveals the end of *Dr. Nelson's Couch?*"

Neal shifted nervously on his feet. Paula laughed. "Running that clip was my idea, I'm happy to say."

Luana clamped a hefty hand on Paula's shoulder. "Good for you, Paula. The more emotion these two show on the screen, the better ratings they're bound to get. Max, you should consider changing agents and letting me represent you. If I handled you and Belle as a team, I could get you both a lot more money on the next contract."

Paula brushed Luana's hand off her shoulder as she might an irritating fly. "Agents. There's only one thing lower in my book."

Luana beamed. "Yeah, I know. Critics. And this pair is probably going to single-handedly save your ratings tail this holiday season, Paula dear. How's it going to feel to owe the lucrative terms of your new contract to a couple of critics?"

Paula looked suddenly like someone with a very bad taste in her mouth. She whirled on her purple pumps and stalked off.

"Stewed in her own juice," Luana said, unconsciously using a mixed metaphor. She turned back to Max. "So, how about it? Want to join my team?"

"No thanks, Luana. I'm happy with my present agent. Besides, you're too eager for this battle between me and Belle."

Neal stepped forward. "But this is what we've all hoped for, Max. Calls are flooding the lines even as we speak. The response has been great."

Max shook his head. Oh, what the hell. Neal was right. Belle's shots at him improved his ratings as much as hers. Not that he had any intention of just sitting there and being her target.

Neal's voice sounded almost apologetic as he seemed to read the look on Max's face. "She's got the counterpoint all sewn up in her contract. She'll always have the last word."

Max shot another look at the program director. "She may have the counterpoint, but that doesn't mean I can't shoot a promo of my own."

Neal's eyes widened. "Your own promo?"

"For you to run tomorrow. A preview of tomorrow night's review. If it's controversy everyone wants, it's controversy they'll get. Round up some technicians tomorrow morning to shoot it."

Max could feel Neal and Luana almost salivating in anticipation. All this unhealthy pleasure they gleaned from his confrontation with his beautiful adversary was really beginning to get on his nerves.

He stood up, determined to go find Belle. He still had a few things to get straight with that lady.

"Your own promo. That's a great idea, Max! Inspired! Why, you can say anything you want without Belle having the last word. This reminds me of—"

Max didn't learn what it reminded Neal of. He'd already moved out of hearing range.

After several minutes' search of the studio, he finally found Belle at the entrance. She'd apparently been recognized and stopped by a tour group while she'd been making her way to her car.

Max stayed back. He didn't want to get surrounded by the autograph hounds, too. They looked like a convention of Christmas elves dressed all in green with bells on the ends of their stocking caps, curled-toe slippers, and masks fitted with pointy noses.

Max watched as several of the elves chatted excitedly away about how they loved her reviews and handed her things to autograph.

One thrust a pen into her hand. Another offered his back as a writing surface.

Looking a bit overwhelmed but giving in gracefully, Belle smiled and clicked the pen. But when she leaned over the offered back and began to write, she suddenly swayed.

Max started forward in alarm. But he was already too late. Belle fell like a stone onto the hard, cold concrete.

Chapter Five

ounds seemed to be coming from far away. A man's deep
oice mumbled something. Belle strained to break through
he mental blanket weighing her down and the painful
hrobbing in her head.

She moaned but didn't know if she had actually made a
ound. Her feet felt cold. And her calves. And the back of
er neck.

Then a faint scent of lilac reached her nose. Paula? She
ied opening her eyes; unrecognizable shapes floated in
ront of them. She lay motionless, waiting until the blur fo-
used into something identifiable.

"Wilde, it's okay. Cancel the ambulance. She's coming
)."

Belle recognized Paula's voice. An instant later a dan-
ling purple earring flashed into clear outline. Then the
tation manager's face.

"So, Breeze. You're among the living again."

Belle turned her head to find herself in Paula's office, ly-
1g on the woman's cold purple-leather couch. Neal and
uana stood behind Paula. Max said something into the
hone, then hung up and came around to stand with the
thers. A look of relief lit his eyes.

Slowly, fighting the throbbing in her head, Belle made an
ffort to raise herself to a sitting position. She felt incredi-
ly disoriented and spacey. Even her lips felt numb. Her

words sounded gravelly and strange even to her own ears.
"How did I get here?"

"Max carried you," Luana explained.

"After you fainted," Paula added. "You scared the people in that poor tour group who were trying to get your autograph."

Belle raised her hand to her forehead as though her fingers might be able to still the throbbing. "I didn't faint, Paula."

"Well, what do you call it when you lose consciousness, crash to the concrete and send everyone into a state of uproar?"

Paula's tone held a decidedly accusatory note to it, telling Belle all too clearly that the woman blamed her for the inconvenience in her day.

Belle carefully swung her legs around the leather couch, seeing someone had removed her shoes. "When you're about to faint you get a cold, clammy feeling and your vision starts to tunnel. This wasn't like that."

Max elbowed Neal and Luana out of the way to grab Belle's suit coat, which had been draped over her and was now heading for the carpet as she sat up. Max caught the jacket, then knelt down next to her to fit her shoes back onto her feet.

Belle felt the warmth of his hands as he took a firm hold on her ankles. Stimulating spikes of heat jabbed through her chilled body. He raised his eyes to hers, bright black pools of concern. "What was it like?"

She took a deep breath and tried to erase the sudden images of being cradled against that bare brawny chest as those warm strong arms carried her to this couch. "One moment I was leaning over to sign an autograph. The next moment my eyes were opening to find Paula bending over me."

"You don't remember falling?"

"No."

Paula turned and circled around her desk, obviously becoming bored with the entire episode now that Belle seemed

all right. "Go home, Breeze. Eat something. You're probably just hungry."

Belle heard the dismissal in Paula's voice. Time to get to
her feet. Fortunately the throbbing in her head had begun
to subside into a mild pulsing. Max extended his arm to help
her up. Her muscles responded to the draw of his warm
strength.

But even the closeness of Max Wilde couldn't detract her
mind from the big unanswered question. She wasn't the
fainting type. What in the hell had happened to her?

"I'll drive you," Max offered.

Belle shook her head.

Luana gave her arm an admonishing tug. "Let him, Belle.
Your being seen together is good for you both."

"Yeah, Breeze," Paula chimed in, although her attention seemed distracted as she scanned some papers on her
desk. "Can't chance your blacking out behind the wheel.
We'd never be able to get a replacement before Christmas."

Neal's foraging hands nervously found his pockets.
"Maybe Max should drive you to a doctor, just in case. You
know, get a checkup? Sometimes brain tumors—"

Neal stopped when he caught sight of Max's dark look.
Max took Belle's arm. "Let's go." He walked Belle quickly
out of Paula's office, holding her firmly to his side.

"You really don't need to do this," Belle said when they
reached the outside hallway. "I'm feeling much better now."

"Well, you might be better, but after the reaction from
your well-wishers back there, I may start screaming any
minute. Sometimes I wonder if anyone in this industry is real
or if they're all escapees from the local loony bin."

She smiled at his shaking head. "You wonder about that
only *sometimes?*"

He chuckled and smiled back. He still held her arm securely in his. Feeling the strength of his support, seeing the
light of amusement in his dark eyes, Belle felt a strange little pull just beneath her diaphragm.

Damn. How utterly, impossibly easy it would be to fall for this handsome man with those bright black eyes and limitless charm. No wonder he had an equally limitless little black book.

A book in which she was *not* going to become an entry.

She steadied herself both physically and emotionally and slipped her arm from his. "I need to wash up before we leave. I'll meet you in front of the guard's station on the first floor in a few minutes."

He nodded. She made her way to the ladies' room, glad to find that with each step her strength seemed to return. Before going inside, however, she couldn't resist a glance back. And then wished she hadn't when a different kind of weakness swept through her as she watched his large, capable hands carefully draping her suit coat over his muscular arm for safekeeping.

MAX WALKED BESIDE BELLE as they left the KALA studios. He was relieved to see her face at least had some color now. When he saw her lying on that cold gray concrete with a complexion to match— He shook the image away. He didn't want to relive his chaotic thoughts and feelings from the moment he'd watched her fall into that crowd of autograph-seekers until she came to on Paula's couch.

"I can drive myself, Wilde. Really. I feel fine."

"We'd save a car if we went together."

A slight frown of wariness knitted her brows. "Look, I appreciate what you've done for me, but you might as well know now that I'm not inviting you up to my place."

Yes, that was better. Her combative spirit was back. And just in time. He had a feeling she was going to need it. He slipped his hand beneath her arm. "When the time comes my Arctic Breeze, I won't be waiting for an invitation. Now try to keep your mind off sex for a while. We're not going to your apartment."

Her eyes flashed as her defiant chin rose so quickly he felt the displaced air against his cheek. "You've got a lot of nerve."

"Which is one of the things that makes us such a good match. Come on. Let's see if he's in."

She frowned. "He? Who? Where are we going?"

"To see our favorite detective sergeant at the Hollywood police station."

"The police station?" Belle echoed.

Max opened the passenger door of the Porsche for her, but Belle stood her ground. "Look, I want an explanation. Before I go anywhere."

"All right." He handed Belle what he had found only a moment before. He'd carefully placed it in a cellophane folder along with the letter that had come from inside it. He watched her immediately stiffen as she saw her name typed on the outside of the familiar long, white envelope.

Her eyes quickly switched to the letter and she read aloud the message he already knew by heart.

"On the third day of Christmas, Santa Claus gave to Breeze
Three poisoned pens.

> The mighty can fall, too,
> Santa Claus."

He watched her face whiten again, could see her struggling to remain calm. He understood the hollowness radiating out from the center of her next breathy words. "Where did you find this?"

"It was in your suit coat pocket. Along with two more pens with your name printed on them—exactly like the one I picked up from the ground where you fell outside the studio."

"Outside the studio?" she echoed as though not able to take in what he was saying.

"You dropped the pen you were signing that autograph with when you fell."

She swallowed as he pulled out the pen she'd used from his pocket. He'd also placed it in a cellophane bag.

Her eyes studied it for a moment. "It does have my name printed on it. I didn't notice before." The previous calmness of her voice began to unravel. "How'd this happen?"

With an effort, he kept his voice calm. "My guess is that the person who typed this stanza deliberately slipped it and two pens into your suit coat pocket while you were distracted with the autograph-seekers. And then that same person handed you another 'poison' pen to use knowing it would knock you out."

Belle blinked as she continued to stare at the pen in the cellophane bag. "Three poisoned pens instead of three French hens in the original song. I blacked out because of a poisoned pen? But how could a pen be poisoned? How could it make me black out?"

"Maybe we can find out by conducting a little experiment."

Max carefully brought the two unused pens he'd found in Belle's coat out of his pocket. Like the one she had used, these were wrapped in a small cellophane bag. He twisted the end tightly. Then he clicked the top of one of the pens to eject the point. He pressed the point against the back of his hand in a single hard swipe. On impact, a visible haze instantly filled the bag.

Belle started beside him. "Fumes from the pen! Something in the fumes knocked me out!"

"So it would seem."

She ran a hand across her eyes as though trying to wipe a haze from them. "This is so insane. How could somebody get these pens and that note into my pocket without my knowing it?"

"I don't know, Belle."

She looked him in the eye then and he saw the confusion and fright there, belying the control she exerted over her voice. "Why? Why is someone doing this to me?"

He exhaled a long sigh as her distress sank deep inside him to fan the embers of his anger at the person behind this sick game. He rested his hand on her shoulder and looked into her eyes.

"Let's go talk to Sergeant Morse."

"MORSE?"

Belle looked over to see a young detective approach Sergeant Morse's desk. The man held out a plastic bag with the pens, and the two cellophane sheets with the paper and the envelope in it. "No prints."

Morse took the bag and thanked the detective as the younger man nodded and walked away. Morse then turned to face Belle and Max, who were seated in front of his desk. "So now we know the guy uses gloves. I expected as much."

"Maybe you can trace the typewriter?" Belle asked hopefully.

Morse shook his head. "Not realistic anymore. Looks like he used a computer, and there are multiple typefaces in every computer software program. I can make some inquiries about the paper, though."

Sergeant Morse waved the end of the bag past his nose. "Yeah, just as I thought. Somebody put a dab of dried chlorine bleach with a dab of dried ammonia on the end of the pen. When the ballpoint was rolled on a surface, the two mixed, producing chlorine gas. Very poisonous."

Belle leaned forward in her chair. "I was poisoned by chlorine gas?"

Morse leaned back and laced his fingers over his belly and squinted at her. "Since you were bent over the pen when the gas was released, you probably inhaled a full dose of it into your lungs. Still, you were in no real danger. You would have needed to be in a small, unventilated room for over an hour with far denser fumes before the effects of chlorine gas could be lethal."

Belle leaned back. "So like the other presents this is simply an attempt to scare me."

"Yes, Ms. Breeze. I'd say that's exactly what this anonymous Santa Claus of yours is trying to do. Did you recognize the person who handed you the pen?"

Belle exhaled heavily, feeling suddenly very tired. "I'm afraid I wasn't really looking. I was in a hurry. On the way to my car. The tour group just sort of surrounded me all of a sudden, shoving things at me to sign. They were all dressed like Santa's elves with those green felt hats with bells on the end and masks with long, pointy noses. All their faces are sort of a blur."

"Mr. Wilde, you said you saw Ms. Breeze fall. Did you recognize anybody in the crowd?"

"No. Their costumes and masks were too concealing. All I can tell you is that they were men and women of nearly all sizes and shapes. But Paula White, KALA's station manager, has to approve any tour groups at the station. She should have a list of who was in this one."

"Does she know about Ms. Breeze's collapse?"

"Yes. But not the reason for it. When I found the pens and stanza in Ms. Breeze's pocket, I thought it best that we discuss it with you first."

Morse nodded. "Who else would have known this tour group of elves was scheduled to be at KALA today?"

"I don't know," Belle answered. "I suppose anyone could have if they asked. Which tours are scheduled to come through isn't something anyone would think to keep confidential."

"Which leaves us with very little to go on."

"Did you have any results from your inquiries?" Max asked.

"No," Morse answered. "That Wacko shop doesn't keep records of who buys what—they take only cash. And although they do sell plastic palm trees, they don't sell plastic vultures like the one you described. Jim Apple, the internal security guard at KALA, didn't remember seeing any strangers lurking around the station. But, of course, he probably didn't even think about tour groups. Obviously if your anonymous Santa Claus is gaining entry through those tour groups, he can probably slip in and out without detection.''

Belle felt the muscles in her neck and shoulders tighten. Sergeant Morse was not relieving her mind. Quite the contrary. Frustration began to build up inside her again.

"There must be some reason for this. Why is he using the 'Twelve Days of Christmas' song for his theme? Why is he calling himself Santa Claus?''

"Ms. Breeze, I've seen these nuts call themselves everything from the Masked Avenger, to the Angel of Death. The fact that this one labels himself Santa Claus doesn't surprise me in the least. The common thread is that each one has taken on a persona that possesses the power to mete out vengeance." Morse's finger tapped on the latest stanza. "Trying to understand the motives that drive someone to write this gibberish and send these warped presents to you is impossible. These people move in a different world than the rest of us."

Belle swallowed uneasily. "You mean you think this person could be insane?''

"From the evidence so far, that would be my judgment call."

Belle rubbed at the new tension jabbing the back of her neck. "Then you don't think it could be someone in the business, like these men associated with *Pound of Flesh*— Russell Ramish and Justin Daark?''

"Experience tells me that a crazed fan would be a more likely candidate. But considering their tie-in to the vulture and palm tree you received and after what you've told me about your confrontation with them, perhaps a visit to Ramish and Daark for an informal chat wouldn't be out of place."

"So you will talk to them, Sergeant?"

"Don't get your hopes up, Ms. Breeze. I really doubt either of these men are involved in this crazy business. But as talking to them is about all I can do until the next time, I'll certainly give it a try."

Belle felt a heavy cold lump collecting in her stomach as she tried to absorb the sergeant's words. "The *next* time?"

Sergeant Morse's squinty hazel eyes regarded her intently. "I'm quite sure, Ms. Breeze, that you haven't heard the last of your Santa Claus."

"BELLE, ARE YOU ALL RIGHT?"

"Yes. I . . . should have known there would be more. I guess I just didn't let myself think about it."

Max draped an arm across her shoulders as they headed for his car in the police station's parking lot. "Sergeant Morse's job has taught him to be a pessimist. He can't know for certain that this will continue. Anyway, worrying about it can't do any good."

Belle raised questioning eyes. "But what *will* do any good?"

Max looked into those clear eyes and found himself wishing to hell he had an answer to give.

"Belle Breeze! And Max Wilde! Hey, everybody, it's Belle Breeze and Max Wilde! Let's get their autographs!"

Max started at the shout, feeling Belle stiffen beneath his arm. He turned toward the direction of the call. Immediately he saw a hefty middle-aged lady leading a group of eager-eyed and obviously starstruck fans on an interception course for him and Belle.

He was just thinking that he and Belle might as well accept the inevitable as graciously as possible when he heard a muffled cry from beside him. He flashed a look at Belle's face only to find she had gone absolutely white.

Max called out his regrets to the surprised fans as he raced Belle quickly to his car and handed her inside. She dropped into the seat like a robot with not a word or a sign of her normal vibrancy. He circled around the car and jumped into the driver's seat, barely waiting for the engine to turn over before gunning the accelerator and speeding away from the police station parking lot.

They were buzzing down Santa Monica Boulevard before she seemed to collect herself. "I'm sorry I overreacted back there. I…they just startled me, I guess. Running at us like that."

"After what happened following the last autograph you tried to sign, I'm not surprised an eager autograph-seeker can spook you."

Her head turned as though she was only now aware they were moving. "Where are we going?"

"Where there's laughter and good food and where everybody's a celebrity so nobody's a celebrity."

"Not a Hollywood party. I couldn't face—"

"No. Not a Hollywood party. Spago."

That gave her pause. She stared at his profile. "We'll never get in! You have to make reservations two weeks in advance to get a table for dinner."

"Unless you're a regular."

"So that's the way it is, is it?"

He looked over at her and smiled. "Did you expect any less?"

He smiled at the shake of her disapproving head, happy to see even that small evidence of her returning spirit. It had certainly undergone a trouncing tonight.

The restaurant was just as Max had hoped—loud with the din of Hollywood's "in" crowd and brimming with the wonderful smells of California cuisine. Max could barely hear himself think much less carry on a conversation with his dinner companion.

But that was as planned. He hoped Belle's senses were equally overwhelmed, because he'd figured that a little anonymity and a respite from her troubles was just what she needed about now.

That and a good dinner. He was glad to see her dive into her plate of angel-hair pasta and shrimp. He gave his own attention to his favorite, baby oysters topped with golden caviar. When he sat back to sip his wine, he was happy to see his companion's color had returned along with the sparkle in her eyes.

They were such clear, lovely eyes. She must have felt him watching her because she looked up and for an instant their eyes locked.

He read excitement in those deceptively cool blue depths. And the promise of unimagined pleasure waiting for him.

His body reacted wholeheartedly to that glimpsed promise.

Then he blinked and the promise was gone—if it had ever really been—and she was coolly gazing around, looking at the movie, television and recording personalities flitting around the famous restaurant like flies, chatting with each other between bites of pizza slices, heaped with exotic toppings.

He wasn't into celebrity-watching tonight. He was too interested in watching her. Twinkling Christmas lights from gaudy decorations cast a soft glow on her peachy skin. Her long thick hair swirled around her face and shoulders, flowing and liquid like golden honey.

She seemed to get more beautiful every time he looked at her and that fascinated him. He'd always found that his initial attraction to a woman waned quickly. This was not true with Belle. Every passing moment imbued her with an additional radiance and increased his hunger for her.

He sipped the last of his wine, then came to immediate attention as he saw a renewed tension stiffening her spine.

Quickly he followed the trail of her eyes to see Russell Ramish at a table in the back. And sitting very close to him was their own station manager, Paula White.

Ramish had his arm around the back of Paula's chair, and he was nibbling on her ear. Paula White was giggling like a schoolgirl.

Max relaxed back into his chair. No wonder the couple had surprised Belle. Who would have thought that the growly bear of horror movies could get the spitting pussycat of TV news to purr?

Max glanced back at Belle only to find she had risen. When he saw the look on her face, he realized she wanted to leave. He nodded his readiness, took care of the bill and followed her out.

"Did you see them?" she asked as soon as they were outside and could hear each other without shouting.

Max signaled for his car to be brought around. "Yes."

"Did you know?"

"About anything romantic between them? Wouldn't have guessed in a million years. This is bothering you, Belle. Why?"

"Well, don't you see? If Paula and Ramish are seeing each other, she's bound to have given orders at the station for him to come and go as freely as he pleases."

Max rested his hand on Belle's shoulder and felt the tension again beneath his fingers. The shadow of fear was back in her eyes. So much for a respite.

Max exhaled a frustrated breath. "Belle, what time are you coming into the station tomorrow for the broadcast?"

She looked surprised at his question but answered readily enough. "Depends."

"On what?"

"On whether I decide to write my review right after that preview we're scheduled for tomorrow morning or wait until after I've tackled some serious Christmas shopping. Why do you ask?"

"Well, it seems pretty obvious that this anonymous Santa Claus must be watching your movements around the station. Right?"

"Right."

"Okay, then what I propose is that I meet you at the guard's desk when you get there tomorrow and that we stay together until you're ready to leave. That way the creep can't get near you to deliver any more sick presents."

She silently studied the crop of parked luxury cars in the lot around Spago as though she was memorizing every license plate. "That is very... gallant of you."

He slowly eased his hand across her shoulder until it came to rest at the back of her neck, gently rubbing his thumb against her smooth, sensitive skin. He purposely lowered his voice to his most seductive tone. "Being gallant has nothing to do with it. I'm just protecting my business and... other interests."

She shied away from his teasing touch. "I don't think it would even occur to you to play Sir Galahad if there weren't a basic core of decency inside you."

"Don't go encasing me in all that heavy hero armor, Belle. It doesn't fit. Open vests and open relationships are my style. I want you and I intend to have you."

Those blue eyes watched him with a steady light. "And you'd like to pretend that's all you're about. Why do men who legitimately care for others try to hide and even deny that most important part of themselves?"

He'd thought her inexperienced and naive. She didn't sound like either at the moment. He searched for one of those easy, charming smiles he normally had in abundance. "Where did you acquire all this pop psychology, Ms. Arctic Breeze? Oprah? Donahue?"

The steady light in her eyes suddenly sparkled with icy fire. Her mouth set into a stiff, straight line. "Experience. I've already lived with four obstinate Neanderthals just like you. And I can't even begin to describe what an enlightening experience that was. I'll get a taxi back to KALA, thank you. Good night."

SANTA QUIETLY WATCHED as Belle stalked back into Spago, leaving Wilde at the entry, hands clenched, looking like he could cheerfully wring her neck. Ha! What a joke it was that the only one around she could turn to was the critic she so despised.

And how well the fear was growing inside her. She was already turning pale and running from autograph-seekers! Pretty soon she'd be running from her own shadow.

Just wait until she saw what Santa had in store for her tomorrow.

MAX WATCHED BELLE yawning beside him as they sat through the final scenes of a made-for-Christmas movie Thursday morning. He didn't know if the yawn reflected her reaction to the content or the early hour they had both had to get up at in order to preview the show for that night's program.

He decided the early hour. Contentwise, Ms. Clean Breeze couldn't complain about this production. Not one four-letter word. Or even a hint of violence. Just lots of mushy tears and a happy ending.

He should be the one yawning.

On several accounts. Very uncharacteristically, he'd had a hard time falling asleep the night before. He kept wondering about those four men she had so flippantly and irritatingly categorized him with. He didn't like being categorized.

He didn't like the thought of them, either. Who were they? Had she really lived with them?

He'd enjoyed his share of women and never thought in terms of one being exclusively his. And certainly their previous sexual liaisons had never been of interest. But he didn't like the thought of those four men. He didn't like it a lot.

His eyes followed the smooth line of her jaw to the small hollow between her bottom lip and her chin. He hadn't noticed that enticing little hollow before. Every time he looked at her there seemed more to discover. He wanted to keep looking, keep discovering.

She glanced over at him when her yawn was finished. He smiled, then remarked, "Hard getting up early when your job makes you a night person, isn't it?"

She nodded as she collected the movie bill in her lap. She looked exceptionally appealing this morning, all soft and sleepy and far less formal in a pink cashmere sweater, slim beige slacks and low-heeled pumps. Of course he was sure she'd look even better out of her outfit. He felt his body react to the thought with far too much enthusiasm.

He took a deep breath and made a concerted effort to reclaim control of those rampant reactions she continued to bring out in him. "So, Belle, you decide to write your review now or after that Christmas shopping?"

She stood up and stretched, the outline of her breasts poking through her sweater—which just about undid all his carefully engendered control. "I think I'll stop by the office and try to knock it off while the story is still fresh in my mind. Then I'll have the rest of the day to shop."

"Good. I'll follow you there and get my review written at the same time."

He stood up next to her and let her special scent waft through him in delicious, seductive waves. His pulse thumped as his hands ached to sample all her warmth and softness. He took a step closer.

"What do you say I treat you to a brunch first at Paty's down the road? They serve a beef stew in a hollowed-out loaf of home-baked bread that's good enough to be sinful. Of course, everything will be purely platonic."

She eyed him pointedly. "You don't mean that platonic part."

He smiled as he moved even closer to whisper in her ear. "Of course not. I'd rather have you for dessert than even their New Orleans bread pudding with hot brandy sauce. Still, you could always fight me off. If you absolutely insist."

She almost smiled as she stepped back. "Well, there's nothing devious about your approach, Wilde. I'll give you

:hat. But I'm not hungry. I'm going to the office to work. Coming?''

Max's smile broadened as he watched her turn and walk away. He liked this crossing of sexual swords with her. Her determination to win almost matched his own. Almost.

His smile became a frown as he hurried to catch up to her. This game would be a hell of a lot more fun if he didn't have to worry about what her anonymous Santa Claus might be planning for her.

AFTER COVERING the more than seven acres of the Beverly Center mall and nearly every one of the two hundred stores, Belle's feet were sore, her charge cards were pushed to their limits and her arms were weighed down with gifts for her parents, her four brothers, their wives and her ever-growing numbers of nieces and nephews.

And she felt light as air.

Luana had been right. Her Christmas spirit had been rekindled. With every carefully selected present for one of those people she loved, she had been filled with that special unmatched joy that only came from this special season of giving.

Of course, the surroundings had helped, too. Beautiful Christmas lights and decorations with fantasy trees soaring through the roof, the smell of crisp pine and caramel apples and heated chestnuts, the happy songs of roaming, rouge-cheeked carolers, the excited squeals of small children as they delighted to the life-size animated reindeer pulling a sleigh of toys—all the trimmings that made Christmas magical were enchanting her all over again.

Ah, the wonder of the modern-day mall.

What did it matter that when you stepped outside your nose was in danger of getting sunburned instead of frostbitten?

Belle was pulled out of her pleasant musing by the shock of hearing a very familiar voice. She whirled in the direction of the sound and immediately saw it was accompanying an equally familiar handsome face flashing from all six television screens in the show window of a video electronics shop. She stopped to watch and listen.

"Hi, I'm Max Wilde, entertainment critic here on KALA's nightly news. Tune in tonight for my down-to-earth review on one of the newest movies coming out this holiday season. Also dropping in from Never-Never Land will be our own improbable Tinker-Belle Breeze, the critic who has obviously been star-dusted one too many times. Don't miss us squaring off tonight here on KALA— L.A.'s hottest station."

Belle greeted the end of Max's promo with a shake of her head. So, shooting his own promo was what he meant by taking the gloves off? Dirty, underhanded trick. Too bad she hadn't thought of it first.

What an arrogant, irritating man. How insufferably pleased he had looked and sounded when he called her Tinker-Belle! Well, he wasn't going to get away with it. She'd think of a proper retaliation for that one.

She smiled. This sparring was fun. A lot of fun.

Belle quickly lost her smile when a rambunctious group of teenagers suddenly barreled by, bumping into her, knocking her hard against the store window.

Belle twisted around to give them a piece of her mind only to find them charging blissfully along, mesmerized by the blaring rap music blasting out of their boom box.

As she bent down to pick up a couple of her dropped packages, she tried to remind herself that she had been a teenager once and probably just as oblivious to all around her.

It was then she noticed the time. "Oh, murder. Four-thirty already. I've got to get home and showered and changed if I want to get to the station by six."

Belle wove her way through the thick crowds of holiday shoppers, making a beeline for the parking lot. She dumped her packages into the trunk and set off at the fastest pace possible in the holiday traffic.

Of course it was barely more than a crawl.

When she finally lugged her booty up to her apartment forty minutes later, she felt as weary and wrung-out as an old dish mop. She dumped her packages on the living-room couch, intending to dash in for a quick shower, when suddenly something fell out of one of the packages and landed on the carpet.

Belle did a double take. Then she leaned down and picked up a foot-high plastic mynah bird. Where had this thing come from? Had she picked up the wrong bag in one of the shops by mistake?

Belle quickly rifled through her purchases. Everything she remembered buying was there. And more. Much to her amazement she found three more of the plastic mynah birds, exact duplicates of the first. She set them on her coffee table, lined up in a row, and looked at them.

"This is crazy. I didn't buy these."

Belle reached for her purse and opened it, intending to go through her receipts to see if she had been charged for the birds. That was when she saw the long white envelope with her name typed on it.

A cold wave washed over her as she stiffened, staring at the envelope. Icy sweat broke out on her palms and under her armpits. She knew now that she would find no receipt for these birds.

They—like this envelope—were from her anonymous Santa Claus.

Belle swallowed into a dry, raw throat as her pulse beat sickeningly fast in her ears. He'd been at the mall. He'd been following her. He must have seen his chance to drop these plastic mynah birds in her bag when she had been jostled by those teenagers.

And somehow he'd even opened her purse and slipped the envelope inside.

A new shiver racked Belle as she dropped her purse. It landed on the carpet and its contents scattered. Perversely, the envelope remained anchored inside.

I must get hold of myself. I must call Max.

Why had she thought immediately of Max? Sergeant Morse was the person she really needed to contact.

She snatched at the telephone and called information for the number of the police station. Then, after two abortive starts where she fumbled over the wrong numbers, she successfully punched in the right digits.

Sergeant Morse answered on the second ring.

Belle took a deep breath and tried to steady herself. She projected a calm into her voice that she was far from feeling. "Sergeant, Belle Breeze. I've received another envelope. And another present. Four plastic mynah birds, each about a foot high."

"Can you bring them down to the station?"

"I'm at my apartment. I'm due at KALA shortly for tonight's broadcast. If I come by your office first, I'll never make it."

"All right, Ms. Breeze. I understand. The show must go on and all that. Let's see what we can do now over the phone. You say you're at your apartment?"

"Yes."

"How was the package delivered?"

"I've just got in from shopping at the mall. The new presents were slipped into a bag containing my other packages, the note into my purse while I was there."

"You didn't see who did it?"

"No."

"Who knew you were going to be at the mall today?"

"No one."

"Did you go directly from your apartment to the mall?"

"No, I stopped by KALA first to quickly write a review after an early-morning screening. Why?"

"I'm trying to understand how your anonymous Santa Claus knew you'd be at the mall. It could be he followed you from KALA. Let's hope so."

"Why should we hope so?"

"Because otherwise he followed you from your home and that means he knows where you live."

Belle swallowed, trying to dislodge the cold lump of fear that was now sticking in her throat. Dear God, did he know where she lived?

"Ms. Breeze?"

"I'm sorry, Sergeant. I didn't hear that last question. Would you repeat it?"

"I asked, what does the note say this time?"

"I haven't read it."

"Go ahead, Ms. Breeze. We already know this guy isn't leaving his fingerprints. Can't hurt for you to touch it."

That's what he thought. Belle actually gritted her teeth as she reached for the envelope. Her hands were icy-numb and her fingers clumsy. Using the edge of her nail, she slit open the flap. She drew out the sheet of paper inside and took a deliberate deep breath.

But when she read it to Morse, her voice shook.

"On the fourth day of Christmas, Santa Claus gave to Breeze
Four mantic birds.

It's your curtain call now,
Santa Claus."

"Mantic birds? I thought you said four plastic mynah birds?"

"I did. Maybe mantic is a typo."

"English isn't my strong suit," Sergeant Morse admitted. "Does mantic mean anything?"

"Mantic is the same thing as prophetic or the power to foretell the future."

"Just in case we're not dealing with a typo here, you have any idea how those plastic mynah birds might be able to foretell the future?"

Belle drew in an unsteady breath. "No."

"Do the plastic mynah birds do anything?"

"Sergeant, I don't know what you mean by 'do anything.'"

"Are they wind-up toys, squeeze dolls, that sort of thing?"

Belle reached out her hand and reluctantly picked up one of the plastic birds. She turned it over.

"They don't have a wind-up screw. Their surface feels smooth. I think they're just plastic images."

"Try squeezing one."

Belle laced her hand around the bird's neck and squeezed.

"Nothing."

"You sure you're giving it a good squeeze?"

"I'll have to put the phone down to grasp it with two hands."

"I'll wait."

Belle laid the receiver on the telephone stand and put both hands around the bird's middle. She gave it a good squeeze this time.

Immediately she let go and jumped back, her heart punching into her ribs as a loud, strident voice screeched into the room.

"I'm going to get you, Breeze. Get you, Breeze. Get you, Breeze."

Chapter Six

Max paced in front of the guard desk at the entrance to KALA and checked his watch for the tenth time in the last minute. Nearly six-thirty and still Belle hadn't shown. Where in the hell was she?

He looked through the glass entry doors, eyeing her empty parking space. Had she forgotten she'd told him he'd be back at the studio at six? No, she didn't strike him as the forgetful type. Had she had car trouble? If so, why didn't she call? Surely this wasn't an attempt to avoid him? He knew she was a stubborn, willful woman, but if she didn't have the sense to put safety before—

Max relaxed his mental tirade as he suddenly saw her beige Saturn pulling into her parking space. He let out a relieved breath.

He knew his relief was premature a couple of minutes later when he saw her white face as she entered the station and walked up to him.

He instantly moved to her side. "Belle, what is it? What happened?"

She flashed her ID at the guard. "Please, not now. I've got to get to makeup. And I really need to try and keep my thoughts on my review. I promise I'll explain everything after our spot."

Max didn't like waiting, but the lady didn't seem to be giving him any choice. And for once he agreed that her normally warm peachy skin definitely needed some coloring.

He led her to the makeup table, stood by while she was blushed and brushed, and then walked with her onto the set.

When he leaned over to kiss her cheek at the ten-second warning, her customary hot, bristly temper barely heated to lukewarm.

For the first time he found himself fighting to keep his mind on his review. With all the control at his disposal, he blasted the mushy movie they had seen that morning with both critical barrels.

Her tally light came on. Of course, she loved the movie. And begrudgingly he admitted that despite whatever was bothering her, her smooth professionalism shone through in her delivery of its favorable review. But there was no sharp professional jab at him tonight.

And Max knew there should have been.

The instant the tally lights went off, he swung toward her. "What's happened?"

Her eyes were too large; her skin was pale beneath the heavy studio makeup. She let out a deep breath that seemed to unfasten the top button of a tight emotional control. " got another gift while I was out shopping today. He followed me while I was out shopping. He said he's coming to...get me."

Belle's voice broke on her last sentence, and Max reached for her hands and held them firmly in his, anger coating his tongue and words. "Sadistic bastard."

"Max? Belle? That was..." Neal Fort's voice trailed off from behind them as he saw the look on their faces.

Max swung in his chair to see Neal shifting uneasily on his feet, as though he didn't know what to do with them, and then Paula White advanced on them all.

"A Sergeant Morse just called, Breeze," Paula said, a flash of impatience in her eyes. "He wanted me to tell you that he locked up your apartment after he and his technician removed 'the evidence.' Says he'll be by the station at eight-thirty to escort you home. What's this all about?"

"You got another package?" Neal asked in his squeaky voice as he took another step toward Belle.

Paula turned on the program director. "You know something about this, Neal?"

Neal looked as though he wished he could scurry into his hole of an office. His mustache twitched as his hands sneaked into his pockets. "I didn't want to bother you with it, Paula."

"You didn't want to *bother* me? I'm the station manager, Neal. It's my business to know everything that goes on, or did you forget that?"

Neal actually winced under the blow of Paula's redress.

Max got to his feet and brought Belle with him. The entire production crew had begun to swarm around them, straining to hear and see what was going on.

"Not here, Paula," Max cautioned. "Let's all go to your office and Belle and I will explain."

PAULA INTERLACED the sharp, purple ends of her fingernails together carefully as she folded her hands on her desk. "So, you've gotten four of these weird deliveries so far."

"Three of them here at the station," Belle confirmed, feeling a whole lot better and knowing that Max's presence and concern had much to do with that recovery.

"And you didn't see fit to tell me before now?" Paula challenged.

Belle wasn't about to allow herself to become Paula's verbal punching bag. Her chin rose as she delivered her words clearly and crisply. "I'm surprised Ramish didn't mention anything about this to you last night."

Belle watched her shot hit Paula square in her cat eyes. Belle would normally have employed a more subtle approach, but she had gotten irritated at the woman's innocent act over the last twenty minutes when she and Max had taken turns going over the details of the stanzas and presents from her anonymous Santa Claus.

Paula's face went very stiff and cold for a moment. Then she surprised Belle by throwing her head back and letting out a loud, sharp laugh.

"You saw us at Spago, of course. I told Russell that was hardly the place to choose if we intended to remain discreet, but, well, you know men. Bulls in china shops, the lot of them. Okay, Breeze. Russell did mention his confrontation with Wilde and you. But your ramblings about poems and presents didn't make sense to him. Or to me. And I certainly had no idea these things were happening at the station."

"Does Ramish visit you here at the office, Paula?"

"He has. A few times."

"You've given him a pass?"

"Naturally."

"So he can come and go without challenge?"

Paula caught on to what Belle was getting at and unlaced her purple-pointed fingers, spreading them out on the desk before her like missiles ready for launch.

"That's enough, Breeze. Russell told you, now I'm telling you. He has nothing to do with this business."

Max leaned forward in his chair. "I'd like a list of everyone who's come through the station on tour for the last few days."

Paula didn't look particularly pleased with the request, but after a moment of mentally rolling it around, she pushed her chair back and stood.

The crepe of her purple slacks and blouse swished together as she walked over to her filing cabinet and began rummaging through the drawer. Her slew of purple bracelets jingled as she extracted several sheets of paper, bumped the file closed with her hip and brought the sheets back to Max's waiting hands.

Max's attention immediately went to the list of names.

Paula turned to Neal. "Get Jim Apple in here."

Neal scurried out without a word. Paula turned back to Belle and Max seated before her. She rested her behind on the edge of her desk directly in front of Belle's chair.

"Look, Breeze, this whole mockery of the 'Twelve Days of Christmas' is obviously distressing for you. But that doesn't give you the right to throw around accusations. What you do and say reflects on this station. As an employee of KALA, you have a responsibility."

Max's head came up from the list of names he'd been perusing. "And as an employee, she's entitled to feel safe at her place of employment. That is your responsibility."

Paula's returning expression toward Max sizzled with resentment.

A small knock on the open door to Paula's office drew all their attention. Jim Apple walked in with Neal in his wake. "You wanted to see me, Ms. White?"

Paula rocked her weight forward onto her feet and faced him. "Yes, Apple. Ms. Breeze is the object of some kook's fancy. He's been sending her notes and presents based on the 'Twelve Days of Christmas' song. She's received four so far and I—"

Apple turned to Belle, interrupting Paula. "You've gotten four now, Ms. Breeze?"

Paula threw her hands up in the air. "What, did everybody at this station know about this damn business but me?"

Neal tried to fade into the door at the anger in Paula's tone. Apple trotted discreetly backward.

Paula shook her head in vexation. "Get back in here, Apple, and listen up. From now on I want you to stay with Ms. Breeze every moment she's in the station. Consider yourself her personal bodyguard. Do not let anyone who isn't authorized approach her. If you see anyone even watching her, grab him. If we've made a mistake, we'll apologize later. You are to take no chances. Do you understand me?"

Apple's dark mane nodded gravely as his body stiffened to attention. "Yes, Ms. White."

"Good." Paula turned to Neal. "Cancel all tours until further notice."

"At Christmastime? But Paula—"

"You heard me, Neal. No buts."

She swung back to Belle. "If you get any more of these little gifts or messages, you will tell me. Immediately."

As Paula had not expressed a question but issued a command, Belle didn't feel obliged to reply.

Not that Paula was giving her a chance. She immediately swung over to Max. "Satisfied?"

He slowly got to his feet. "For the moment."

Belle also rose to her feet. "Thank you, Paula. Your decisive handling of this problem is very much appreciated."

Paula impatiently waved away Belle's thanks as she swung around her desk and into her chair. "This is nothing personal, Breeze, so don't get carried away. A threat against you is a threat against my station's programming. I will not tolerate it. Now, I'd appreciate it if you'd all get lost. I have work to do."

ONCE THEY WERE BACK in her tiny office, Belle plopped into her chair.

"Don't get too comfortable," Max warned. He handed Belle the tour lists he had gotten from Paula. "You've got work to do. Read through these and tell me if any of these names are familiar."

"No rest for the weary, I see." Belle took the lists and started through them. Max sat on the edge of the desk beside her, his attention wandering to the sweep of her lashes, the curve of her cheek, the light fragrance that was so distinctly her.

But what he was enjoying most was the return of her spirit.

Finally she raised her head. "Not even one familiar name. I paid particular attention to the names of the tour group of elves from that bowling league in town for their tournament."

"Well, it was a long shot," Max admitted, taking the sheets from her. "If this creep's gotten into the station by joining a tour, I doubt he used his real name. Or her name. We shouldn't be jumping to sexist conclusions."

"I suppose not, but if this really is a crazed viewer, would it matter if he or she used their real name? I mean, even their real name probably wouldn't mean anything to me."

Max nodded. "That's a point. Did Sergeant Morse have any words of wisdom to offer on the meaning of this last stanza or present?"

Belle paused to take a deep breath. She let it out slowly, soundlessly. "He said that he didn't like its implied threat. He said I must be very, very careful."

Max read the fear in her eyes, heard it in the cracks in her voice. He reached down and captured her hands. He could feel her pulse—quick and light against his palms.

"Morse had no business telling you to squeeze one of those hideous mynah birds. Where was the man's head? Couldn't he figure out the damn things had to be booby-trapped in some way? Fool!"

She exhaled heavily. "He said he was sorry afterward. He even dropped everything and came right over to get them out of my place. If I had taken them directly to the station as he told me to in the first place, it never would have happened. But it was already so late, and I was afraid I would miss the show."

"You could have called me."

She looked into his eyes, very deeply into his eyes. "Yes, I believe I could have."

"Ms. Breeze?"

Max let go of Belle's hands and straightened to see Jim Apple standing stiffly in Belle's doorway.

"You need something, Jim?" Belle asked.

The security guard shuffled on his feet. "I'm sorry to bother you, Ms. Breeze, but as I'm now your bodyguard here at the station I thought it might be a good idea if you could give me your schedule so I'd be sure to be here at the right times and all."

"That is a good idea, Jim. I'll write it down and drop it by the guard's desk downstairs when I leave tonight."

Apple nodded but lingered. "Is it true what Mr. Fort just told me? You got three of those packages right here at the station?"

"Yes."

Jim Apple snorted as he shook his heavy brown mane. "This is terrible, Ms. Breeze. I feel responsible. I'm supposed to be preventing things like this from happening."

Belle smiled at him. She got up, walked over to him and rested her hand lightly on the sleeve of his uniform. "Well now that you're my bodyguard, maybe you can."

Apple's sallow complexion colored. He nodded as his right hand went to the holster on his belt, massaging the butt of his revolver, something Max recognized as a nervous habit with him. "I'll keep my eyes open, Ms. Breeze. You can count on me."

"Thanks, Jim. I feel safer already."

Max turned to Belle as soon as Jim had trotted off to wait outside her office. "How long have you known that guy?"

"Since the station hired him a couple of months ago. Why do you ask?"

"He seems a little too willing and eager to please for a security guard making minimum wage. I don't find his attitude a comfortable one."

Belle looked at Max in disbelief. "You're not comfortable with someone willing and eager to do a good job? Boy, if you're typical of an L.A. native, I'm glad Jim Apple and I are from the Midwest."

"How do you know Apple is from the Midwest?"

"We talked when he first came on board. I've forgotten the little town he said he hailed from, but I haven't forgotten that back there people take pride in a job well done. Look, it's almost eight-thirty and Sergeant Morse is probably waiting for me in the parking lot. I better go."

Max waited as she collected her purse and gloves. They slowly walked together out of her tiny office. Max felt her nearness in every cell of his body as she brushed against him going through the entry arch. He wanted to take her in his arms. He wanted to feel her warmth and her response to him again. He wanted—

"I imagine you're relieved now that Jim has replaced you as my bodyguard around the station."

Max eyed Belle silently for a moment, wondering how she could possibly look so beautiful and be so blind as to all the churning desire for her that was building up inside him—a desire that was rapidly slipping past his control. "Is that what you imagine?"

And then, because he was afraid of what else he might next say and do, Max just turned and walked away.

"WELL, IF IT ISN'T Tinker-Belle from Never-Never Land. What are you doing in the waiting room of a rival TV station? Are you a spy? Have nothing else to do this fine Friday morning?"

Belle winced as she heard the address. She looked up from the script she was reading to find herself face-to-face with Luana's happy smirk.

"Could you keep your voice down, Luana? I'm just reading over a script for a friend. She thought it might be dragging a bit and I could give her a few pointers."

"Well is it and are you?"

"No it's not and no I'm not. It's a wonderful script."

"A wonderful script? Well, well. Why don't you introduce me to this talented lady. Maybe she needs a new agent."

"Sorry, she's happy with the one she has. Why is it that every time I turn around lately, I'm running into you?"

"Thanks, Belle. I'm glad to see you, too."

"Well, I didn't mean it that way."

Luana laughed. "Come on. I'll treat you to lunch. I've just negotiated a lucrative contract, and I'm in an expansive mood. Besides, I've been meaning to talk to you about this hate mail you've been receiving.''

Belle started in surprise as she closed the script and got to her feet. "What have you heard?''

"You mean apart from that confrontation with Ramish the other night?''

"Oh, that's right. I forgot. You were there.''

"And you two have been the topic of conversation ever since. I can't tell you how many calls I've received from nosy folks wanting the rundown.''

"What have you told them?''

"What can I tell them? I don't have the rundown. A condition I'm determined to rectify. No use trying to drive anywhere. We'll never find a parking space. Come on. Let's foot it over to the Columbia Bar & Grill. It's the only decent place to eat at on this side of Tinsel Town.''

Once more Belle found herself hurrying to keep up with her juggernaut of an agent. "Why do you always seem to be running, Luana?''

"It's all relative, Belle. I'm not running. Everybody else is crawling.''

They chugged along Melrose Avenue on their way to Gower Street. A bag woman, muttering to herself, nearly ran into Belle with her shopping cart of worldly goods. Belle watched her next nearly collide with a concrete wall covered by graffiti. Glamorous Hollywood.

Belle exhaled a lungful of smog and car exhaust as they ducked into the cool, tiled restaurant. Belle followed Luana to the large, lovely atrium-style central dining area.

They both ordered the same—the Grill's famous crab cakes. When they had finished cleaning their plates, Luana leaned forward expectantly.

"So, Belle, give. What's it all about?''

Belle once again repeated the story of the stanzas and presents she had received from her anonymous Santa Claus. Luana leaned back and listened, quietly sipping her coffee until Belle had finished.

Her agent's blunt cut hair bounced from side to side as he shook her head. Her tone held a vehemence Belle had not noticed before. "World seems to be producing more and more of these crazies in it every day. They watch and wait until we're alone and then sneak up on us and slit our throats before we even have a chance to raise a hand to defend ourselves."

Of course her agent was right, but Belle could have done without that throat-slashing image at the moment. "Thanks, Luana."

Realization flashed through her companion's eyes. "Damn, I'm sorry, Belle. Believe me, I understand how frightening this must be for you. I've gone through it myself."

Belle leaned forward in total surprise at her agent's unexpected admission. "You had someone terrorize you, Luana?"

"Yeah. Nearly two years ago now. Only my crazy did it over the telephone at night. Nasty little man with a nasty little mouth. I changed my home number twice. All three numbers were unlisted. Didn't matter. Crazy still managed to find them out."

"But it stopped?"

"Police finally authorized a tap and caught him. I was never so grateful in my life. Turned out to be a dissatisfied would-be actor who had applied to me for representation and been turned down. Hell, I turn down all those silly hopefuls who come traipsing through my door, clutching pathetic little portfolios of them playing the lead in their high school play. Who'd figure one would take it personally?"

"Apparently, taking it 'personally' is spreading. Sergeant Morse thinks my crazy is a viewer who's gotten a fix on me somehow and is angry at some imagined wrong I've done to him."

"So Morse is handling your case? Well, at least that's one point in your favor, Belle. He knows the industry players

and the crazies that are likely to attack us. Not that ever
experience helps sometimes when a crazy gets a fix on hi
victim."

"You almost sound like you know someone that hap
pened to?"

Luana sipped her coffee and thought a moment before
answering.

"I do. Be careful, Belle. Keep your eyes open. At al
times. I'm afraid for you."

BELLE PUSHED OPEN her apartment door to hear the ring
ing of the telephone. But when she rushed up to answer it
her hand paused over the receiver as Luana's shared expe
rience of that afternoon came back to her in far too vivi
recall.

What if her crazy had gotten her number? What if it wa
him on the telephone now?

The phone jarred its ringing demand.

Belle gave herself a mental shake. *You can't stop answer
ing your phone. Come on. Where is your backbone? Pic*
it up.

"Hello?"

"Eight-thirty again tonight, Ms. Breeze. I'll be waiting i
the KALA parking lot to see you safely home."

Belle sank into her living room sofa, a sense of relief als
sinking into her chest. "That's good of you, Sergeant."

"It's a small step, Ms. Breeze. The bigger ones are up t
you. Like I told you last night, having one of KALA's se
curity guards with you at all times while you're at the sta
tion is a good move. But don't let it make you becom
complacent. Be on guard at all times. Keep looking aroun
you. Notice everyone. Everything. You mustn't let you
guard down for a second."

Belle's momentarily eased nerves jagged back to instan
attention. "Do you really think this person intends to... t
get me?"

Sergeant Morse exhaled heavily in her ear. "No way to tell for certain what this madman means by these presents and stanzas, or what he's after. But I don't like the way this one feels, Ms. Breeze. Call it experience. Call it a sixth sense. I think this guy is serious. I'll see you tonight."

Belle hung up the phone. She immediately jumped up to throw the safety bolt on her front door. Then she returned to the couch and tried to quiet her now shaky hands.

First her agent. Now Sergeant Morse. Nothing but dire predictions. Terrific. Didn't anybody offer hope anymore?

She thought of Max. The warmth of his hands as they held hers. The reassurance in his eyes. She had an overwhelming impulse to call him.

Of course she couldn't. For one, she didn't have his number. For two, even if she did, what would she say? Come over to my apartment and hold my hand because I'm scared?

Damn. Where was the woman who had stood face-to-face with Hollywood's kingpins and told them their movies weren't worth the cellulose they were printed on? Where was the valiant heart that had so long been hers to command?

Was it now ruled by fear? What a bitter pill that was to swallow!

But anyone can be legitimately afraid of a madman, can't they?

A madman. A shiver ran through Belle. She wrapped her arms around herself, trying to find some warmth for the chill in her chest. No matter what Sergeant Morse said she had to stop thinking about this. If she dwelt on it twenty-four hours a day, *she'd* go mad.

What she needed was to talk to someone who didn't know anything about this awful business—someone who'd chat about holiday plans and the weather and all the wonderful, boring, commonplace, everyday-life events that meant nothing and everything.

Belle's eyes swept the room, coming to rest on the Christmas tree and the presents she had carefully wrapped and placed beneath it for her family. The biggest was tied with a red velvet-and-satin bow. It contained the softest, sweetest, warmest pink robe Belle had ever seen.

She picked up the phone and punched in the familiar number. It was answered on the first ring, as though the person on the other line had been sitting and waiting for her call.

Belle smiled. "Hi, Mom."

"So, MAX. What do you think of your new office?"

Max looked up from reviewing his copy to flash the program director a smile.

"Well, Neal, I feel as if I'm sitting in the middle of a movie set. Two hours ago this was just a corner of the newsroom. Then two guys with metal-and-glass partitions arrive and enclose an eight-by-ten space, shove in a desk, chair, computer and telephone, and hang a couple of pictures on the one solid wall, and presto—an office is born. I almost expected you to say 'action' when you walked in just now."

Neal chuckled as he made himself comfortable on the edge of Max's desk. "We use our stage crews to create and uncreate office space to save on overhead. Did you see your promo on the air yet?"

"Yes. That 'Tinker-Belle from Never-Never Land' went over very well. I think our Clean Breeze is getting another handle—although I doubt it's one she'll wear with relish."

Neal chuckled. "We got a slew of phone calls yesterday. And a bundle after each night's broadcast. Only three nights' running this new point-counterpoint and the advertising department is already getting calls from advertisers asking to sponsor the news program. This controversy you two have going is hot! Watchers love to take sides."

"What's the split?"

"Popularitywise, you and Belle are running neck and neck, although Monday night there were a few more calls in favor of her and last night a few more for you. 'Entertainment Today' definitely wants to go ahead with an interview next week.''

''Does Belle know yet?''

''Haven't seen her today. But she must be scheduled to come in shortly. Jim Apple is waiting for her at the guard station downstairs. Max, can I ask you something?''

''You can ask. Whether you get an answer or not is another matter.''

Neal's mustache twitched. ''Do you have something going with Belle?''

''What do you mean by 'going'?''

''Rumors have been spreading like wildfire. My phone's been ringing off the damn hook for the last two days.''

''Yeah, I've gotten a few calls, too.''

Neal shifted on his feet again. ''I've tried to keep a lid on this thing, but I don't know how successful I've been. And it's not just this anonymous Santa Claus business. They're saying you and Belle are an item.''

Max shrugged. ''Hell, Neal. The gossips in this town have linked me with every woman who's even purchased a TV, much less been on one. They've built a reputation around me I couldn't live up to if I were a hundred men.''

''You're saying you two haven't . . . gotten together?''

Max stayed relaxed in his chair but there was nothing relaxed in his tone. ''Neal, what Belle Breeze and I have or haven't done together outside of this station is none of your business or anyone else's. Is that clear?''

Neal nodded reluctantly. He looked uncomfortably suspicious at Max's refusal to confirm or deny. Max couldn't care less.

''It's getting close to show time,'' Neal said in a more formal tone. ''Do you have any copy for the TelePrompTer tonight?''

Max felt a quickening of his pulse as Belle walked past the glass partitions of his office and headed toward her office on the other side of the newsroom with Jim Apple dogging her footsteps.

Thoughts of her had interrupted his concentration all day. Even while he wrote his review, he could almost hear her response to every word—see her disapproving glower at every point.

She stopped just before she got to her office and turned around, almost as though she knew he watched. Unerringly, across that crowded, busy room, her eyes instantly found his. And held them.

Max's heart hammered against a sudden constriction. It continued to labor, even when she turned away and entered her office.

"Max?"

With an effort Max refocused his attention back to Neal. "What?"

"I asked if you had any copy for the TelePrompTer."

"No, Neal. I make mistakes, but never the same one twice."

"Mistake?"

"I'm not going to let her get an advance look at my copy again."

"You're memorizing your review, too?"

"You got it. Now, leave me in peace so I can concentrate."

Belle stepped through the archway of her office and hung up her jacket as always. She strode over to her chair and plopped down onto its comforting bulk.

She felt better. Much better.

And pleasantly excited over that heated look she'd just exchanged with Wilde. Damn, but that man could get her blood going. Not that he was solely responsible for her improvement.

Her call home had helped her regain her equilibrium. Feeling the strength of her family's love had done a lot to regenerate her flagging spirit. And as she looked up now to see Jim Apple standing on guard outside her office and reminded herself that Sergeant Morse would escort her home, her heart was light, indeed.

She rummaged around in her shoulder bag until she found the key to unlock her computer. She called up the file that contained her review for tonight. She already had it almost memorized, but she knew it wouldn't hurt to review it before airtime.

And it was a good thing she did. As the storyline and characters came back to her, she realized that the clip she had chosen to illustrate her points wasn't really as good as another scene from the movie would be.

She'd better get a correcting note to the control room to let them know to change that scene.

She scooted her chair back to open her recessed middle desk drawer to take out the proper form. She reached down and tugged the drawer toward her. But it wouldn't budge. She tugged harder. No luck.

What was wrong with this stupid drawer? It didn't have a lock. Must just be stuck. She clasped the handle and rattled the drawer, trying to see if she could release whatever was jamming it shut. It stayed stubbornly closed.

Belle frowned, both frustrated and determined to get the drawer open. She stood up, pushed her chair aside, placed one hand beneath the drawer and the other on the handle and yanked for all she was worth.

She felt something give. The drawer rushed open so fast it slid completely off its railing and crashed to the gray carpet.

Belle crashed with it, her momentum landing her unceremoniously on her behind.

She blinked, somewhat stunned. Then she sucked in a horrified breath as a small swarm of huge, angry hornets flew out of the now-open drawer, heading directly for her face.

Belle instinctively raised her hands to shield her face from their stinging attack, screaming at the top of her lungs.

Chapter Seven

Max sprinted across the newsroom the instant he heard Belle's scream. He plunged through her open archway on Jim Apple's heels, just in time to deflect the biggest buzzing hornet he'd ever seen in his life. He batted at it as it whizzed past him out into the newsroom. Apple was waving his hands at another one in front of Belle's desk.

But Max couldn't see Belle.

She screamed again.

Max's eyes located and locked on a stockinged foot sticking out from behind her desk. His heart gave an uncomfortable lurch as he rushed toward it.

He found her lying on her side, beating what was left of a hornet into the carpet with her shoe, a look of utter horror on her face. Another hornet carcass lay pounded into the carpet a few feet away.

He dropped to his knee beside her. "Belle, are you all right?"

She flashed scared eyes at him, her voice a terrified whisper. "Did you see the others? Did you get them?"

"One was near the doorway when I came in."

Belle started at a sudden thumping sound. "Got one," Apple called out.

She shuddered. "That leaves one." She came to her knees and stared around warily, ready to do battle, shoe poised in her hand. Max would have laughed if he hadn't seen the look in her eye. This was no laughing matter.

Max got to his feet to look for the remaining hornet. Apple came around the desk. "You say there's another one, Ms. Breeze? You want me to try to trap it?"

"Trap it? This isn't 'Wild Kingdom.' We don't have to bring them back alive. That's a damn hornet!"

Max would have felt a lot better hearing her anger if the fear hadn't also been stacked beneath it.

A buzzing sound against the glass partition in the far corner alerted him to the position of the last hornet. He quickly dispatched it and returned to her side.

He rested his hands on her shaking shoulders and eased her into her chair. "It's okay now, Belle. The last one is dead. Tell me what happened."

She sunk beneath the slight pressure of his hands, still clutching her shoe, as though she couldn't quite let herself believe she was safe yet. Another shudder swept through her body. Her voice sounded small and uneven.

"My middle drawer was stuck. When I yanked it open, the . . . the hornets flew in my face."

Her voice cracked on a sob. Max sank to his knees beside her chair, his heart twisting painfully. He gathered her in his arms and rested his head against hers as another shudder shook her body. "It's okay. It's over now."

"Can I do something for you, Ms. Breeze?" Jim Apple asked, shuffling back and forth on his feet, looking rather at a loss.

Max motioned to the news people, whose faces were plastered against the glass to Belle's office, looking in, whispering back and forth. "You can get rid of them for a start," he said.

Apple nodded and exited through Belle's archway. "It's all over, folks," he called as he began to peel some of the squashed insects off from the glass. "Give the lady some privacy, please."

Reluctantly, they backed away. Max dismissed them as his eyes drew again to Belle's face.

"Better now?"

She took another deep breath and he watched her reaching for control. The increased volume in her voice reflected her partial success. "Yes. Thank you. But I don't understand. How did they get in my desk?"

Max released his hold on her. He was pretty sure he knew the answer to that question, but he didn't want to volunteer anything without proof. He picked up the desk drawer lying on the carpet and examined it. He wasn't surprised to find a small, triangular cone in its center, a bulky-enough object to have restricted the drawer. He knew instantly that it had also housed the hornets.

Anger at the cleverness of this nasty trap flared through him. A rattling drawer could only have added to the hornets' fury at being imprisoned inside. And made them ready to fly out ready to sting.

Then Max saw the long white envelope with Belle's typed name, sticking out from beneath the cone. This did not surprise him, either. He slipped it out and slit it open.

The instant she saw it, he heard the startled intake of her breath beside him, could sense the stiffening of her muscles.

He read aloud the newest stanza.

"On the fifth day of Christmas, Santa Claus gave to Breeze
Five angry stings.

> This year it's my turn,
> Santa Claus."

SERGEANT MORSE SCOOPED up one of the hornet carcasses from where Belle had pounded it into the carpet and slipped it into a waiting envelope.

Jim Apple clopped forward, his long nose positioning itself over the evidence. "Yes, the one I killed was just the same. Now, how could your Santa Claus have gotten hold of them?"

Max leaned toward Apple in interest. "What do you mean?"

"Well, insects like these hornets are dormant during the winter. At least here in our northern latitudes."

"So?"

"Well, that means these hornets don't belong here, Mr. Wilde. Somebody had to go to some trouble to bring them here from south of the equator. Maybe Ms. Breeze's Santa Claus is from another country."

Max watched Belle's head lift hopefully toward Sergeant Morse. "You think you could check on that?"

"Ms. Breeze, I'm sorry, but even if what Apple here says is true, looking for a foreigner is a bit too vague to be a clear line of inquiry."

Sergeant Morse sent her a small regretful smile before turning back to Max. "Can I see you outside for a moment, Mr. Wilde?"

"Of course." Max turned to Belle. "Be right back."

She nodded and looked down at the shoe she'd been holding in her hand for the last hour as though just becoming aware of it. Slowly she replaced it on her foot.

"Apple? Perhaps you wouldn't mind joining us?" Sergeant Morse added.

Apple nodded and followed Max and the sergeant. Paula was right on their heels. Morse didn't seem to care one way or the other. "Mr. Wilde, I'd appreciate it if you'd see Ms. Breeze home tonight. She should be safe enough. The guy's already delivered his present for today."

Max nodded solemnly. "So there's no way to find out how these hornets got into the country?"

Sergeant Morse held up his empty hands. "I certainly wouldn't have a clue how to even begin, although I'm certainly open to any suggestions.'' He turned his squinty eyes on the security guard. ''You have any?''

A muscle twitched in Apple's jaw.

Paula turned to the security guard. ''What in the hell were you doing during all this, Apple? Didn't you see Breeze having trouble opening her desk drawer?''

''Well, yes, Ms. White.''

''Then why didn't you go in and help her with it?''

''I didn't think it was suspicious—''

Morse rested a fatherly hand on Paula's purple shoulder and another on Jim's bony one. ''Berating one another won't help. Being more alert is the ticket. If Ms. Breeze had been more alert, she would have immediately suspected the drawer had been tampered with and called for help, avoiding much of the resulting unpleasantness. Keep her alert and keep yourselves alert.''

Paula's bracelets jangled in nonverbal irritation.

Morse immediately seemed to pick up on it as he dropped his hands and squinted at the station manager. ''Ms. White, with four of these presents showing up in and around KALA, it does begin to make one wonder.''

Max could see Paula's back curl as though her fur was standing on end. ''Wonder what?'' she demanded.

''If Ms. Breeze's anonymous Santa Claus might be gaining entry through someone connected with this station. Now, if you'll excuse me, I'll be returning to my office.''

''What a preposterous idea that someone from this station would be helping a maniac,'' Paula spat, but Max noticed that she had waited until the sergeant was out of hearing range first.

Neal came scurrying up. ''Max, we need you and Belle on the set immediately.''

Max shook his head. ''Belle can't go on. Not after this.''

Neal's mustache twitched. ''But I just talked to her and she said she could.''

Max looked over to see Belle coming out of her office, carefully slipping her fingers into her gloves. She was still white and shaky, but there was a resolute look in her eyes that he was coming to know quite well.

"Good," Paula said. "Get her to makeup, Neal. And tell them not to skimp. Right now one of those squashed hornets looks like it has more life to it than our Ms. Clean Critic."

"BELLE? ARE YOU READY TO GO?"

She didn't look up at Max's call, just sat in her chair and stared at her hands in her lap. All things considered, she'd held up her end of their conflicting ratings on the movie so far. But just barely. With not a hint of a jab at him.

And after watching her sitting motionless for nearly fifteen minutes since returning to her office following the show, Max was becoming newly alarmed.

Quickly he circled around her desk. "What is it, Belle?"

As he moved closer, she gave a small shudder. "A couple of them stung me. It . . . hurts."

Max dropped to his knees beside her chair. Gently he gathered her hands in his and saw what her gloves had hidden on the set—two angry red welts, big as quarters, one on the back of her hand, one on her wrist.

"I'm allergic to hornet stings. Always have been."

Max looked at her face to see its grave expression, the fear behind the brave acceptance in her blue eyes. Her voice was barely a whisper. "It's not going to stop, is it? Whoever is doing this is going to keep writing these stanzas and sending me these presents. And soon he's coming—"

Anger and fear rose like a choking bile in Max's throat. He grabbed her arms, pulling her to her feet, deliberately stopping her from saying more. He couldn't bear to hear the words that were already going through his mind.

"No! We'll stop whoever is doing this, Belle."

"But how?"

Max took a deep breath, fighting his anger and frustration, looking around for something, anything, concrete to

do. "This damn office is too exposed. You don't even have
a door, just an open archway. Anyone can walk in here."

She took a deep breath. "I can't give it up. I really don't
have any other place to work."

"Well, then, we'll just have to fix this one, won't we?
Neal!" he called over his shoulder. "Would you step in here
please?"

Neal looked up from his conversation with Jim Apple just
outside Belle's office. He stepped through the open archway. "You need something, Max?"

"Yes. A door on this office with a good lock. Can you get
your set crew in tonight and have it fixed by tomorrow?"

Neal looked at his watch. "Not a prayer for tonight. But
I could probably have it done by noon tomorrow."

"Good."

Max turned back to Belle and firmly took her arm in his
with a tone that brooked no quarrel. "Come on. I'm going
to drive you home. And you might as well know right now
that I'm inviting myself in. Your review tonight was about
as exciting as warmed-over oatmeal. You're not going to
fold under this terror campaign, Belle. I'm not going to let
you."

"But what can you do?"

"What can I do? Just watch what I can do!"

MAX FOUND THE LIVING ROOM of Belle's Hollywood
apartment spare and functional. The muted tones of a large
painted toile hanging of young girls in the long dresses from
another century harmonized with the black-and-beige print
sofa and Louis XV chairs, all gracefully proportioned and
well-scaled to the dimensions of the large living room.

A classy, clean style. Reminiscent of times both gentler
and tougher; it fit her.

In the far corner, the deliberately quiet ambience was
challenged by a fragrant, real Christmas tree, eight feet high
and decorated with sparkling tinsel, strings of multicolored
lights, heavy-looking antique glass balls and a large, smil-

ing angel on the top. Beneath it sat two dozen different-size packages, all elegantly wrapped.

Max made himself comfortable on the print sofa. She paced uneasily. Despite his forceful insistence on why he had invited himself into her home, now that he was here he found himself delaying the pursuit of the business he professed he'd come to discuss.

Part of his delay stemmed from his desire to give her time to recuperate from this latest episode, and himself some time to think up a plan of action.

The other part came from the distraction he felt from being here, surrounded by the things she had chosen to be part of her life. They both answered questions and raised many more in his mind.

Max pointed to the presents underneath the tree. "Who are those for?"

She followed his pointing finger and the ghost of a smile set on her lips. "My family."

"You must have a big one."

"I do."

"Any here in L.A.?"

"No. All in Minnesota."

Belle moved over to put on the Christmas tree lights and some background music of the season in the CD player.

Nat King Cole sang the "Christmas Song." Her all-time favorite. She thought about her home in Chanhassen. Jack Frost nipping at her nose. Folks dressed up like Eskimos. Los Angeles had hit seventy-two degrees today. But it wasn't just the weather difference that made Minnesota seem so very far away.

"What's Minnesota like at this time of year?" Max asked, as though reading her mind.

She eased herself onto the couch cushions beside him. "A lot like that song. Freezing."

"And during the spring, summer and fall?"

"We only really have two seasons in Minnesota. Winter and mosquito."

He smiled. "But you miss it sometimes?"

"Sometimes. Christmastime. My whole family gets together every Christmas at my parents' home. My brothers, their wives and kids. Even my aunts and uncles and a slew of cousins. It's absolute bedlam."

"And you love it."

She smiled, wondering just how transparent her face had become. "Yes, I guess I do. Christmas wouldn't be Christmas unless I'm with the people I love. I'm flying back Christmas morning to be with them."

Max had no family to miss. He felt a small pang of envy. "You'll take all those presents with you?"

"The airline tells me that what I can't carry, they'll let me check. I'm sorry—I haven't offered you anything to drink because I don't have anything alcoholic. I do have coffee if you're interested."

"Fresh ground?"

"Freeze-dried."

Max made a face. "I guess I could choke down a cup."

She got up. "Milk? Sugar?"

"Sugar, never. But considering it's freeze-dried, yes, by all means drown it with milk. Or better yet, I'll come with you and do it myself."

He followed her into a kitchen with pale, natural wood cabinets, copper kettles hanging from hooks and light lemon appliances gleaming with polished care. It felt crisp and clean and sunny. He watched her scoop out the coffee into delicate Lennox china cups and then place each in turn under an instant hot water dispenser.

He shook his head. "You need a proper coffee grinder and bottled water. How can you put such swill into such beautiful china?"

She almost smiled at the horror in his tone. "Change your mind about having a cup?"

Max opened the refrigerator, reached in for the quart of milk and scowled in instant distaste. "Half a container of plain yogurt. A dented apple. Two scrawny leftover chicken legs. Wilted lettuce. The label on that freeze-dried coffee jar looks more tempting than the contents of this refrigerator."

"So you won't be inviting yourself to dinner, too, I take it?"

Max smiled internally at the light sarcasm in her rallying tone. He dumped some milk into his coffee and replaced the container in the refrigerator, slamming the door shut with mock emphasis. "Not if you begged. I'm calling out for Chinese. Where's the phone?"

"Behind you. The telephone directory is in the first drawer. But you won't find a place that delivers after five."

"I don't have to find one. I already know one."

Max dialed the number from memory and spoke with the proprietor of his favorite Chinese restaurant, happy to converse with his old friend. When he told him what he wanted and where he wanted it delivered, his friend readily agreed to have it on its way immediately.

When he hung up the phone, Max turned to see Belle staring at him, a startled look in her eyes. "Where did you learn to speak Chinese?"

"In China. Come on. Let's take our coffee back into the living room. Do you have a pen and some paper?"

She blinked, as though having a difficult time keeping up with the conversational changes. "Well, yes. In that same drawer with the telephone directory you just didn't use."

"Good. I'll get them. You carry the coffee. We are about to put our heads together, Belle. Get prepared to be brilliant."

An hour and a half later, Belle felt far less than brilliant, but she did feel one hell of a lot better with a hot meal of the best Chinese food she'd ever tasted in her tummy and sitting next to the most exciting man she'd ever met.

And one of the nicest, too. Although he'd probably run for the door if he knew she was thinking that about him. But she felt the concern behind the gentle verbal nudging he had kept her engaged in since he insisted on driving her home.

He was tugging her out of her fear by getting her to focus on other things. He was being a friend. In the real sense of that word. This strong, handsome, exciting man was being her friend.

And now he had insisted they get down to examining the specifics of this terror campaign against her—as though there really was something they could do about it. And with each passing moment Belle spent at his side, the hope rose in her heart.

"You really think there is some logic behind these notes and presents?"

He sent her one of his confident smiles. "I'm a great believer in there being a reason for everything—even if the reason is a warped one. Come on, Belle. Concentrate. There's got to be some connection in your past to this business."

Belle wondered if that could possibly be true. She reread their list yet again. "A vulture in a palm tree. Two bloodied gloves. Three poisoned pens. Four mynah birds. Five angry stings. I wish I could tell you that these things—any one of them—meant something to me or reminded me of someone, but I can't. They don't make any sense at all."

He shrugged those broad, resolute shoulders, undaunted. "Okay. We've still got the altered stanzas to work with."

"But even Sergeant Morse called them gibberish. And I've read each one and none of them brought anything to mind."

He pursed those sensuous lips as he stared at the sheet of paper in front of him as though willing it to cough up the answers. "Individually, perhaps not. But maybe we've been looking at them wrong."

"Wrong?"

"Yes. Let's cross out the part that deals with the 'Twelve Days of Christmas' song and the reference to the presents and just look at the personal messages that are contained in each note. Here goes. Ready?"

"Ready."

"The first one is 'I'm reviewing you now.' "

"Reviewing me? That is a curious wording, isn't it? Maybe it means that in the way I reviewed someone in the past and found fault with their performance, this Santa Claus is now reviewing me and finding fault with mine?"

"Good, Belle. I like it. Let's take the next one. 'You've blood on your hands.' "

"That was a reference to the bloody gloves."

"What if it wasn't? Forget the gloves for a minute. Free associate. What does 'you've blood on your hands' mean to you?"

"Well, I suppose being told you have blood on your hands generally means that you're being accused of injuring someone. So maybe this Santa Claus is accusing me of injuring someone's career with my review?"

"Another logical interpretation. Let's take the next one. 'The mighty can fall, too.' "

Belle leaned forward as she felt herself becoming more involved with the possibilities of this analysis. "Hm. If this Santa Claus really does think I've caused someone's career to fall, maybe this terror campaign is designed to scare me so badly that my professional performance also plummets?"

His black eyes flashed at her as a small smile lifted his lips. "You're on a roll. Now the next one. 'It's your curtain call.' "

Belle did feel as though she was finally beginning to glean some sense out of this madness. "A personal threat that he intends this terror campaign to end my career?"

"That would get my vote. Now the last one. 'This year it's my turn.' "

"This year? But that must mean..." Belle paused to wave her hands excitedly in the air. "Max, the review he's angry at—the one he thinks I've hurt someone with—is one I did last year!"

Max clasped her waving hands with his and brought them to his lips, brushing her fingertips with a feather-light kiss. Belle felt the warmth of his touch wrapping around her in excited swirls. Her heart began beating wildly in her chest.

"Now, let's take this stanza analysis further," he said as he released her hands.

Belle's thoughts had already taken her further. But not in the direction of their analysis.

Max's attention, however, seemed to be right back to business. "This Santa Claus of yours is pinpointing last year as the time when your unfavorable review occurred. Agreed?"

Belle rubbed her still-tingling hands over the quilted fabric of the couch. "If I'm interpreting the stanzas right."

"Don't start doubting your logic now. You were working at KALA last year at this time, isn't that right?"

"I'd just started."

"Then our next step is obvious. We've got to take a look at the reviews you did and see whose career could even remotely be considered hurt by them. Would the station have copies?"

Belle bounced off the couch excitedly. "I do. I set my VCR every night to record my spot. The tapes are in a hall closet. I'll get them."

She was back in less than a minute carrying three VCR tapes in her hand, holding one up. "I had applied for the opening with KALA along with four other hopefuls from other parts of the country. We all flew in to review a film, *Major Change,* as a kind of test. Our reviews were taped, and Paula picked mine out of the bunch. I was offered the job and my review went on the air."

"Paula picked it? Didn't Neal have a say?"

"Neal was in another department at KALA at the time. Advertising, I think. Paula was between program directors. She promoted him into the position a few weeks later."

Belle walked up to an unobtrusive Italian-Renaissance-style entertainment cabinet. She opened its doors to reveal

VCR and a twenty-five-inch-screen TV. She slipped the
first tape into the machine and picked up the remote con-
trols for both the VCR and the TV before returning to the
couch to retake her seat next to Max.

"You didn't review *Major Change,* did you?" she asked.

"No. Last year about this time I was at the Kahala Hil-
ton in Oahu on vacation. But I did see it later. I liked its
realism."

His smile and musky, masculine scent drifted to her, en-
folding her in a potent embrace. With an effort, she sum-
moned up an appropriately distasteful frown. "What a
surprise."

He chuckled at the sarcasm in her tone, then grew immediately quiet as she flipped on the TV and VCR and the
review flashed on the screen.

"And now we present our new entertainment portion of
the news hour, introducing our own very lovely and talented critic, Belle Breeze. Welcome, Belle."

Max watched her taped image on the screen, acutely
aware of her warmth and nearness beside him.

Watching her slice up the film's focus on the corruption
and death of the human spirit, Max could see why she had
been selected for the job at KALA. Disagree with her as he
might, the lady had a straightforward way of speaking her
mind that made it easy to believe she meant every word she
said. And honesty, he knew, had an immense appeal when
it could be caught like that on camera.

Or caught in person like he was doing now. He found her
rejection of "offensive" movie messages both rather naive
and brave. Her integrity was heartfelt, direct and amazingly attractive. He had the sudden impression that if he
looked long and hard enough into those clear eyes, he could
see through to her very soul.

Her attention focused on the empty tape holder in her lap.
"The movie, you may recall, didn't do well at the box office. I attach a list of credits from each movie I've reviewed
to the tape's folder. This is the one for *Major Change.*"

He took it from her hands, letting his knuckles lightly brush hers. "Remember anything special about these people?"

"The producer went on to do that woman's buddy movie that did so well this past summer. I gave her a good review on that one. The director and scriptwriter teamed up again and made a hit, too, despite my thumbs-down."

"Doesn't sound like any of their careers suffered from your unfavorable review. What about the actors?"

"Most of *Major Change*'s cast including the female lead, Trina Cork, were previous unknowns. I don't recall seeing them or hearing about them in anything since."

"We should try to track them down, Belle. See where they are now. Might be one of these young actors took hot exception to your cool review and has been simmering ever since, waiting to strike back."

"But I didn't single out the acting. On the contrary. I purposely kept my unfavorable comments directed at the distasteful storyline and the sadistic sex and violence."

"Still, if you give a movie a bad rating, it can't help but reflect on everyone associated with it."

"I suppose that's true," Belle agreed.

"Let's take a look at the next tape."

She got up to put it into the player, then returned to her seat. He was immediately distracted by the gentle sway of her hips, the curve of her calf as she tucked a foot beneath her, the unconscious way she had of throwing her thick hair over her shoulder when gravity rustled it across her cheek.

"Ready?" she asked.

He shifted his position on the couch, trying to ease a sudden uncomfortable constriction in his jeans and hoped she wouldn't notice just how ready he was. "Roll 'em."

She flipped the Play button.

This review proved to be a very articulate blast at a Russell Ramish Christmas horror film of the year before called *You'd Better Be Good*. Max heard Belle use the now-familar "brain dead" label for all those who could seriously be onsidering seeing the movie.

Belle's eyes rested on Max the moment the tape shut off. "I didn't notice it before but Ramish always seems to be roducing horror movies that have a vengeful theme."

"Yes, I think you're right. Both this one and *Pound of lesh* use revenge as their action impetus. I wonder if your nonymous Santa Claus purposely selected a symbol from *ound of Flesh* to send that message to you?"

"You mean a message that he was going to get back at me or some wrong I was suppose to have done him. Seek his wn revenge?"

"I think it's a possibility, Belle."

"Yes, I do, too. And maybe that makes Ramish a strong ontender for that Santa Claus role."

Max nodded. "Your review must have gotten to him, therwise he wouldn't have remembered your 'brain dead' omment. Also, there's something very staged about the way hese notes and packages have appeared. Do you sense hat?"

"Like they're part of a production? Yes. And who would now better about planning such a production than a di-ector?"

"Except we're both forgetting something. Ramish wasn't urt by your unfavorable review. *You'd Better Be Good* ent on to make a bundle."

"So it did. You think that takes the spotlight off of Ramish?"

"Well, let's just say it dims it a bit. Let's look at the last ape."

Belle inserted it and they settled back to watch.

Her final review was of a scary thriller written, produced nd directed by Justin Daark.

Hell Dwells Within was an extremely black story both vi-ually and messagewise. Because it was a Daark story, evil aturally triumphed. And because it was Belle reviewing it, Daark naturally ended up viscerally denounced.

Belle shook her head as soon as the review was over. "Can you imagine what it would be like to have to focus your mind on images like that every day and night for months on end in order to give cellulose substance to such grotesque nightmares?"

Max smiled. "You have to admit he does it well."

Belle snickered as she crossed her arms over her chest. "You would say that as though it was some grand achievement. At least I'm happy that particular piece of his mental garbage didn't do well at the box office and Daark lost his shirt on it."

"Not his shirt, Belle, but close enough. He lost his home in Beverly Hills that he put up as collateral against the future box office receipts."

Belle released her arms from around her chest and sat forward in interest. "He did? Then Daark was hurt by my review."

"I doubt your review had that deadly an impact. I think the film just proved a bit too murky even for his fans. He might have done better if he'd managed to release it just before Halloween instead of just before Christmas. Anyway, the flop of that film was what made him decide to get out of producing and directing and just stick to the screenwriting."

She leaned closer as her tongue darted over her lips. "If my review didn't have that big an impact, then he can't blame me for his trouble surrounding the film."

She was so close. Max clasped his hands behind his neck because he was afraid if he didn't, he might be too tempted to reach out for her. "Don't be so sure."

"But you just said—"

"Belle, one thing I've found in my years covering the Hollywood scene is that many of its talented people possess a common trait—a fragile ego that yearns for unconditional love."

"Unconditional love? You mean like the love a parent gives its child?"

"Early child-parent relationships are probably the closest expression of unconditional love we as human beings ever experience. That's what some of these people crave as adults, to be loved no matter what they do, only they want to be loved by everyone. They see becoming famous in the entertainment world as that kind of adoration."

Belle's brow furrowed as she considered Max's words. "Are you saying this unconditional love thing has something to do with Daark and an unfavorable review of his work?"

"Or Ramish, or any of them. An unfavorable review is a rejection—a distinct lack of that love these people crave. And that love is an addiction, Belle."

"But people like Daark and Ramish face rejection all the time simply because of the volatile and fickle nature of the entertainment business."

"Yes. But consider the nature of that rejection. If the public doesn't flock to their movie, they hurt, but it's hard to get mad at a faceless public. If the Academy Awards don't honor their work, again they hurt, but too many voting members exist to be the recipient of their focused disappointment. They really have only one target to focus on."

Belle was suddenly beginning to see what Max was driving at. All too clearly. "The critic who didn't like their work," she said.

"Yes," Max replied. "The critic. You. Ramish is still burning over your 'brain dead' comment, remember? And it's no secret that *Hell Dwells Within* had Daark's ego tied up in it much more so than anything else he's done before or since."

"So Ramish or Daark could be trying to get back at me."

"Or some actor in that *Major Change* movie. Most likely we can restrict this vengeful Santa Claus to that time period. Otherwise, we'd run out of ink and paper trying to list all the suspects."

Her eyes flashed at him. "And so we might. But if the lis contained a hundred thousand names, I would not change a word of any review I've given."

Max smiled as he watched his deliberate provocation re new the combatant sparkle in her eyes. He inhaled the smel of the perfume from her hair, her skin, from her. He leaned forward, letting the warmth of his breath rub against he cheek as he whispered her name. And then he scooped he into his arms and claimed her lips with his.

Belle acknowledged he'd given her warning. But after tha brief warning he struck like lightning, fast and sure and shocking in one scorching stroke. She felt his experienced mouth seducing her lips open as his hands branded her neck her back, her shoulders.

With a response that totally stunned her, she melted un der those heated demands. Her mind felt like an undone knot on the end of a balloon, all her thoughts whooshing into the air as she spun round and round in glorious sensa tions.

His taste! Only now did she realize how much she missed it, craved it. No other man could possibly taste this good. O feel this good. His hands—smooth, firm, confident, insis tent—slipped beneath her blouse, circled under her bra. Her breasts swelled with need, her nipples suddenly erect and aching beneath the focused attention of his deft, practice fingers.

She moaned in pleasure as her hands plunged inside hi vest, eager to feel the hot skin of his hard muscles stretch ing beneath her fingers. Her hands traveled up the corde strength of his neck, became lost in his thick, clean hair. A she had become lost in his scent, his touch, his taste, his feel As she never again wanted to be found.

Then suddenly a loud bang vibrated in her ears, an Max's strong hands pushed her away just as quickly as the had crushed her to him.

In less than a second they had both jumped to their fee stiff, alert, listening.

She heard only the laboring of his quick breaths. And hers.

"What did that sound like to you?"

The icy seriousness in his tone sliced a warning up her spine. "Maybe the stairwell door. It's just outside. The spring broke on it last week. Now anytime anyone goes through it, it slams."

"Who uses the stairs?"

"I do. But I thought everyone else on this floor used the elevator."

"Stay here. I'm going to check. Lock and bolt the door behind me. I'll call out to you when I return. Don't open the door until you know it's me. Got it?"

He was giving her orders. Belle surprised herself by not arguing with even one of them. In the blink of an eye, Max had silently let himself out of her apartment. She slid over to the door and slipped the bolt into place behind him.

And listened with her ear to the door. And waited.

Seconds crawled into minutes. Long, endless minutes.

She started when she heard something that sounded like scraping on the outside of the door. She raised her hand to release the bolt in anticipation of Max's return.

"Max?"

The scraping suddenly stopped.

Belle dropped her hand from the bolt, her muscles tensing in uneasiness. She peered through the peephole, but the previous tenant had so badly scratched the glass than it was virtually useless. She wished now she'd remembered to mention it needed replacing to the landlord.

"Max, is that you?"

She listened to the quiet on the other side of the door.

And then the scraping sound again.

Belle took a deep breath and let it out slowly. Tension burned between her shoulder blades. The dinner she had enjoyed so much a mere hour ago now hung like lead in her stomach.

She tried to take another deep breath but felt a constriction around her lungs, preventing them from filling. She listened intently, her ear plastered to the door. Sweat rolled down her back, collected in the creases of her palms and her underarms. She swallowed into a dry throat.

And then she heard that scraping sound again. But this time, something else, too. An eerie, breathless laugh.

Chapter Eight

The sweat froze on Belle's back as the tension sliced icy and rigid through her muscles. Her heart pounded in her ears.

Unbidden images flooded her mind. She saw a dim Santa Claus waiting on the other side of the door, the belt buckle of his outfit scraping against the wood as he rocked back and forth, laughing through an evil smile.

Belle shook her head, trying to shake away the awful images. Her eyes locked on the doorknob as though she expected to see it turn any second and that awful image walk in.

Reason fought to resurface in her brain. She told herself the door was locked and bolted. She told herself she was safe as long as she stayed behind it. She told herself Max would be back soon.

But she couldn't quite believe any of it.

An eternity passed.

A numbness replaced the rigidity of her muscles. Her legs ached. Her body slumped against the door.

"Belle?"

She nearly jumped out of her skin at hearing her whispered name coming from the other side of her door. She stiffened, pulled away from it, her heart racing like a thoroughbred.

Her throat felt so dry, she barely managed a choked hopeful reply. "Max?"

"Yes, Belle. It's Max. Everything's okay. You can open up."

She gulped as a wash of relief left her shaky and weak. With clumsy, fumbling fingers she released the security bolt and opened the door.

As soon as Max saw the look on her face, he secured the door behind him and gathered her into his arms. He rested her cheek against his chest and gently stroked her hair. "Belle, it's all right. It was just a visitor to one of your neighbors down the hall who got impatient with the elevator and decided to use the stairs. I caught up with him in the parking garage. Nice old guy about seventy. Driving this vintage Porsche I'd give my eyeteeth for. He let me have a look at the engine. Spotless."

Belle couldn't believe her ears. Her protest squeaked out. "You've been gone all this time because you've been looking at some nice old guy's vintage Porsche in the parking garage?"

Max lifted his chin off the top of her head and leaned back to look in her eyes. "What is it, Belle? What happened?"

She sucked in a shaky breath, angry to find herself so close to tears. "I heard a scraping sound at the door. And something that sounded like an awful laugh. I called out. No one answered."

"When did you hear the sounds?"

"I'm not sure. A few minutes after you left. I'm not even sure how long you've been gone."

His brow furrowed. "Five minutes. I didn't make any scraping sounds. And I didn't laugh. Are you sure about what you heard?"

She licked dry lips. Was she? Now that she was safe in Max's arms, her earlier fears seemed so hazy and far away. Had her overwrought senses imagined everything?

"Max, I honestly don't know now. I was straining so hard to hear something, maybe what I really heard were sounds coming from inside the apartment across the hall. I can't be sure.''

He leaned down and kissed the top of her head, slowly, softly. His hands stroked her back, then her arms, pressing gently against the taut muscles, easing and relaxing them with a warm firmness.

Belle sighed and leaned against him, feeling the tension being taken from her with each long, luxuriant stroke. Ah, he had a magic touch! And he knew just where to touch, too. Her head rolled back against his arm. He drew her more firmly to him.

His scent was clean and all male. His mouth scattered warm kisses across her chin, then grazed leisurely up to her lips.

Shimmers of incredible sensation streamed through Belle. Every movement he made seemed to be in such absolutely slow motion.

His tongue circled around her mouth, engaging and inviting. Belle felt her body responding to the provocative, deliberate slowness with a heightened and tingling sensuality. Slowly, deeply, his mouth took hers as though this kiss alone was to be the ultimate fulfillment.

And it *was* fulfilling, as Belle had never before knew such fulfillment from a kiss. It suffused her from head to toe with a glowing passion. And then like a wave that had flooded a beach only to retreat, it suddenly left an enormous throbbing emptiness and ache in its wake.

He'd done it so expertly, she was aroused before she had a chance even to entertain a thought of resistance. And he was still moving slowly, in perfect control and command of this simmering seduction.

He whispered her name as his breath caressed her neck and then her ear as his teeth scraped against her earlobe. His hands inched down her spine, his fingers pressing her ever so gently against his body in lazy, wide, circular undulations.

His chest lightly brushed her nipples. They responded eagerly, straining against the bonds of her bra. His muscled thigh grazed hers. Hot, wet need coiled between her legs. She sucked in a desperate breath.

At this moment she wanted this man more than she had ever wanted anything.

Yes, she had had a few relationships before. With nice, sane, attractive men. Who made nice, sane, attractive love to her. But none of them had made her feel like this. No, nothing like this.

This taunting taste told her that making love with Max Wilde would be all-claiming fire and passion—the kind that would singe her very soul.

If she had ever doubted that, she certainly didn't doubt it now. But if she gave her body to him, he'd be getting her heart along with it. And this man did not know what to do with a woman's heart.

An ancient, primitive fear, one only a feminine heart could understand, had her denying her physical desires, moving back, out of his arms.

"I'm . . . still shaky. Tired," she lied, not looking him in the eyes.

He didn't press, but let his hands rest gently on her shoulders. She stared at the baseboard at the edge of the carpet. Damn him. He didn't even seem to be breathing hard.

He leaned over and kissed her lightly on the temple. "I'm not surprised. Your nerves are probably as raw as red meat. You need to get some rest. The screening for tomorrow night's spot is in the early afternoon. Sleep in. I'll pick you up here late morning."

She turned with him to the door. He put his hand on the knob, but then turned to stare at her for what seemed like a very long moment. "Don't open your door to anyone in the interim."

She raised her eyes to his. "You think he knows where I live?"

"Even if he does, you're in a secured building, so he's not going to have an easy time getting to you here. Still, don't take any chances."

She sighed. "It's not knowing what he plans next that I think is the worst. If I just knew who and what I was up against, it would be so much easier to face."

When he spoke again, a fierceness sparkled in his black eyes. "We're going to fight this creep, Belle. I told you I wouldn't let you give in to this terror campaign, and damn it, I won't."

He scooped her up into his arms then in a hard embrace, crushing her to him. Gone was the smooth, experienced seducer. This kiss was blunt and bruising and thrilled Belle to the bone.

And then just as suddenly as he had grabbed her, he released her and was out the door, closing it carefully behind him.

Belle threw the security bolt into place and stared at that closed door a long time. Exciting, dangerous, out-of-control feelings coursed through her, putting a sheen of perspiration on her skin.

And a spear of new terror through her heart.

If he had even suggested staying after that last embrace and kiss, she'd be in bed with him now. Heaven help her. She never knew she could lose herself so completely or so quickly in a man's arms before. Have her body burn like this. Want like this. Ache like this. Her hands shook as she leaned her back against the door and closed her eyes.

And at that moment she didn't know what danger was greatest. The one from her sadistic Santa Claus or the one from Max Wilde.

"MAX, THIS ISN'T THE WAY to KALA. If I'm going to get this review written and ready for tonight, I've got to get to my office and get at it."

"This won't take long, Belle."

"Where are we going?"

"To the offices of the Screen Actors' Guild. My friend Chris works there. Maybe their records can help us."

"I see. You think your friend can help track down those actors and actresses from *Major Change*. But this is Saturday. Aren't the offices closed?"

"Don't worry. I called first."

Max stole a look at her, just as he had been stealing looks at her all morning long. She was so incredibly sexy and desirable.

It had taken every ounce of his control to leave her the night before. She'd been heaven in his arms, as responsive as any dream.

But she was a woman terrorized, and there were rules about taking advantage—and Max Wilde had never violated those rules.

And there had been fear in her eyes when she'd pulled back. Just as there was a palpable tension about her now, as though she was a doe skirting the edge of the meadow, ready to run at the first sign of danger.

He turned his eyes away, angry and frustrated to see her fear, wishing there was something he could do about it as he concentrated on the traffic before him.

He knew he could easily strangle the sick bastard who was putting her through this terror. What's more, he wanted to. With his bare hands. He'd twist his neck until—

"Max, didn't we just pass the building that houses the Screen Actors' Guild?"

Tardily, Max came to attention and swung the wheel of the Porsche toward the right lane. "I'm going to circle the block to see if I can find a parking space on the street."

He wondered if she knew the idea of parking on the street had just come to him.

WHEN BELLE WAS INTRODUCED to Max's friend, Chris, she did a double take. The name had conjured up a Christopher, but Chris proved to be short for Christine, a buxom and beautiful redhead with flashing teeth and a terrific tan.

The instant Belle saw Chris greet Max by kissing his cheek, Belle knew that Chris and Max knew each other intimately.

Belle felt the jab of that knowledge pass through her heart. And then she saw Max's cool response, and she understood that whatever had existed between Chris and Max was in the past. At least for Max. She wasn't so sure about Chris.

She clasped Chris's hand and gave it a warm shake, already feeling a bond with her. She got a warm shake in return.

"It's good to meet you, Belle. I admire a woman who speaks her mind. Too few of us around. Sit down. Sit down. It seems like everywhere I go these days I'm hearing about Max Wilde and Belle Breeze. Maybe now I'll find out the real scoop?"

Chris had left a question at the end of her sentence that Max acknowledged with a polite smile and then promptly ignored. "We need your help, Chris. Belle's become the target of some crazy creep's sick little game."

"This is about that twisted 'Twelve Days of Christmas' business?"

Belle felt a small surprise at Chris's immediate understanding, but then reminded herself that by now everybody in Hollywood must have heard and be buzzing with rumor.

Max seemed prepared for his friend's knowledge and didn't so much as raise an eyebrow. "Belle's received five warped stanzas and presents over the last five days. We think maybe the person who's sending them to her could be associated with a movie she reviewed last year called *Major Change*. Remember it?"

"Vividly."

"You do? Now, that surprises me, Chris. Why? It wasn't exactly a box office sensation."

"No, but every one of its young actors and actresses were picked from off the street, without so much as a minute of previous acting experience. I'll never forget the day the whole cast came marching through my door waving applications for Guild membership when they found out they got the parts."

"Why did the casting director select unknowns?"

"He was on this realism kick. Wanted real college students to play college students. Didn't want them to have acting experience. Didn't want them to act like anyone but who they were. Even the lead was a local girl—a freshman out of some private girls' college, I think. Can't remember her name offhand."

"Trina Cork," Belle supplied.

"Yes, that was it. Nice kid. Unspoiled. Real excited about the part. They all got a bit starstruck, if you know what I mean. Being pulled out of anonymity like that and thrust into a major motion picture raised their expectations into outer space."

"Do you know how they reacted when the picture flopped?"

"I can imagine those falling expectations landed with all the noisy dramatics of youth."

"Do you know what happened to them specifically?"

Chris shrugged her soft, round shoulders. "Not offhand."

"Can you help us try to locate them?"

"I can pull out the paperwork of their Guild membership and check addresses and telephone numbers if that will help. But you aren't really serious about one of those kids being behind this psycho business, are you?"

"Belle's life could very well be at stake here, Chris. I intend to take every possibility seriously."

Chris's large brown eyes seemed to open in some surprise as she looked from Max to Belle. She treated Belle to a look that Belle could have sworn was envious. "Oh. I see."

BELLE CLUTCHED the telephone receiver to her ear in some frustration. "But Sergeant Morse, don't you think the messages in the notes sound as if someone is angry at me for a review I did last year?"

"I admit you and Mr. Wilde have given me something new to think about, Ms. Breeze. But even if those messages mean what you think, it doesn't necessarily follow that someone involved in the movies you reviewed is behind this stunt."

"But two of those movies involve Russell Ramish and Justin Daark. Don't you think it a bit too coincidental that they are also the principals in *Pound of Flesh,* whose billboard is that vulture in a palm tree?"

"Yes, that is a tie-in, I agree. But I've talked to Ramish and Daark, Ms. Breeze. They were both cooperative. They're successful men doing well in a fickle business. My experience still leads me to believe that your Santa Claus is more likely to be a crazed viewer or possibly a fan of those movies."

"But someone like that could be—anyone!"

"Yes, I understand how frustrating and frightening that thought must be. I'm sure you'd much rather have a list of identifiable suspects who could be cornered and questioned. But I have to be honest with you, Ms. Breeze. I very much doubt that's going to happen."

"Won't you even look into the possibility that this person is connected with those three films I told you about?"

Sergeant Morse exhaled wearily in her ear. "Yes, I've made a note of them and I will look into it. But please don't get your hopes up. Now, I'll be there tonight as agreed. Wait for me. Stay with someone at all times until then and remain on your guard."

Belle hung up from her conversation with Sergeant Morse and leaned back dejectedly in her office chair. Damn. And she had felt so good after she and Max had uncovered all those potential clues hidden in those stanzas the night before. Except, were they really valid clues? Or had she just been engaging in wishful thinking?

"Here are the keys to your new office door, Belle," Neal said as he walked up to her desk and held them in his hand.

"Now, don't lose them, because not even Apple or Paula or I have a duplicate."

Belle leaned across the desk and clutched the keys in her hand. "I won't lose them. You really worked fast to get this door and lock installed so quickly. I appreciate it."

Neal's mustache twitched as his hands foraged nervously into his pockets. "Well...uh...I suppose it's the least I could do. After those hornets yesterday..."

Belle shrugged away a shiver as she relived that moment when she saw those awful hornets flying out at her from the drawer. And then she remembered the steady, reassuring feel of Max's hands as they held hers. She glanced over at his office on the other side of the newsroom.

His dark head was bent over his computer screen, no doubt feverishly working on a glowing tribute to the absolutely terrible movie they had screened earlier, bless his warped little brain cells.

She smiled. He'd driven and bossed her around all day, but she'd ended up with the last word. She would be driving herself home from the station and to the premiere they were both attending that evening.

He didn't like it. He made it obvious he didn't want her out of his sight for a minute. But logic had won out. He couldn't wait around her apartment while she got ready and still have time to drive to his town house in Pasadena, get ready and make it to the premiere.

Besides, Sergeant Morse had agreed to follow her home and wait while she dressed, then to follow her to the premiere. She was going to be perfectly safe.

Not that Max had accepted defeat gracefully. He still had growled and acted just like a bossy, put-out male. And every growl had made her feel very special and cared for.

"Belle?"

"What?"

"You haven't been listening to me."

"No, I haven't. Sorry, Neal, my mind wandered. What were you saying?"

"I said that Apple will still continue as your bodyguard here at the station today, but tomorrow, Sunday, he's got to have off. Union rules."

"That's not a problem. I don't plan on coming into the station tomorrow."

"Good. Now, we've adjusted his shift to correspond to the hours you gave him. If you deviate from them, Belle, try to give him at least twenty-four hours' notice. Okay?"

"Okay."

"Okay, Apple?"

Jim Apple's brown mane nodded.

Neal turned back to Belle. "Naturally when you're away from your office, he'll be also. Lock your door behind you when you leave and no one will be able to get in."

Belle took a deep breath and let it out in relief. She looked around at the small space, feeling for the first time in days that its sanctity had been returned to her.

Her eyes returned to the program director. "Thank you, Neal. Very much."

Neal's mousy little hands flicked nervously. "Just promise me that you'll be careful and won't forget to lock up. I don't want you scared by any more of this craziness."

Belle felt touched by the message in Neal's words. She swallowed a small, sudden lump in her throat as she sent him a smile. "I promise."

"Good. If anything happens to break up this successful new critic's spot, Paula will have my head. See you on the set in five minutes."

And with that Neal scurried off.

Belle almost laughed as she realized she had misread the program director's concern. After a year in Hollywood, she should have known. The show was everything. Individual players were merely necessary props.

"Ms. Breeze?"

She turned at the security guard's address, having almost forgotten he was still standing at the new door. "Yes, Jim?"

"Your hands . . . those welts . . . the hornets did that?"

Belle took a deep breath as she looked down at the now-golf-ball-size swellings on both hands. "Yes. Good thing I have an extra-large pair of gloves for my spot tonight. Makeup couldn't hide these knobs."

"They look like they hurt."

Actually they hurt like hell. But Belle liked to think she could keep a stiff upper Minnesota lip when necessary. "A bit." She looked over at the resulting frown on his horsey face. "It's okay, Jim. I'll survive."

"But if the hornets had gotten to your face, your eyes..."

Belle swallowed. Jim's concern was gratifying, but she could have done without these images. "They didn't. It's past. Come on. I need to get on the set."

Belle picked up her gloves and purse off her desktop and exited her office, pausing to close her new door behind her. She felt good turning the key in the knob and hearing the lock fall securely into place. Good and safe.

"So, Max, don't tell me you're attending this gala premiere by yourself?" Luana Halsey bellowed as she lumbered up to him with a glass of champagne in her hand and a gleam in her eye.

Max turned to the hefty woman, looking all the more tanklike tonight in a green sequined dress that fell from her square shoulders to her toes in an uninterrupted line.

"Reviews are a business occasion to me, Luana. Not a social one."

The agent waved her hand in dismissal. "Everything in Hollywood is business. Doesn't mean you can't inject a little socializing in, too. Which reminds me. I have someone with me who wants to meet you."

She turned and let her eyes survey the crowd through the potted palms lining the lobby of the old Egyptian Theater, still sporting its ornate decor despite the fact that United Artists had converted it into a triple-screen facility for first-run movies several years before.

Luana beckoned to a tall, slender, bearded twenty-year-old whose clumps of wavy blond hair stuck out in front of his ears. He lumbered up to Luana's side like the disjointed, long-nosed Afghan he resembled.

"Max, this is Terry Stut," Luana announced as though she were particularly proud of her pedigree puppy. "Terry, meet Max Wilde, the critic you're always raving about."

"Real pleasure," Terry said, holding out his hand.

Max returned Terry Stut's hearty shake. Although he was sure he had never met Stut before, Max knew something was familiar about him.

"Are you in the busi—" Max began.

"New leading man, Luana?" Paula White interrupted Max's question as she walked up, all decked out in her traditional purple; tonight's ensemble was low-cut and very tight.

Luana coughed nervously as she made the introductions. Max was a bit surprised. He didn't think the indomitable agent had a weak spot. Seemed as if he was wrong. And he wasn't the only one who immediately picked up on Luana's uneasiness.

Paula positively purred as she clasped Terry Stut's hand. "I'm so glad to see you don't go in for those tanned, muscle-bound, beach-bum types, Luana. Why, Terry here looks so personable and pleasant, just like someone you could pick up in the average college dorm."

Max watched the age-difference dagger find its mark in Luana's eyes. He saw a flare-up of hot anger. Then her expression amazingly cooled as Luana caught sight of something over Paula's shoulder.

Luana circled her arm possessively through Terry's and brought him to her side, like a mother protecting her offspring. "I've never appreciated the hairy, old, fat types, either, Paula. You know the ones whose brains and bellies are just full of beer?"

"Oh, here you are, Paula," Russell Ramish bellowed on cue as he strode up, his belly too big to allow the jacket of his tux to be buttoned. From the way he was swaying, the bottle of beer in his hand was obviously not his first of the evening.

He smacked a wet, sloppy kiss against her cheek. "Sorry, babe, but I had to go out and get my own brew from the car. Can't even get a real belch out of champagne."

Paula stiffened, knowing full well who Luana had just described. She grabbed Ramish's arm, her voice more like a growl now than a purr. "Come on, Russell. Let's find our seats."

Max shifted to avoid Ramish's spilling beer as Paula jerked him away.

Luana chuckled. "A perfect pair."

Max looked past Luana's not very nice smile to catch sight of Belle just entering the lobby, a high-collared, floor-length gold lamé dress hugging her tall, statuesque form to perfection. Her hair was piled high on her head in thick golden sweeps. She looked regal, exquisite. She took his breath away.

With that unerring antenna she seemed to possess, her eyes swung almost immediately to his across that crowded lobby. And held for the space of a heartbeat.

Something passed between them then that Max couldn't describe. All he knew was suddenly he felt a pull in his chest so strong that it knocked the breath out of him.

And then she looked away, and the moment was gone and he sucked in air, wondering if he hadn't just imagined it. A producer who Max knew Belle respected had called her and strolled up for a chat. Several other people then began to crowd around her.

"She draws attention, that's for sure," Luana said from beside him, her arm still curled possessively inside her young date's.

"Too much," Max said meaningfully.

"She get any more gifts lately?" Luana asked.

Max glanced back at the agent. "One a day since Monday. You've got any ideas about them, Luana?"

Before Luana could respond, Terry Stut surprised Max by offering a comment. "Someone obviously is trying to get back at her for what she said about their movie."

Max turned to Terry, his interest piqued. "You know about all this?"

"Luana mentioned it."

"Why do you think it's someone in the business who's harassing her?"

Terry's thin neck straightened nervously, as though his collar had suddenly gotten too tight. "Well, makes sense doesn't it? She's a critic. She gives bad reviews. Someone didn't like their bad review."

Luana gave Terry's arm a definite tug. "Shall we go in now? Looks like most everyone is heading for their seats."

Max watched Luana and Terry stroll off, uncomfortable with two things. One, why did Terry Stut seem so sure Belle's tormentor was someone in the business? And two, where had Max seen him before?

Max's thoughts and eyes returned to Belle. She was chatting with several people as she angled down the theater's aisle. He was just about to move forward to join her when suddenly from out of the corner of his eye, Max spied Justin Daark behind a potted palm, less than five feet away from Belle.

Daark stood alone, drinking a glass of champagne. And staring intently at Belle. Very intently. Something that looked almost like a smile played at the corners of his mouth. Max got an uneasy feeling in his gut.

"ARE YOU STILL HOPING to see something wonderful?" Max asked, a gentle nudging in his tone Belle had come to recognize.

Even before he spoke, Belle knew Max had moved beside her as she followed the crowd to their seats. From the moment she'd entered the Egyptian Theater that night, his presence had reached out to her like a caress, even from the other side of the room.

He looked so absolutely sensational in that black tuxedo. And when their eyes had met earlier, she could feel his approval as he took in her dress and hair.

Every fiber of her being vibrated with awareness of him. She let out a sigh as she reached for a rallying tone. "Better to expect something wonderful than awful. What attitude do you assume when you're about to see a movie?"

"I work to make my mind a blank."

"You have to work at it?"

He chuckled, deep and warm and familiar.

They settled back in their adjoining seats and the movie began. But over the first few minutes, Belle had to keep yanking her attention away from the man beside her in order to concentrate on the screen.

Fortunately, the movie proved good enough to finally claim her interest. It was a heartwarming tale of a lonely little girl whose life started taking some quite unexpected and delightful turns when she received a rambunctious piglet for Christmas. Belle laughed and cried and enjoyed every minute, sorry to see it end. But as the credits began to roll up the screen and she looked over at Max, he had already sprung to his feet and was standing over her.

"Finally it's over. What a boring piece of mush. Come on. I'll walk you to your car and see you home."

Belle took a deep breath and tried to fight down her irritation. What had ever possessed her to think she wanted this man? Their tastes were universes apart. Was this some kind of temporary insanity she was going through?

And then she put her hand into his offered one and felt the heat flow through her like fire. She let out a long soundless sigh.

"You're disappointed, Belle. What's up?"

His question surprised her, both because she didn't realize he could read her so well and also because his tone didn't have its normal kidding edge. "I guess I wonder sometimes how we can both be from the same species."

He smiled one of his devastatingly handsome smiles as a mischievous gleam entered his black eyes. "The biological proof of the same species is the ability to mate. I'm ready and willing to offer my services."

She tried not to smile but it was already too late. They jostled through the crowds to make their way outside.

Max kept close to her side. "Don't tell me you're really surprised because I didn't like the movie?"

"No, not really," Belle admitted as she walked out into the cool evening, stepping away from the leisurely moving crowd and heading at a brisk pace for the parking lot where she had left her car. "I wonder what would happen to our point-counterpoint spot if we ever did agree?"

He grinned beside her. "I don't think you should worry. The chances for that range from zero to zilch. You headed for the smaller parking lot around the corner?"

"Yes. Sergeant Morse thought it was better lit. He directed me to park underneath the brightest lamp on the lot because he said thieves and such generally will shy away from a well-lighted area."

"I agree. That's why I parked my car in that lot, too. Did you happen to mention any of our conclusions to Morse when you talked with him today?"

"Briefly. He didn't seem too enthused, although he said he'd do some checking. He's still convinced it's some crazed viewer. He all but told me we'd been wasting our time."

Max stopped and put a restraining hand on Belle's arm. Gently he turned her toward him. "Belle, you don't think we're wasting our time, do you?"

Belle bit her lip, trying to hold in her frustration and very much afraid she was doing a rotten job of it. "Oh, Max, I felt so sure we were really on to something last night. But maybe that's because I just wanted to believe there was some logic in all this."

He raised his hand to her shoulder. "There is logic in this, Belle. I'm convinced the personal messages in those stanzas are the clue. Someone associated with one of those three reviews you did last year at KALA is behind this insanity directed at you. You believe it, too, don't you?"

Looking into that concerned, handsome face and feeling the confidence in his words and the warmth in his hand, Belle knew she wanted to believe anything and everything this man told her.

She sighed. "Yes, Max. I believe it, too."

He gave her shoulder a gentle shake. "That's the spirit. Look, I've got a few friends who owe me favors. I called them this afternoon and I'm going to meet with them tomorrow morning to see what I can do about putting round-the-clock surveillance on Ramish and Daark. We're going to get to the bottom of this business, Belle. Now, come on. Let's get you home."

Max undid the restraining button of his tuxedo jacket with one hand as he draped his other casually over her shoulder and steered her in the direction of the parking lot.

Belle felt the warmth of his arm and his confidence seep through her as she resumed her pace. A weight she didn't even realize she'd been carrying seemed to lift from her shoulders.

His voice was deep, assured. "Getting Ramish and Daark under close scrutiny is just the first step. Chris hasn't gotten back to me yet, but when she does—"

Max was interrupted by the sudden blast of an unusually loud car alarm. His head shot up as he quickly scanned the parking lot. Belle felt him stiffen. "Damn, sounds like someone's trying to steal my Speedster. Quick, Belle. Get your keys out."

Obediently, Belle dug into her purse and pulled out her keys. She'd barely gotten them into her hand when she felt Max grab her arm and begin hurrying her toward her Saturn parked under the bright parking lamp at the close end of the lot.

The second they reached her vehicle, Max grabbed the keys from her hand, unlocked the driver's door, shoved her side, threw the keys in her lap, and locked and slammed the door shut.

"Stay put until I get back," he yelled over the sound of the blasting car alarm before sprinting off to the other end of the lot.

Belle twisted in the driver's seat to stare at his rapidly receating form. Both the loud car alarm and the sprinting man had caught the attention of the small number of attendees to the premiere who had also chosen to park their vehicles in this smaller, out-of-the-way lot. They turned as one and headed for the action unfolding on the other end of the lot.

Leaving Belle alone in her locked vehicle.

Belle twisted and twisted, trying to get a better look, but Max had quickly disappeared into the far recesses of the lot and she could no longer see anything, although she could still hear the loud alarm blasting steadily.

Her attention was focused out the back of the window. Her thoughts followed Max and the plight of his Porsche.

When the first blow landed on the Saturn's windshield, Belle swung toward it, taken totally by surprise.

And immediately stared into the face of terror.

There he was—her Santa Claus, grinning at her from behind a fake white beard and wig—a hideous, fiendish form multiplied a hundred times through the tiny cracked pieces of safety glass that had seconds before been her windshield.

Belle's heart froze. The blood in her veins solidified into ice. Horror, primitive and raw, ripped the fierce scream from her throat.

The Santa's mouth opened in a monstrous, soundless laugh, a grotesque light glittering off the perspiration on its brow, as it swung the crowbar again, a thunderous, savage blow that caved in the window completely, burying Belle beneath it.

Belle threw her arms over her head, instinctively trying to protect herself. Another thunderous blow cracked the driver's window, its force rocking her seat. Then another and another in rapid succession as the monstrous demon viciously pounded at her car.

Belle screamed and screamed and screamed until she was deaf from the sounds of her own terror.

Chapter Nine

Sergeant Morse's boots crunched with the sound of broken glass as he rejoined Max where he stood surveying the damage to Belle's beige Saturn.

Spiderwebbed sheets of broken glass, glistening under the parking lot lights, surrounded the car, giving the immediate impression that it had been showered in sheets of ice. Except, of course, it wasn't ice.

Every single one of the six windows of her SL2 had been smashed, the shattered glass strewn over its hood, its bumper, inside on the seats, all around the pavement.

Morse shook his head as he exhaled heavily. "It's a wonder she only suffered a few cuts."

Max instantly turned his head to where the paramedics attended to Belle's injuries a few feet away. She sat on the back of the paramedics open unit, her knees together, her expression blank, her face ghostly beneath the blue-and-red flashing lights. They had cut the long sleeves of her beautiful gold dress in order to check her arms for injury.

Her arms were so white it was hard to tell where the bandages began and ended.

Pain more acute than Max had ever felt shot through his chest. He'd let her down.

He couldn't look at her anymore; he couldn't let himself feel this way anymore.

Resolutely he swung back to Morse, shoving away the unfamiliar emotions and replacing them with a much more familiar one. His words came out clipped and short. "You found another envelope, didn't you?"

Morse nodded as he slipped it out of his suit coat pocket. "On the floor in front of the passenger seat. He must have thrown it into the car after he smashed the windows. Here, you might as well read it."

Max took the sheet of paper out of the envelope and opened it.

On the sixth day of Christmas, Santa Claus gave to Breeze
Six windows a-smashing.

> Here's my smash hit,
> Santa Claus

Fire burned in Max's gut.

"Too bad Ms. Breeze didn't get a better look at this Santa Claus of hers. If she could have even told me it was definitely a man or a woman it would have helped."

Max shoved the stanza back into its envelope and flipped it back at the sergeant. "She was a bit occupied at the time trying to protect herself, if you'll recall."

"Hey, easy, Wilde. I wasn't finding fault. I was just hoping for a break. We're on the same side, remember?"

Max took a couple of deep breaths and let them out again. He wasn't used to anger getting the better of him. He'd always been known for keeping cool under fire. He'd have to regain that cool, and quick. Losing it wasn't going to help Belle.

"Sorry, Morse. I'm a bit . . . edgy. The guy played me for a fool. He deliberately tripped that alarm on my car to get me out of the way and distract everyone else's attention so he could get her alone. I didn't even hear the glass smashing or her screams over that damn alarm."

"Unfortunately, I've found some of the most unbalanced minds are also some of the cleverest."

"If he knew about me, he's got to be watching her, Morse. Every minute."

"I have that feeling, too. I've talked to the lieutenant. Unfortunately, manpower-wise, we're hurting. I can't get an officer released to stay with her on any shift. But I will have the patrol car assigned to her neighborhood make extra sweeps of the street where she lives. And the one around the KALA station."

"That's all?"

Morse rubbed his face as though trying to wipe away a layer of weariness. "Wilde, the force is in a budget-crunch nightmare. I've got thirty other open cases on my desk and no help. I should be off duty in fifteen minutes, but I'll probably be stuck here most of the night while the crime scene investigators do their thing. When I followed Ms. Breeze home from the studio last night and again tonight and to the premiere, it was all on my own time."

"So what are you saying, Morse? It's hopeless? That there's no way to identify this guy and stop him? That Belle's supposed to just wait until he—"

Max stopped himself. He wasn't going to give sound to the words revolving inside his head. He turned away from Morse and stamped over to where Belle sat.

She looked up at his approach, a pale woman with mussed honey hair, deep saucer-blue eyes and lips that trembled. A frightened woman. A stranger.

"There, all done," the cherub-cheeked paramedic announced in so cheerful a tone Max nearly slugged him. "Do you have transportation home, Ms. Breeze?"

Max reached down to claim her cold hand, capturing it within the warmth of his. "I'm taking her home."

BELLE DIDN'T REMEMBER much of the ride home. It just seemed as if suddenly she and Max were exiting the elevator and he was getting the keys out of her purse and letting them inside her apartment.

He led her to the couch and motioned her down. He left only to come back moments later with a steaming cup of hot milk. She took it into her hands. Sipped it. She didn't know if it had any taste. The world inside and out was a cold, swirling fog. Her thoughts, her feelings—nonexistent.

He took the empty cup out of her hands. Set it on the coffee table. And then she felt his arms closing around her, warm strong arms that drew her back to rest against his chest.

Gradually, his warmth seeped into her, and with it, the cold numbness began to recede. One by one, her senses re-awakened.

First she shook—deep, violent quakes. And then she cried—soft, silent tears. And all the while he held her—held her as though he never intended to let her go.

And finally, after a long while, she stopped crying and fell peacefully and dreamlessly asleep in his arms.

BELLE WOKE to an insistent ringing. Sunlight streamed into her bedroom window. She stretched and yawned and read Sunday 11:00 A.M. flashing on her nightstand clock. She reached for the telephone.

But it wasn't the telephone that was ringing. It was her doorbell.

Belle swung her legs over the side of the bed. Something was poking her uncomfortably in the back. When she realized it was the hook to her bra and that she had been sleeping in her slip and bra and panties, confusion swarmed over her. Then she noticed the bandages on her arms, and her eyes glanced over at the chair to her dressing table and she saw the remnants of her gold lamé dress.

Memory flooded back in rushing waves. The premiere. Walking toward the parking lot with Max. The loud car alarm. The dreadful blows that smashed her windows. That awful face of her maniac Santa Claus looking down at her through the cracked glass.

Max had brought her home. Max had held her. She had fallen asleep in his arms. He must have removed her dress and put her to bed. Her second bed pillow had not been mussed. Nor had the sheets on the other side of her queen-size bed.

So he'd slept on the couch? A small smile circled her lips. Had he gone for food after discovering her cupboard was bare? Was that him at the door now, arms full of coffee and sweet rolls?

The doorbell rang again.

Belle jumped up and rushed to the closet for a robe. She snatched at a light cotton one and wrapped it hurriedly around her as she raced for the front door.

But when she raised her hand to the knob, a sudden thought made her freeze.

What if it wasn't Max?

All her previous happy expectations halted in a wave of unease. She looked through her peephole, but the scratched glass was as unrevealing this morning as it had been the night before.

The doorbell rang again.

Its shrill vibration reverberated in her chest.

She swallowed, trying to clear the sudden collection of phlegm in her throat. "Who is it?"

A response, low, muffled. Definitely not Max's voice.

Belle's muscles tensed as she swallowed again, trying to keep the growing panic under control as she called out again. "I can't hear you. Who is it?"

"Donna. It's Donna from down the hall."

Belle exhaled in relief as she opened the door to her neighbor. She blinked in surprise. Donna's waitress uniform and sensible low shoes had been replaced with a classic black sheath and heels. One hand balanced her baby in her arms, wrapped in a pink lace blanket, the other extended downward to hold on to her energetic four-year-old boy, Eddie, who looked painfully scrubbed and combed.

Donna took one look at Belle in her robe and an expression of absolute dismay flashed over her face. "You didn't forget the Christmas party?"

Damn. The Christmas party for the graduates of the Literacy League and their families. Belle had completely forgotten.

Belle opened the door wider and stepped aside. "Come in, Donna. It's all right. We'll make it. Just going to get a late start. I had some...uh...car trouble last night. We'll need to take a taxi over to the center."

Donna's expression lightened perceptively. "You're sure you still want to go? You're not sick or anything?"

"I'm fine, Donna. Just need to wash up a bit and put on some makeup."

Belle took Eddie's hand and led the way into the kitchen toward the cookie jar. She reached in and brought out a gigantic Christmas tree cookie, generously decorated with chocolate chip ornaments, and the little boy beamed as his hands eagerly grabbed it.

She turned back to Donna. "Why don't you make yourself some coffee while you wait?"

"Okay. I could do with a cup. It's been a hectic morning getting myself and these two ready after having to work overtime last night. But, I wouldn't have missed today for the world."

Belle looked at the pride and excitement in Donna's eyes and smiled. For the entire past year she had tutored this hard-working, single mother several afternoons a week, helping her to learn how to read. This Christmas party in celebration of her achievement and that of the other graduates of the Literacy League meant a lot to her. And to Belle.

"I'll just be a couple of minutes," Belle called as she headed for the bathroom. But as she hurriedly washed and slipped into her clothes, even the anticipation of the party couldn't keep the frown off her face as she wondered why Max had just left her without a word.

Fifteen minutes later she reemerged into the kitchen. "As soon as I find where I put my keys we'll be all set. I called for a taxi from the bedroom. It'll probably be arriving any minute."

Donna smiled, stepped over to the sink to wash out her cup and set it on the drain board, one-handed as always as she cradled the sleeping baby in her arms. But when she looked over at Eddie, her smile vanished.

"Oh, no. You've got chocolate all over your face. How is it you always manage to wear more food than gets into your stomach, young man?"

Eddie looked pleased, obviously considering the observation a high compliment.

Belle reached for a paper towel and quickly ran it under the water. "It's okay, Donna. Won't take a moment to wipe off. There. Now, let me see your hands, Eddie."

But Eddie stubbornly shook his head as he continued to hold his hands in back of him.

Donna circled behind her uncooperative son. "Just what I thought. You've got something in those grubby little paws of yours. Come on. Give it up."

Eddie did, but with much reluctance. Donna took the piece of paper out of his hand, and after a careful scrutiny, handed it to Belle.

"I'm sorry. This note is addressed to you. I don't know where Eddie found it. I'm afraid he's sort of fascinated with paper that has any kind of writing on it. I think it's because my excitement over our lessons this past year has infected him. I've even found some of my homework papers hidden under his pillow."

Belle was barely paying attention to Donna's explanation as she eagerly took the chocolate-smeared note from her hand, suspecting immediately who it must be from.

Belle,
You were sleeping so soundly, I decided not to disturb
you. I've gone to meet with those friends I told you
about last night. I took your keys so I could lock the
bolt in place on your front door behind me. I'll be back
early afternoon to take you to brunch.

Try not to poison yourself with what's growing in
your refrigerator in the meantime.

Max

Belle smiled. Well, that explained why she hadn't been
able to find her keys. A frown quickly replaced her smile.
Max was going to expect her to be here when he returned.
All things considered, she really shouldn't leave.

She looked over at Donna's face. No. There was no way
she could back out from going now. Only one thing to do.

Belle grabbed for the pen in the kitchen drawer, turned
Max's note over and quickly scribbled out where she would
be and what she would be doing. She included the telephone number and address for the Literacy League center.
Then she set the note in the middle of the kitchen table and
anchored it with the jar of freeze-dried coffee.

She turned back to Donna, who had been watching her
with undisguised interest. "It's a note for a friend who'll be
dropping by," she explained. "He...uh...borrowed my
keys. I'll get my purse and an extra set and meet you at the
door."

MAX KNOCKED on Belle's apartment door after the doorbell failed to rouse her. Still no answer. After waiting several minutes, he shifted the bag of coffee and croissants
under his left elbow and put the borrowed key in the lock.
The second the door swung open, he called out so as not to
frighten her.

When he got no response, he checked the bedroom and
then quickly searched the rest of the apartment. Belle was

gone and so was his note. He dumped the bag he carried onto the kitchen table. His pulse began to pound in alarm. She wouldn't have just left like this with no word. Unless... Had that sadistic Santa Claus come to the door? Had he somehow lured her out?

The phone rang. Once. Twice. Was it her?

Max grabbed and answered it after the third ring.

"Mr. Wilde?" an unfamiliar female voice asked.

"Yes. Who's this?"

"I'm a switchboard operator at KALA. I have a message from Ms. Breeze for you. Here, I'll read it. She says she had a family emergency and had to leave. She says she'll be back very late tonight, so don't wait."

"That's all."

"Yes, Mr. Wilde. That's all."

Max thanked the woman and hung up the phone. So that explained it. He thought it had to be something serious to have gotten her to leave. Relieved, Max sat down at the kitchen table and drew out a coffee and croissant from the bag. The croissant was halfway to his mouth when he remembered Belle's family were all back in Minnesota.

If she really had a family emergency, wouldn't that mean she'd be at the airport boarding a plane about now? And if she was soon going to be in Minnesota, how could she possibly be back "late tonight."

Max's croissant dropped untouched to the table.

BELLE WAS DELIGHTED to find the somewhat utilitarian hall that was the heart of the Literacy League had been transformed with wreaths, lights and holly circling its drab walls, and a large, decorated Christmas tree sitting at its center. The season's music and the happy voices and faces of families gathered around the buffet table added to the spirit of the festive occasion.

After everyone had sampled the homemade dishes that offered everything from turkey tamale pie to the traditional fruitcake, the ceremony began. One by one, the adult grad-

uates proudly came forward and shared their individual
stories of the hardships they had endured by not being able
to read and write. As each received their diplomas, Belle
clapped and cheered as loudly as any of their family members.

When the formalities ceased, the group gathered around
the Christmas tree to chat and sip eggnog. It was then that
Donna surprised Belle by waving her hand for attention.
The group quieted down to hear her speak.

She handed her sleeping baby into Belle's arms and
beckoned Eddie to her knee. As her son cuddled up to his
mom's side, Donna drew a small book from out of her
purse.

"Since my Eddie was born four years ago, I have dreamed
of this day, this moment. Thanks to the Literacy League and
my tutor, Ms. Belle Breeze, it has arrived."

Then with bright happy tears in her eyes, she opened the
book and began to read.

'Twas the night before Christmas when all through the
house
Not a creature was stirring, not even a mouse...."

The room was absolutely still and not an eye was dry as
the proud mother read to her child their very first story together.

And at that moment, Belle knew she'd just received a
priceless gift that would remain with her all her Christmases to come.

Belle was wiping her eyes after Donna had finished reading her story when the Literacy League's secretary moved up
to hand her a note. "This message was called in for you a
little while ago."

Belle thanked the secretary and opened the slip of paper

Stay inside the center. I'll pick you up there at five. I could be a few minutes late. Do not leave under any circumstances before I get there. Important.

Max

Belle looked up. The group was finishing their eggnogs and some were making moves to leave. She checked her watch. Going on four. Oh, well. Not too long a wait.

She corralled the busy vice president of the League, knowing she lived only a few miles from Donna and Belle's apartment house, and got her to agree to give Donna and her brood a ride home. By the time Belle had said goodbye to the last of the stragglers, she and the League's secretary had completed the cleanup.

"Thanks for your help, Belle. I'll be locking up now."

Belle glanced at her watch. It was a quarter to five. "Someone's picking me up here in fifteen minutes. I really don't feel safe waiting out on the street. Would you mind if I took your key and locked up after I leave? I could return it to you tomorrow."

"Sure, no problem. Here it is. Good night."

Belle made sure the door was securely locked after the secretary left. She listened to the click of the secretary's heels as she descended the one flight of stairs and then opened the door that led onto the street. It, too, clicked closed as the secretary set the latch, automatically locking the door behind her.

Belle turned to face the now-quiet hall. She flipped off the room's overhead fluorescents and the lights that trimmed the walls, but left on the multicolored strands of Christmas lights that decorated the tree in the center. Then she stepped over to the window to look out at her second-story view of Los Angeles, a city whose night scene resembled an enormous lighted Christmas tree, its branches flattened and spread out as far as the eye could see.

It sparkled and bustled and rustled beneath her—vibrantly alive—ever growing, sending out new shoots. Mute and shiny from this viewpoint, the sprawling giant could certainly be impressive.

Belle was so totally engrossed in the sights before her that when she finally became conscious of the faint plaintive sound, she realized it had been a part of the background noise for several minutes.

Belle turned back to face into the room. She looked around, actively listening now. The cry came again, faint but distinctive. She walked to the tree at the center of the room. Stopped. Listened again.

Again the cry. To her left. She angled toward the store room.

Yes. Seemed to be louder here. More distinguishable. A kitten's plaintive mewing.

A kitten? Had one of the children smuggled a kitten into the Christmas party? Had it gotten loose and inadvertently scampered into the storeroom?

Belle checked her watch. Five after five. Max would be here any minute. She'd better find this kitten quick.

Belle ran to the front of the hall, where she switched on the overhead lights. She raced back to the storeroom. She twisted the knob on the door and pushed it open. It was pitch-black inside, the light from the hall barely penetrating. Holding the door open with one hand against its spring loaded hinge, she felt for the light switch with the other hand. Found it. Flipped it. Flipped it again. Nothing. Great. The bulb must have burned out. Now what?

Then she heard the plaintive mewing again. Much louder. No doubt about it. That kitten was in this long, dark, narrow storeroom somewhere.

She called out. "Here, kitty, kitty. Come on. Come on out."

The plaintive mewing continued.

Poor thing. Probably scared to death. She knew how it felt. She'd always had a somewhat claustrophobic fear of dark, closed-in places herself.

Belle hesitated as she tried to remember what the storeroom looked like. Steel shelving lined the walls. A copier sat in the center. If things hadn't been moved around since she was last in here.

The cry continued. Mournful. Aching. Entreating. Belle bit her lip as she stared into the dark. Although she couldn't see it, she knew somewhere in there that kitten sobbed for help.

She reached for a nearby chair and propped open the door. She tested out the chair's resilience by rattling the door against it. The chair had rubber grips on its legs. It was anchored on the wooden floor and wouldn't budge. Good. She faced the dark storeroom and then resolutely, cautiously, step-by-step, started forward.

"Here, kitty, kitty."

The plaintive mewing continued. Just ahead? Must be at the very back of the storeroom. Naturally. She banged into the copier. Ouch. Well, at least she knew she was in the center of the storeroom. Meant she was headed in the right direction. Gradually her eyes began to adjust to the darkness. The faint light from the hall was just enough to reflect a faint line on the edges of the metal shelves.

Black turned into gray and dark gray shadows. Her eyes strained, trying to see the kitten's form or some movement. No distinguishable form. No movement. Nothing. The mewing echoed loudly in her ears. Where was this blasted kitten?

Barely she began to make out the small black lump on the floor. Against the back wall. She moved toward it. Called to it. Leaned down slowly so as not to frighten it.

She wasted her effort. Not a kitten. Her fingers slid over a cool, rough edge of plastic. Perplexed, Belle picked up what was obviously a small tape recorder. She pressed a button. The mewing stopped.

What craziness was this?

She started uncontrollably at the sudden noise of the storeroom door slamming closed. Darkness instantly shrouded her.

Belle's stomach clenched in cold and sudden fear. She stiffened, unable to move, desperately blinking to try to get her eyes to adjust to the darkness. She strained her ears, but all she could hear was the frantic beating of her own heart. Perspiration slid down her spine, popped out on her palms.

Seconds or minutes passed. She wasn't sure in that absolute blackness. She was blind, deaf, dumb with fear in her airless, windowless tomb.

Everything flashed crystal clear in her mind. Somehow her anonymous Santa Claus had gotten inside this building. The plaintive cries of the kitten had been just a ruse to get her to enter the storeroom. So he could close the door on her. And now he waited on the other side of that door.

Dear God, he was out there.

Unless he was in this storeroom with her now? Belle's stomach somersaulted in new terror as she listened intently, desperately, for any movement. The quiet beat against her ears.

She collapsed to her knees in ragged relief. She was imprisoned, but alone. At least she was alone.

For the moment. But he could come in at any moment!

The thought made Belle begin to shake so badly her teeth rattled. Her chin sunk to her chest. She wrapped her arms around her and tried to fight down the rising wave of new panic.

If only Max were here! If only he'd come!

The thought of Max brought Belle sitting up straight.

Her tormentor had to realize she wouldn't have stayed in the building unless she was expecting someone to pick her up. He had to realize he couldn't stay around after his latest sadistic trick.

Yes, yes, of course, he would have to realize those things! He couldn't be waiting for her on the other side of that door.

He ran too much of a risk of getting caught. He had to be long gone.

She could get out of here.

Relief steamed some needed warmth into her cold-starched muscles.

She tried to remember exactly where she was in relation to the copier and the door. All she had to do was carefully make her way to the door and let herself out.

He probably thought she'd be too panicked even to try. He probably was counting on it. Damn. He'd almost been right.

She tucked the tape recorder into her sweater pocket, reached out blindly with her hands until she felt the back wall. She pressed against it, using its solid support to get herself back on her feet. Slowly she swiveled until her fingers scraped against the edge of the metal shelving. She grasped its cool edges like she would a lifeline, knowing if she followed the shelving, it would eventually lead her to the door.

Baby step by baby step she groped her way through the blackness, relying only on her sense of touch, concentrating her mind only on the fact that she was getting out—she was getting out!

When she finally felt the smooth grain of the wooden door, relief and exultation washed through her. Her hands fumbled eagerly now to locate the doorknob. Grasp it. Turn it. Push.

But the door didn't open. She turned again. Pushed again. Nothing.

Belle's hands began to shake. This couldn't be happening. The storeroom doorknobs didn't lock. They were just like the doorknobs on closets.

In a panic of sudden denial, she twisted the knob and threw her weight against the door. The impact reverberated through her arm and hip. She ignored the bruising pain as she once again threw herself against the door. It didn't budge.

Tears welled in her blind eyes, spilling onto her cheeks. She was trapped, trapped! She pounded on the door with her fists, pushed against it with her full body weight. "Help! I'm locked in here. Help! Let me out!"

But the door remained stubbornly closed.

Belle's muscles gave out on her then. Her fists sunk to her sides. She sagged against the door, sobbing.

And then she heard it. On the other side of the door came a distinctive scraping noise and an eerie, breathless laugh.

Belle's sob froze in her throat. A strangled scream ripped through her lungs. She jumped back from the door she had been so urgently trying to open, now fervently praying it would stay closed.

He is still out there! Dear God, he's waiting right on the other side of that door for me!

The blood in her veins froze into ice, her petrified heart heavy inside her chest.

Waiting for what? What did he have planned? Was he going to come in after her? How long would Belle have to wait to find out?

She reached into her sweater pocket and grasped the small tape recorder in her hand. It wasn't much, but it was the only weapon she had.

She no longer had any hope of Max coming. She no longer had any hope at all. She was alone with the terror that stood on the other side of that door. Alone. Waiting. For whatever was to come.

The nerves tightened to steel in her neck. Down her back. What was that sound? The turning knob on the other side of the door? Or merely the beat of her own blood?

Every pore in her skin oozed in sweat, clammy and swimming in fright. Time stretched, compressed, swirled, stopped. Seconds, minutes, hours—indistinguishable.

Over and over the noises came. And went. Huddled in the dark, wincing at every one, Belle no longer knew which were generated by the sounds of her tormentor or by the fear that raged through her heart.

And in that unbearable time warp of terror, she even began to pray he *would* come and end it.

Then suddenly her ears picked up the clicking of soles on the hall's wooden floor. Circling. Then coming closer and closer to the storeroom door. Her prayer was being answered.

Belle's exhausted muscles tried to rally to the new surge of fear pounding through her heart. She jumped at the unmistakable sound of the doorknob turning, her oversensitive ears picking up even its barely perceptible click. The squeak of the opening door. The blinding flash of light after so many hours of darkness.

This was it. Finally, the end. Belle dropped into a crouch behind the slowly opening door, her sweat-soaked body shaking, every nerve ending tensed for action, her paltry weapon grasped tightly, defiantly, in her hand.

Chapter Ten

He stepped cautiously into the darkened storeroom, instantly sensing the charged atmosphere, feeling the presence within the shadows. He propped his shoe against the door to keep it from slamming shut. He didn't move forward, but waited for his eyes to adjust. His nerves stretched out to the darkness. He listened for the sound of breathing. His muscles tensed for action.

"Belle?"

The barely audible sigh came from behind the door. Max swung it aside, his eyes staring unbelievingly to find Belle crouching behind it, perspiration beading on her skin, her eyes enormous, her face a ghastly pallor.

Immediately, he leaned down, took hold of her shoulders, brought her to her feet. Profound, stupefying relief turned his voice into a harsh, grating sound. "Belle, what in the hell are you doing in this damn storeroom?"

Her voice wobbled like a wounded whisper. "Max, I'm so glad it's you. I thought—"

The tape recorder fell from her hand to the floor with a cracking, splintering sound. She collapsed against his chest, quivering violently, a mass of boneless flesh. Max wrapped his arms around her, held her close, never feeling so grateful that he'd found her after so many tortured hours of searching. Feeling her safe in his arms, he knew a prayer had been answered—one he hadn't even realized he'd said.

He raised a shaking hand to stroke her hair. Mumbled soothing, incoherent things. Rested his cheek against the top of her head. Drank in the warm sweetness of her scent until it was a part of him.

He knew something had scared her, something to do with why she'd been cowering behind this storeroom door. It surprised him a bit to realize he wasn't in any hurry to get the details. All that was important at the moment was that she was safe. And in his arms.

She felt so damn good in his arms.

After a while her shaking eased. Then stopped. Her heartbeat slowed. She rested quietly against his chest for a moment or two more. Then slowly he felt her drawing back. Reluctantly he eased his hold until his arms rested loosely around her waist.

She looked up at him. The fluorescent light from the hall streamed across her face. The Christmas tree lights flashed colors onto her cheeks. Her voice was still barely a whisper. "You were so late in coming to pick me up."

Her words confused him. "I didn't know where you were, much less that you needed me to pick you up."

Her whispery voice took on some volume of insistence. "But you called and left a message for me here this afternoon. You told me to wait for you, that you would be by for me around five."

Max took in a deep breath and tried to keep his voice even. "Belle, I didn't call. I didn't leave a message. When I got back to your apartment, a switchboard operator at KALA called me with a message from you about some family emergency."

"I left no such message."

"That I figured out. I've been searching for you all day. The police wouldn't listen to me until Morse came on duty this evening. He finally got them out looking for you."

"But I left a note telling you where I was."

Max exhaled. "Yes. I know that now. But I didn't get your note saying where you were until an hour ago when your neighbor Donna stopped by your apartment with it."

"Donna had my note? I don't understand. I left it on the kitchen table."

"She delivered it with apologies. Said someone named Eddie picked it up. Said you'd understand."

Her head nodded slightly. "Oh, I see. Eddie." Her eyes returned to his face, still confused, as though it was hard for her to take in more than one message at a time. "You didn't know I was here until an hour ago?"

"I came by as soon as I found out, but the outside door was locked. I thought you had to be in here when I saw the lights still on. Donna had to help me find a member of the Literacy League to borrow a key. Belle, why didn't you just answer the door when I knocked?"

She took a breath that still barely seemed to fill her lungs. "He must have been the one who called and left that message. Both messages. He wanted me here alone, Max. He lured me into the storeroom, then locked me in."

Max looked closely at the doorknob he'd so recently turned. "This door doesn't have a lock, Belle."

She swallowed as though her throat was swollen and sore. "He must have been holding it closed when I tried to open it from the inside. When I couldn't get it open he...he scraped against the door and laughed. They were the same sounds I heard the other night. Max, he was outside my apartment door the other night."

She had begun to shake again. He brought her back into his arms and drew her away from the storeroom where she'd endured such horror. As his foot released the spring-loaded hinge on the door, he noticed the long white envelope lying on the floor with her name typed on it.

He bent down to pick it up. She gave a little start beside him when he rose with it in his hands. Max glanced at her face. The fear still threatened to overflow the thin veneer of her composure. She wasn't holding it back by much.

She seemed to read the question in his eyes and nodded in response. He slit the envelope open with his fingers, took out the paper inside and read it aloud.

"On the seventh day of Christmas, Santa Claus gave to Breeze
Seven hours a-cringing.

Now you're locked up,
Santa Claus."

Max gripped the paper in his hand. He had to keep himself from giving in to a strong urge to tear it into pieces, which was what he wanted to do to its author. Only her presence beside him maintained his reason. He knew reason, not emotion, would be the only way they could lick this thing. He reached for his slipping control and snapped it resolutely back into place.

He reread the stanza more calmly, forcing himself to look at it with logic this time. And it paid off. "Belle, when did you get locked in that storeroom?"

"Just after five."

Max checked his watch. "It's nearly nine-thirty. Four and a half hours. Yet the stanza says seven. Can it be your sadistic Santa Claus has just made his first mistake?"

Belle looked up, a flash of something like hope creeping into her eyes. "Mistake?"

"Yes. He expected you to stay cringing in that storeroom for seven hours. What does that tell you?"

She was trying to concentrate in the wake of her exhausting mental terror. He was pushing her, he knew. But this was a scrap of hope. If she was going to make it through this madness, she had to have hope.

She took a couple of shallow, unsatisfying breaths. "He didn't expect me to get out in four and a half hours. He didn't expect you to come by and find me."

"Yes. But that's not all. Seven hours from five o'clock means that he somehow planned for you to be released from that storeroom at midnight. How was he going to do that?"

He watched as the implication finally formed in her thoughts. The hope in her eyes grew stronger as her voice raised with excitement. "Max, he's coming back here. He scared me into staying in that closet. He's got to have planned on coming back here at midnight to let me out."

Max felt a wave of relief at the returning color in her cheeks. He raised a hand to one of them and gently caressed it with his fingers. "With some nasty new trick, no doubt. Well, let's show the bastard we've a few tricks of our own. Come on, Belle. We're going to call Sergeant Morse, let him know you've been found and have him station some men watching the doors. When your anonymous Santa Claus comes by this place at midnight, we'll be ready."

She nodded eagerly, her eyes shining trustfully into his.

He couldn't help himself. He kissed her then, softly and tenderly, first on the cheek he had caressed, then on the lips so tantalizingly nearby. She melted beneath his touch with a liquid sigh.

An ache to gather her in his arms and make love to her right then and there tore through him with such force that he began to shake. He moved quickly back and resisted its overwhelming temptation.

And it troubled him. Not because he denied himself. But because the reason he denied himself was that he suddenly couldn't stand the idea of doing anything that might make him unworthy of that trust he found in her eyes.

"WHAT TIME IS IT?" Belle whispered.

"Eleven-fifty-nine," Max whispered back.

They crouched beside Sergeant Morse, peering out the slightly ajar door to the custodial area at the back of the first landing. Three pairs of eyes watched the open stairwell leading up to the Literacy League's offices on the second floor of the building.

An emergency light barely illuminated the stairs. Belle could just see the door to the sidewalk outside, the street lamp's light glowing through the opaque glass.

Upstairs, just inside the Literacy League's hall, she knew two of Sergeant Morse's men waited in a similar silent vigil.

A bead of perspiration trickled down her back. Morse had his pistol drawn, pointed at the ceiling. Moments before, she'd watched him snap a full clip into it. Now she could smell the oil from the well-cleaned weapon, the sweat from his clutching hand.

The seconds ticked by in her head. Slowly, very slowly. The tension tightened in her spine, her neck, made her bent knees begin to ache.

Morse checked his watch. "Midnight. He's late."

Belle shifted beside Max, tried to ease the tension splintering through her. Where was her tormentor?

Then, as though in answer to her silent question, she saw the shadow suddenly cast across the glass door to the building.

She felt Max tense beside her. She could hear the approaching footsteps, leather slapping on concrete. The footsteps echoed in her ears, getting louder and louder like the beats of her heart. She tried to make out if they came from a man's heavy step or a woman's lighter one. The footsteps stopped. She heard the front window lock being rattled.

She swallowed, remembering just how terrified any noises, even those she had imagined, had made her feel in that dark storeroom prison. She didn't even want to think how she would be feeling now if Max hadn't come by when he did to release her from it.

As though he'd read her thoughts, Max's hand clasped her shoulder. She felt his touch flood through her, warm and reassuring.

The footsteps started up again. Closer. Again a pause. A step up to the door, the jangle of keys, one fitting into the lock. Soon he'd be in sight. Soon she'd be face-to-face with this sadistic tormentor.

The knob turned. The door opened. The shadow stepped inside.

Belle felt the tension mounting in Max. Sergeant Morse inched slightly forward. His pistol no longer pointed at the ceiling. He held it straight in front of him.

The intruder started for the stairs.

Sergeant Morse jumped to his feet and darted out into the stairwell. "Police! Hold it right there!"

The door at the top of the stairs banged open as the two policemen waiting behind it also barged out into the stairwell, guns drawn.

Belle felt a scary excitement as she got up from her crouched position with Max and moved into position behind Morse. Was she about to confront Ramish...Daark? She blinked in startled disbelief at whom the policeman had pinned in their sights.

He was a young, uniformed security guard with a blond beard and long wavy hair gathered in unusual clumps in front of his ears.

"Spread them against the wall. Now!" Sergeant Morse commanded as he advanced on the man.

Once the officers from the top of the stairs had secured the man in handcuffs, Morse holstered his pistol and turned back to Belle and Max.

"Recognize him?"

Before Belle could say anything, Max responded.

"Yes, Sergeant. His name is Terry Stut. I met him at the premiere we attended at the Egyptian Theater last night, a couple of hours before Ms. Breeze's windows were smashed."

Morse's eyebrows shot up. "Well, well. I find that very interesting."

Belle stepped forward. "It gets even more interesting. This man was also one of the leads in a picture I reviewed last December, Sergeant. Perhaps you remember my telling you about it. It was called *Major Change.*"

"I KNEW I'D RECOGNIZED him from somewhere," Max said as he drove out of the parking lot of the Literacy League building. "He played the college boyfriend of the coed who becomes a prostitute. I should have remembered."

"It took me a moment to place him," Belle admitted. "His hair was short a year ago and he didn't have that beard. If you hadn't gotten me thinking about that movie the other night and who played in it, I doubt if I would have even made the connection."

"Still, I'm pretty good at names. I wonder why the name Terry Stut didn't ring a bell?"

"It doesn't ring a bell with me, either. He probably used a stage name. I suppose his adamant denial he had anything to do with this terror campaign is a typical response."

"Very typical," Max agreed. "I'm just surprised he didn't also demand to talk to a lawyer, too."

She was shaking her head, still struggling with acceptance. "He seems to know so much about me. Where I work. Where I live. Even about the party at the Literacy League today. And the fact that I'd stay there if you told me you'd come by to pick me up. How can he know so much?"

"He'd obviously put considerable effort into this. He must have been watching you a long time—maybe since right after your review last year."

"But why did he wait so long to get back at me?"

"A sense of the dramatic, perhaps. Maybe because he suffered through a holiday season, he wanted you to suffer through one."

"I wish I knew exactly why he did this to me."

"A failed career. A need to blame and punish someone. You may never know for certain, Belle. *He* may not even know for certain."

"Do you suppose he's insane?"

"If not in the legal definition of the word, certainly in the moral one."

She sighed, long and deep. "I can't believe it's over. I'm still shaking inside."

He rested a hand on her forearm for a brief second. "It'll take time for it to sink in. Now, no more dwelling on it tonight. Or I should say morning. It's nearly one o'clock. And I'm having trouble of thinking of anything but food. I haven't eaten all day and I'm starved. How about you?"

She touched the flyaway strands of hair around her face and glanced down at her wrinkled pantsuit, smudged with dust and perspiration. "I am hungry. But I'd be lucky if they let me into a twenty-four-hour Denny's the way I look now."

He laughed. "Not to worry. There's no dress code where we're going."

"Not my place. I haven't done any shopping since your critical assessment of the contents of my refrigerator this morning."

"No, not your place. My place."

She looked over at him.

He extended a finger to lightly trace the small worry line in her forehead. "It's okay. I know what you've been through, Belle. I'll be on my best behavior. Promise."

BELLE WALKED INTO Max's Pasadena town house, expecting to see lots of heavy macho furniture emphasizing the virile image he projected with that magnificently muscled body so prominently displayed beneath those open vests and formfitting jeans.

The last thing she expected was to be greeted by shining black walls in the entry, setting off an enormous pure white alabaster statue of a graceful dolphin leaping out of a sea wave.

The sunken living room had the same gleaming black walls and a solid black carpet—dramatic backgrounds to the streamlined stark-white sofa and chairs resting elegantly within. Straight ahead was a wall of glass leading out onto a balcony. On either side, two enormous floor-to-ceiling mirrors covered the walls—reflecting the room's simple contents into images of infinity.

Belle thought such a combination of black and white should feel austere, even claustrophobic. But amazingly it didn't. Rather than confine, the black gave an illusion of endless space. The room reminded her of a well-made black-and-white film, one that often retained more real warmth and sensuality than a color rendition because it concentrated more on the dialogue between the characters than on the scenery and special effects.

"You decorate this?"

"If you mean did I tell someone what I wanted, yes."

"Is the black and white a statement about how you see the world?"

"No. I just like a simple, unobtrusive background. People should be the highlight of any room, not the furniture. You have your choice, Belle. You can relax out here with a drink and some soothing music, or you can join me in the kitchen and watch me throw something together."

"I'll watch. But I'd like to wash up first."

He showed her the bathroom and pointed in the direction of where she'd find him in the kitchen.

The bathroom was like the rest of Max's place, spacious, simple and elegant, displaying a mixture of white and black in its tile and porcelain fixtures. On her way back to the kitchen, curiosity had her ducking into his study for a quick look around. More black-and-white decor. And a trophy case in the corner. Filled.

She read a few of the inscriptions. Journalism awards. There were pictures, too. Unposed shots of well-known personalities.

It began to sink in that she really didn't know much about Max. And she suddenly wanted to know everything.

She left his study and headed for the kitchen.

He smiled as she entered. "What can I get you to drink?"

"Nothing alcoholic. Some orange juice, if you have it."

"That 'clean-living Minnesota Viking' constitution, I suppose?"

"More like that 'I get sick on alcohol and disgrace myself every time' constitution."

He chuckled appreciatively. The kitchen was gleaming white. The walls, the ceiling, the floor, the cabinets, the appliances.

He held out a white leather bar stool for her, which he withdrew from the center island counter. She sat down and he poured them both a glass of orange juice from a chilled juice container he retrieved from the refrigerator.

Then he surprised her completely when he put on a utilitarian white apron and took a bag of flour out of the pantry.

"What are you going to make?"

"Some biscuits. I thought they'd go well with an omelet."

"You make biscuits from scratch?"

"Just a little flour, baking powder, salt, shortening and water. Good cooking is no more work than bad. I've been making my own meals since I was a kid."

She took a sip of the orange juice. It tasted wonderful, as though it had been freshly squeezed. "Your mother taught you?"

He dumped the ingredients into a ceramic blue bowl without measuring. "I never knew my mother."

He didn't say it with any regret. Actually, he didn't say it with any emotion at all.

Belle sat forward. "Did she die?"

He mixed the ingredients with his bare hands. "She left my father and me when I was about two. Ran off with some guy from Buenos Aires."

Again no emotional inflection in his tone. Belle's curiosity deepened. "Your dad never remarried?"

"No. Enjoyed playing the field too much. And it was a large field. Can't remember the same woman ever staying over twice. From the time I was seven I knew how to get my own dinner when I came home from school, retire to my room and keep my bedroom door closed.''

Belle wasn't sure she felt comfortable with the images that kind of father-son understanding evoked. ''What does your father do?''

''He was an airline pilot.''

''Was?''

Max turned the dough onto the kneading board. ''He died a couple of years ago. Heart attack.''

''I'm sorry.''

''No reason to be. Brought it on himself. Smoked like a chimney. Still, he enjoyed his life. Last thing he said to me was he wouldn't change a minute of it. That's the way to live.''

''You have any other relatives?''

''My father was estranged from his family. Never talked about them. And of course my mother wasn't around to talk about hers.''

Belle frowned. ''You seem so nonchalant about your parents and their . . . unusual life-style choices.''

He looked over at her, his black eyes deep, endless wells. ''Do I?''

She saw it then. The barest flicker. There had been pain. He'd just faced and come to terms with it.

Belle shook her head a little sadly as she circled her index finger around the edge of her glass of orange juice. ''My parents always played a prominent role in my growing up. They've shaped so much of who I am. I can't imagine their placing me on the back burners of their lives.''

''Like mine did with me?''

She looked up to see his eyes focused directly on her and immediately felt uncomfortable with her hastily shared thoughts. ''I'm sorry, Max. That was . . . inconsiderate of me.''

''No. Just blunt. And accurate.''

Max's eyes returned to the dough in his hands as he dug his fingers deeply into its formless bulk.

He wasn't a man who opened up easily. She sensed those things that were the most important to him would be the most difficult for him to discuss.

She tried another question. "What did you do before you became a movie critic?"

"I was a foreign correspondent."

"Why did you change focus?"

"I've always been a movie freak. Used to live in the theaters when I was a kid."

"You don't miss doing hard news?"

His eyes flashed to her face. "Miss flying to some wartorn country to interview men balancing AK-47s with banana clips on their arms, telling you the reason they want to slaughter their neighbors is because they believe in a different religion?"

She felt the strength of the emotion in those words, and she knew then that this was a man who felt deeply, however infrequently he displayed the power of those feelings.

She watched his attention revert back to the dough between his hands, the impressive muscles in his forearms flexing as he kneaded it. A strong man. In so many ways a very strong man.

He asked the next question. "Why'd you become a critic?"

She took another sip of her orange juice, enjoying its sweetness trickle down her throat. "I grew up just a mile or so down the road from the Chanhassen Dinner Theatre complex."

"I'm not familiar with it."

"It's very well-known where I come from. The majority of professional actors in the Midwest have performed full-length plays in its four theaters at some point in their careers. I remember every month, sometimes twice a month, we attended as a family. *Hello Dolly!*, *South Pacific*, *The*

ound of Music, West Side Story, Fiddler on the Roof—I
w them all, and lots more."

"You sound like you enjoyed yourself."

"I did. I thought they were wonderful. Still do. I thought
ie entire entertainment business was wonderful. Until I
arted going to see motion pictures."

"And they didn't measure up."

"Instead of entertaining, they offended. It seemed the
iore offensive they were, the higher their critical acclaim.
decided then that new critical voices needed to be heard
nd mine was going to be one of them. And it is."

He smiled at her. "The stalwart voice of Middle Amer-
a."

Belle raised her chin. "You might be surprised to learn
iat my Middle America, as you call it, extends to both the
ist and west shores."

He chuckled. "No, I wouldn't be surprised."

Belle's toes tingled at the kidding warmth in his tone. He
idn't agree with her, but he accepted her for who she was,
nd the realization left her warm and breathless.

They ate right at the counter, the fragrance of the freshly
aked biscuits making the kitchen smell heavenly. Heav-
uly, too, was the omelet he whipped up with cheese and
eshly chopped vegetables, baked into a puffy French style.

Sadistic stalkers and threatening notes receded into a dim,
araway past.

Belle didn't know how hungry she was until she looked
own to see her plate was clean and realized between them
iey'd polished off not only the six-egg omelet but also all
f the biscuits.

"Glad to see you like my cooking."

She leaned back, took a sip of the rich, freshly ground
offee and sighed. "What other talents have you been hid-
ig?"

He smiled slightly over his coffee cup, enough to look
ioroughly pleased, disreputable and irresistible. "I'd be

delighted to show you, Belle, but I've promised to be o good behavior tonight."

She smiled back at him. He was honest. He was himsel Yet she had to admit that as strongly as he kept his ow opinions, he still allowed her to keep hers.

Belle watched him sip his coffee and felt her world ex panding. She'd always thought she had to agree with man's philosophy in order to respect him. She did not agre with Wilde. Not for a minute. And yet she respected him The revelation intrigued her.

He intrigued her. She wondered what had gone throug his young mind when he found out his mother had deserte him. When he saw his father with different women all th time. Is that why he had never married? Is that why h himself went from woman to woman?

His brow had furrowed into a frown as he stared at h coffee cup, deep in thought. A single tendril of black ha had fallen across his prominent cheek. Belle had a sudde desire to touch that tendril, feel it curl around her finger To feel herself curled within his arms. Her heart beat lighte faster.

She put down her coffee cup, slipped off her bar stoo and for one of the few moments in her life, gave action t her feelings without weighing the consequences. "I haven really thanked you for what you've done for me. Last nig you were so wonderful. And today. Actually, all throug this terrible ordeal."

Max watched her approach with a quickening of his pulse The glistening look in her blue eyes was one he'd never see before, although it did sort of remind him of the way hungry tiger had once stared at him from behind the bars the Los Angeles Zoo.

She came right up to his bar stool. He sucked in his breat as she leaned between his parted thighs and bent down kiss his cheek.

Slivers of excitement rocketed through him. Her scen touch and warmth filled him so fully he felt the air mome tarily pushed out of his lungs. He had an instant vision of being that hungry tiger now, watching the trainer tempt him with a juicy morsel while he strained against his inhibiting chains.

And he was straining. He gripped the edge of the bar stool to keep himself from grabbing her and pulling her to him. And all the while he told himself this gesture of gratitude on her part would be over soon.

It wasn't. Her lips brushed down his cheek to his mouth, planting kisses along the way. Soft, infuriatingly stirring kisses that raised havoc with every nerve ending in his body. In an instant she totally aroused him.

He dragged some much-needed breath into his lungs, hearing the hoarseness of his voice in his ears. "Belle. You're welcome. That's enough."

She leaned away, slightly, the innocent look on her face totally at odds with the gleam in her eyes. "Is that really enough, Max?"

His knuckles were getting white from his ever-increasing grip on the seat of the bar stool. His jaw clenched. "Step back, Belle, while I'm still willing to let you. You've got two seconds."

She didn't even take one. She melted into a mass of soft, pulsing heat against him, stripping him of his thoughts, of anything but her scent, her taste, her feel, as her arms circled his shoulders, pulled him closer. Desire pounded through him, hot and heady and instantly out of control.

He moaned and grabbed for her, her silky hair tangled in his hands, imprisoning them, imprisoning him. Her hands groped beneath his vest to his bare flesh, her touch eager, hot, branding. Greedily he tasted her chin, running his lips down the smooth silkiness of her neck, unbuttoning her blouse to run his hand over the hot swell of her breasts.

He grew breathless from the incredible, sweet heat and taste of her. Somehow, she'd wiggled out of her slacks, raised a naked, silken thigh to circle around his leg.

She pressed her mouth to his, her body against the full length of him. A sigh that sounded like surrender and victory all in one escaped through her lips into his, quivered through him like a sharp, deadly arrow, perfectly aimed to pierce.

And rend. His senses reeled. He hurt. A hurt full of want. A hurt full of need. The want was familiar. The need was not.

With sudden shock he pulled away from her, slid off the bar stool, ready to battle an enemy only his rawest instinct had sensed.

He dragged in a ragged breath. His heart hammered against his chest as he looked at her leaning against the counter, all soft and rosy and ready to be his. And to make him hers.

Her eyes, blue and blurry with passion, swam into his, robbing him of breath, of speech. She slipped onto the bar stool, her lips still wet and flushed from his ardent attentions, her blouse open, her taut nipples straining against her bra, her honey hair flowing over her shoulders and arms in silky, seductive waves. She crossed one long exquisite satin leg over the other.

He'd never seen a more beautiful, desirable, intoxicating woman in his entire life. Or a more dangerous one.

Her voice was low and husky, a siren's call. "Max?"

He reeled with his want of her, his need of her. He could already feel that need dragging him to the edge of a cliff; beneath it were sharp rocks and deadly seas. Panic as he had never known panic shot through every cell.

He clutched at the tiny frayed edge of survival instinct still hanging within reach. "There's a guest room. Find it. Use it."

He tore out of his own kitchen as though the very fires from hell were at his heels.

SANTA SMILED AS THE TAXI pulled up in front of Max's town home, Belle got in, and it sped away. Apparently even the "wild man" hadn't been able to warm the Arctic Breeze.

But because of Wilde, she'd gotten off without full punishment tonight.

That would not happen again.

Santa followed the taxi from a safe distance, always close, always watching.

She thought she was safe tonight. She thought it was all over. Tomorrow she would find out she was wrong. Dead wrong.

And if Wilde interfered again, Santa was just going to have to eliminate him. Permanently.

Chapter Eleven

Neal came running up to Belle as soon as the taxi dropped her off at the entrance to KALA Monday afternoon.

"Belle, I've been waiting for you. Max just told Paula and me the good news about Terry Stut being unmasked as your anonymous Santa Claus. I've got a TV news reporter and camera crew getting ready right now to interview you for an exclusive."

"Forget it, Neal. I appear on the movie review portion of KALA—not the hard news."

"Belle, this is great copy. I've kept our station's reporters and the others away from you while it was going on, but now that it's over, you have a responsibility to our ratings...."

Belle didn't hear the rest of Neal's lament. She was distracted by the long black hearse with heavy tinted windows that was pulling into the nearest parking space to the entrance, the one normally reserved for the handicapped.

"Belle? Are you listening to me?"

She turned back to Neal. "No, and I'm not going to. If I say anything that can later be construed as prejudicial to this Terry Stut, his attorney might be able to use it to get him off. I wouldn't risk that for all the ratings in the world."

"But you don't have to say anything about Stut or the movie he was in that you panned. Concentrate on the poems and presents and how you felt getting them from your anonymous Santa Claus.''

Belle felt her patience being tried. "Look, Neal, I've just endured a particularly nasty week, and I'm not eager to re-live it on camera just for prurient viewers who get off on that kind of thing. Let them go see one of Daark's horror movies.''

"Well, well, did my ears hear right? Is Ms. Clean Breeze now recommending my movies?''

Justin Daark's sudden breathy voice so close behind her had Belle nearly jumping out of her skin. She spun around in uncomfortable surprise, her pulse racing.

Daark's light green eyes glittered at her from behind his thick glasses. "If I had known a recommendation would result from only a few lines of a song and a few presents, I would have sent you some myself.''

Belle gritted her teeth. "What are you doing here?''

"Didn't Neal tell you? I work here now. I hear the police caught your anonymous Santa Claus?''

"Yes.''

"Hmm. I'll have to drop by the county jail later to see him. I know a very good lawyer. Maybe I can help spring him.''

He turned his bland expression to the program director and dropped his car keys in his hand. "Someone has parked in my slot. Have their car towed. Then move mine to where it belongs.''

Neal frowned in irritation as he tried to hand back Daark's keys. "That's not my job, Justin. Talk to the se-curity guard inside the doors there.''

Daark didn't take the keys back. "I don't want to talk to the security guard. I've already talked to you. Take care of it.''

And with that Daark turned and pushed open the glass doors to the offices of KALA.

Belle shook her head. "What a thoroughly nasty little man.''

Neal's mustache twitched. "It's all a facade, Belle. He acts like he thinks people expect him to. Sinister, arrogant. But really he's very insecure and shy. Like so many in Hollywood, he craves attention and adulation. And he just dies inside when he doesn't get it."

Belle was surprised at Neal's words and the absolutely serious look on his face. "You say that as though you really know Daark well?"

Neal's hands foraged nervously in and out of his pockets, as though he was looking for something he had misplaced. "I've...ah...been around Hollywood types long enough to recognize the signs."

"Is he really working here at KALA now?"

"Well, yes. I thought everyone knew. He's punching up the scripts for a new vampire series over in Studio Six that's airing next spring. Scary as hell. He's a great talent. Everybody says so."

"Not everybody, Neal."

Neal's fingers raked his mustache. "Well, I suppose you never would. But, Belle, KALA cannot exist on the news alone. Particularly since a certain critic will not allow herself to be interviewed for one of Hollywood's exclusive and hottest stories."

"Dead horse, Neal. Put the whip away. Come on. I've got a review to write."

"RAMISH PICKED UP his two sons from his ex-wife and took them to see a football game Sunday afternoon. Returned to his place about eight. Daark stayed at home as far as we could tell."

Max leaned back in his office chair as he cradled the phone to his ear. "I'm not surprised to find them in the clear. It seems the guy who's been responsible for terrorizing Ms. Breeze was caught last night by the police."

"Then we can stop following them. Great news, Max. My stewardess is coming in on a flight this evening. Now I can get back to important things. She has this dynamite room-mate. Used to be Miss Orange Squeeze. Want to join us?"

"I'm not in the mood, Greg."

"Max Wilde not in the mood? You sick, buddy?"

"My mind's just elsewhere."

"Oh, I get it. Already got someone lined up, is that it?"

Max shook his head. "Yeah, that's it. Thanks for the help."

"Any time."

Max replaced the receiver on its base and looked up to see Belle approaching her office. She unlocked the door and walked inside. She reached across her desk to answer her phone, stood with her back straight, shoulders held high, her vibrant color returned.

He ached for her, just as he had ached for her all night and morning and afternoon.

If she had stayed at his town house the night before, he would have ended up in that guest room with her. He would not have been able to stay away.

He was glad she had left.

She was the kind of woman he'd thought purely mythical until now—the kind who could drive a man so insane with need that he'd say and do anything to have her. And that scared the hell out of him.

He knew now the signs had been there all along. She wasn't just a beautiful woman. She was smart and challenging and brave and a million other things he vowed he'd no longer notice. Wanting her had been one thing, but he wasn't going to let himself need her. And that was the end to that.

But there seemed to be no end to the unsatisfied ache in his gut that reminded him so forcibly that a man lived less in the rational mind than he did in the reality of his flesh and bone and blood.

"YOU LET TERRY STUT go, Sergeant? How could you?"

Belle nearly dropped the telephone receiver in her hand as

she flopped into her office chair, feeling as though someone had just pounded her on the back and knocked all the air out of her lungs.

"Ms. Breeze, I had to. An hour after we got him to the station last night, his date on Saturday came charging down on us with a lawyer. She swears Stut was with her steadily from an hour before the premiere until eleven-thirty that night. Your parking lot attack took place around ten-thirty. That puts him in the clear."

"But he was coming for me last night. Right at midnight. Just as the last stanza said. You were there. You saw him!"

"I have also just seen a group of owners of the commercial buildings in that neighborhood. They confirmed they hired Mr. Stut as a security guard a couple of days ago because of some trouble with vagrants or vandals breaking in at night. Stut is supposed to begin his rounds at midnight and at the building where the Literacy League is housed. He had a perfect right to be there."

Belle leaned her elbow on her desk and rested her forehead against her hand. "But, Sergeant, don't you see? He must have taken that job as part of his plan. This can't be coincidence. He was in that movie I panned. It has to be him!"

"Ms. Breeze, please calm down. I can imagine how frustrating this must be. But Stut's reason for being at the Literacy League has checked out. Plus, he has that ironclad alibi for Saturday night."

"How do you know you can trust this woman's word? How do you know she isn't lying to protect Stut?"

"Your own agent?"

"Who? What did you just say?"

"I said your own agent, Ms. Breeze. Yes, that's right. Terry Stut's date Saturday night was Luana Halsey."

Belle didn't know how long she sat at her desk, staring into space after hanging up from Sergeant Morse's call.

Her thoughts popped around her brain like burst kernels of corn. Luana dating was not an image that came easily to mind, but Luana dating Terry Stut totally boggled her imagination.

Yet it had to be true. Sergeant Morse would not, could not, have made up such a thing.

Luana dating the man who had run this terror campaign against her? Luana so in love with him she lied to protect him?

Lying? Luana? No. Belle couldn't believe Luana would do that. Luana had been the object of a terror campaign. She knew firsthand what it was like for a woman to be so frightened. She wouldn't be able to protect someone instigating such a sadistic act, not even if she loved him.

But if Luana wasn't lying, that meant that somehow, despite all the evidence, Terry Stut *was* innocent. And her anonymous Santa Claus was still anonymous and still out here.

An icy chill spread from Belle's stomach to her arms and legs, making her shudder. She swiveled in her chair and looked over at Max pounding away on the computer keyboard in his office, instinctively turning to him in her growing fear. Then turned away again.

She couldn't look to Max. Not anymore. Not after literally throwing herself at him the night before and having him reject her. Why had he done it? He wanted her. She was damn sure he wanted her.

The pain of a long night full of unanswered questions swelled anew in her breast. Naturally she hadn't been able to stay in his guest room as he'd so dismissively ordered her to do. She'd called a taxi and fled back to her apartment.

And told herself she should be glad it had turned out this way. He'd done her a favor. He hadn't added her name to his little black book. She should be thanking him.

"Ms. Breeze?"

Belle rose from her unhappy thoughts to see Jim Apple standing at the edge of her desk. "Yes, Jim."

"I wanted to tell you how happy I am that they got the guy, Ms. Breeze. Mr. Fort just got finished telling me all about how they arrested him last night. It must be such a relief."

"It would be if they hadn't let him go again."

"Let him go? How could they let him go?"

Belle met the look of distress covering Jim's horsey face with silent gratitude. Nice to know someone cared. "Seems he may not be responsible, after all."

"Ms. Breeze, I'm truly sorry. Mr. Fort has assigned me to other duties at the station this afternoon and this evening. But I'm sure once he hears that you're still in danger he'll want me back at your side. I'll go right now and tell him."

"I'd appreciate it."

But Jim Apple hesitated. "Ms. Breeze, if you should need someone to accompany you when you're away from the station, I would be happy to offer my services."

Belle found herself seriously considering his offer. Without Max to turn to, she felt very much alone. "Actually, I could use some company. But wouldn't I be taking you away from your family?"

"I've got no family out here, Ms. Breeze. Not anymore anyway. When might you need me?"

"'Entertainment Today' is taping an interview of Mr. Wilde and me over at their station after our broadcast here at KALA tonight. Neal will be driving me over there. But I could use an escort home afterward."

"Of course. If you call me here after you've finished, Ms. Breeze, I'll come by and pick you up and see you safely home."

"That's...very good of you. Thank you."

Apple stiffened, his hand once again coming to rest on the holster of his revolver. "No reason to thank me, Ms. Breeze. We're from small towns, you and I. We know how to be good neighbors."

As BELLE TOOK ON BOTH the movie they were reviewing and Max that night, Max couldn't help but notice that her hands still quivered a bit and the sparkle he'd thought had returned to his lovely co-critic seemed quite a bit dimmer.

He wanted to ask her if everything was all right, but afterward she shot out of her chair and disappeared until he saw her getting into Neal's car for the drive over to the "Entertainment Today" studio.

He followed. Disquieted. Uneasy. Frustrated. Irritated.

He watched Al Nash, the "Entertainment Today" interviewer, ogle Belle from the moment she entered the set. Al completely ignored Max as he took her arm and led her to the desklike position already set up with her name. He sat beside her. Insisted on putting the miniaturized mike on her collar. He kept shifting his chair closer to hers as the cameras and crew adjusted lighting and got into position. He leaned over her shoulder. Whispered into her ear.

Max clenched and unclenched his hands, knowing if this interview didn't start soon, he was going to punch this guy's lights out.

Finally the countdown was given, the interviewer rolled his chair back, and the tape began to roll. After a short introductory sentence or two, he turned to them.

"Welcome, Belle, Max. Your head-on opposing viewpoints of movies over this last week has made Hollywood hot with controversy. Is that what you aim for, Belle?"

"My only aim is to tell the truth as I see it, Al."

"But you will admit that most other critics disagree with the truth as you see it?"

"Of course they disagree. The problem with most critics is they're bogged down in the mechanics of filmmaking. They judge films by how realistic the acting, sets and visual effects are. They totally ignore the most important aspect of story-telling."

"What aspect is that, Belle?"

"They should be asking themselves the question 'Is this an uplifting story filled with wonderful characters that an audience will want to get to know and root for?'"

"And that's how you judge a film?"

"I think that's how people with sense judge films. For too long, those people have had no critic to represent their view. Finally, they have one. Me."

"Still, not all viewers agree with you. As a matter of fact, word is around town that you've been getting some heavy-duty threats recently. What's it all about?"

Max watched Belle swallow uneasily. "All people in the public eye get threats of one sort or another. Just comes with the territory. I bet even you've gotten a few, haven't you?"

Al shrugged noncommittally. "There's also a rumor that you and Max here are an item, Belle. Any truth in it?"

"Now, come on, Al, you can't be serious. You've seen our reviews. Two more different people you could never find. I'd have more in common with Rambo."

As the interviewer laughed along with Belle, Max's gut tightened in annoyance. But what was even more annoying is he knew he had no reason to be annoyed.

The camera and microphone swung in his direction. "So, Max, we've heard about Belle's criteria for judging a movie. What's yours?"

"I think I have to agree with how Alfred Hitchcock put it. I think the best movie is life with all the dull parts cut out."

"Word is that your life doesn't have too many of those dull parts. Want to share with the viewers who the lady is you keep company with these days? Or should I say, ladies?"

Max leaned back and crossed his arms over his chest. "No."

Al looked a bit disconcerted but persevered, probably realizing that what didn't sound good could always be cut.

"What about your costar here? Belle denies there's anything between you, but everybody's still talking about your shaking up a certain producer who you thought might be threatening her?''

Max gritted his teeth, reminding himself that before he did another interview, he'd get a list of the questions first. "The incident was blown all out of proportion, Al. You know Hollywood. Always ready to find a scandal especially when none exists.''

"But you did rough up a director the other night? Because of Belle?''

Max felt like roughing up an interviewer at the moment. Still he knew the only way to handle this situation was to control it, not let it control him.

Max deliberately leaned back in his chair, letting his open vest fall to his sides, displaying the smooth, powerful chest he'd made part of his image. He flashed the camera his most charming and disreputable smile. "A man should always be ready to defend a woman. From other men.''

"So you were defending Belle? Does that mean—''

Max started as he caught a sudden movement out of the corner of his eye. He twisted his head just in time to see Belle scoot her chair back from her position and jump to her feet, a look of utter horror on her face.

Max stiffened in immediate alarm.

Then he heard her scream beside him in unbelievable, blood-chilling clarity.

Max ripped the microphone off the side of his vest and shot to his feet. She screamed again, her eyes riveted below her skirt line as she bent over trying to pull at something. He stepped to her side and stared in disbelief at the slithering snakes circling her ankles, striking lightning fast at her with their fangs, as she desperately and frantically was trying to kick them away.

He dropped to the carpet, grabbed her legs, snatched the cold, wiggling, clinging things off her as fast as he could. He ignored their strikes against his arms. He worked in a frenzy of speed, as the awful vibrations from her continuing screams ripped through his chest.

Within the slowest moving seconds of his life, he finally managed to pull the snakes off her. He picked her up, cradled her in his arms and carried her off the set.

Lights and noise and movement flickered all around him. The stage manager shouted. People at every corner yelled and screamed and jumped out of the way as snakes slithered around the floor and cameras pushed forward and back to catch the action. Technicians scurried in all directions trying to catch the fast-moving snakes.

As Max dashed through the door, he heard the tape that someone had started to play, blasting through the stage's speakers.

"...Santa Claus is coming to town. He sees you when you're sleeping. He knows when you're awake...."

BELLE'S MEMORIES of the hospital's emergency room hazed over in her mind. Even the reassurance of the young doctor that the snake bites hadn't been poisonous barely registered on her consciousness. Vague, too, were the faces of Neal, Paula, Luana, Apple and Sergeant Morse as they came and went from the emergency room. As Morse confided wearily that no one at the "Entertainment Today" studio could shed any light on how the snakes got on the set.

Just two things remained crystal clear in her mind: The slithering serpents wrapping around her legs, sinking their fangs into her flesh as they circled around her legs. And Max's warm, strong hand tearing them off her, carrying her safely away from that terrible nightmare, staying close by every second since, until he had stripped off her suit coat and skirt and gently laid her in his bed mere minutes before.

She thought she had lost him. But he'd been there again. He'd come through for her.

"Hot chocolate is here."

She curled the black satin sheets of his bed around her waist and watched him reenter the room, carrying a large tray containing two mugs and a plateful of sandwiches in those big, strong hands, and her heart cartwheeled inside her chest like the silly brainless thing it was.

He sat on the edge of the bed as she sipped chocolate and ate a roast beef sandwich, both of which were probably excellent, but neither of which she tasted. She had room in her thoughts only for the strong, protecting man sitting on the edge of the bed, quietly polishing off the rest of the sandwiches.

He took the mug out of her hands when she'd finished and put it back on the tray, then set the tray on the nightstand.

"Better?" he asked.

"Much."

He studied her silently, quietly for a minute. "How much?"

"Very much."

Instantly the calm look on his face metamorphosed into one of fury. "I'm glad, because that means now I can yell at you, you fool! Why in hell's name didn't you tell me Morse had released Terry Stut and you were still in danger?"

Belle blinked in astonishment at the complete change in Max. Her chin went up in hurt and anger. "Well, excuse me, but sometimes we 'fools' get funny little ideas in our heads like maybe the pigheaded man who throws us out of his house one night just might not give a damn whether or not we're in danger the next!"

His teeth clenched harder. "I didn't throw you out of my house. I told you to use the guest room."

Belle sat up straighter in the bed. "Told me? You ordered me to!"

Max grabbed her arms, his steel fingers like vises around her skin. "All right, I ordered you to. You should be thanking me!"

His grasp had begun to set her heart to drumming. "Thanking you? Is this ordering of people to your guest room some sort of kinky California hospitality I'm unaware of?"

"You fool! I was trying to keep you out of my bed!"

He was so close. His heat. His scent. She wanted, needed, him so much she hurt. She took a shaky breath that vibrated with that need. "Well, you lose. Here I am."

Belle watched a battle waging in his black eyes—eyes that flashed with a fire much deeper and deadlier than anger. Its flame burned into her from his tightening hands.

His next curse broke into a tortured groan as he pulled her to him.

Belle cried out as her own hunger answered the strength of his molten aggression, measure for measure. She pressed firmer against him, parting her lips beneath his, shivering as his strong, capable, expert hands branded her body with their hot touch.

She knew this time she wouldn't be pulling back. And this time neither would he.

Sensations wilder and freer than any she'd known before burst beneath the hard, demanding, ruthless force of his lips.

He laid her back against the pillows, knelt above her, and tore at her blouse and slip as she tore at his vest and jeans.

When they were naked he kissed her—hot, wet, branding kisses—running his teeth lightly across her neck, arms, legs and breasts, making her moan and wither and gasp.

He grasped her arms and spun with her until suddenly he had her held securely above him. Slowly, he positioned one breast and taut nipple above his mouth, then sent out his tongue to pay it homage.

The pleasure rocketed through Belle as the sensations of that undivided attention shot through her hips, setting her on fire. And just when she thought he had drawn every pleasurable feeling possible, he switched to the other breast and nipple and started over.

She moaned and whimpered and felt his laugh of triumph against her nipple create even newer and deeper quivers of delight.

By the time he laid her on her back again, she gasped with the warm hum that vibrated throughout her body and refused to let her eyes focus properly.

She reached for him in one very quick, efficient move, and took him in her hands. "I'm not complacently submitting to any more of this torture. This isn't a spectator sport."

He laughed as the gleam deepened in his black eyes. She ran her fingers up and down in slow, sensual strokes. He swallowed and closed his eyes as his breath caught at the sharp sensations of need slamming through him.

He opened his eyes to see her staring at his fully aroused body with hungry eyes. And he almost lost it right there. With an urgency, his hands moved feverishly over her body as he branded her beautiful bare flesh with hot wet kisses that had her moaning and withering again beneath his touch. Then he buried himself between her legs and she took him in one powerful thrust with a cry of joy.

Belle fought for sanity and lost. His touch and her responding feelings became all that was left of reality. He pushed her closer and closer to the edge until suddenly she felt the intensity reach its peak and burst through.

Sensations she'd never felt before ripped through her, so violent she cried out. At that final glorious moment, his lips fused with hers and she felt his own cry of fulfillment rumbling like thunder in her breast.

She had thought she knew the heights of passion. She had been wrong. Swirls of warmth coursed through her blood like a delicious, intoxicating drug. The tension in her muscles relaxed as her body sunk bonelessly into the bed.

Dazed, she opened her eyes and saw him through a filmy mist hovering above her, his powerful biceps sparing her the full brunt of his heaviness. She reached for those powerful shoulders. Brought him down on top of her. Luxuriated in the solid weight and size of him.

Formidable. Firm. Hers. New desire rose within her like an insatiable hunger. Strength raced back to tighten her muscles. She wrapped her arms around him, her legs around him, squeezed him inside and out.

His breath broke against her ear. She laughed, contracted around his hardness. Then rolled him over. Got on top, controlled the renewed thrusts he made so urgently. Taunting him. Tantalizing him. Until her own reason shattered as she drove them both beyond the brink.

Afterward, she lay across his chest listening to the beat of his heart, too weak to move.

His heated breath blew on the back of her damp neck, the warm roughness unmistakable in his tone. "Damn woman. Should have known you'd insist on having the counterpoint in this, too."

Belle let out the sound that could only be described as the primitive sigh of the thoroughly satisfied and sated female, wrapped securely in the arms of her mate.

She did not kid herself, of course. She had a long way to go before she could call this mate domesticated. And in the blackness of this December night, an anonymous, sadistic Santa Claus still waited and watched, toting a bagful of terror.

But something strong had entered Belle's heart this night—something capable of conquering even wild men and fear.

Belle was full of love.

SANTA WATCHED THE BEDROOM light go off in Wilde's town house. So Breeze was spending the night this time? Well, well. How the mighty had fallen. And with the wild man, no less.

Santa's brow furrowed. Of course, the wild man hadn't looked all that wild tonight. On the contrary. He'd looked positively tamed by the woman, holding her hand, insisting on being with her every minute. Sickening.

Still, Santa knew Max Wilde would not be able to help her. Nobody would be able to help her. Santa would make sure she learned that, too.

Santa's eyes lifted again to the darkened window. "You and I have a very special date tomorrow, Breeze. You could say we'll be bumping into each other."

Santa laughed.

Chapter Twelve

On the eighth day of Christmas, Santa Claus gave to
Breeze
Eight snakes a-clinging.

> I'm striking back,
> Santa Claus

Max watched Belle reading the stanza again as he poured
her another cup of morning coffee. His pulse quickened as
he saw the flushed, vibrant color to her cheeks. Not even this
latest evidence of this terror campaign against her was able
to dim the spark and sparkle in her eyes.

Several times during the night they had awakened in each
other's arms and made love. And still this morning he could
barely keep his hands off her.

She looked up at him then, and he felt the force of his
desire knock the breath out of him. He didn't know who he
was or what he wanted anymore, except that he wanted her.
Breeze, nothing. Storm was a far more descriptive word for
the way she was sweeping through his life, overturning everything.

"Max, the coffee."

He started as he looked down to see the coffee overflow-
ing from her cup. He put down the coffeepot and reached

for a napkin to wipe up the spill. Did he say storm? Make that tornado.

"So Jim Apple found this taped to the new door of my office?"

"Yes. Neal had sent him over to the newsroom to check on something. When he saw the envelope, he rushed it over to the 'Entertainment Today' studio, but it was too late. We were already on the way to the hospital by then. He gave the original to Morse, and Morse ran off that copy so you could see it."

She exhaled as she dropped the stanza onto the table. She picked up her coffee cup and took a sip. "So it's back to Ramish and Daark."

"No, Belle. I had both Ramish and Daark followed from about three o'clock Sunday afternoon until way past midnight. Neither of them went anywhere near the Literacy League building in L.A."

She put down her coffee cup. "I'm confused. If it's not Terry Stut or Russell Ramish or Justin Daark, then who is it? Could Sergeant Morse have been right all along? Is this sadistic Santa Claus some crazed fan?"

Max shook his head, disturbed by the shadows back in her eyes. He tried to imbue his tone with confidence. "I'm betting we've read those first five clues in the stanzas right. Now we should be looking at the last three to see what they're telling us."

He sat down next to her and got out a pen and paper. "'Here's my smash hit,' 'Now you're locked up,' and 'I'm striking back.' One by one, Belle. You know the drill. Go."

She nodded. "'Here's my smash hit.' Again a reference to the movie industry. And maybe the fact that the movie I reviewed that this Santa Claus is angry about wasn't a hit? If that's true, Max, then that lets Ramish out for certain, because his movie did well at the box office. What's the next one?"

"'Now you're locked up.'"

Her brow furrowed. "That almost make me think Morse is right when he says this maniac is a crazed viewer."

"Why?"

"Well, doesn't that phrase give you the impression that this guy has been locked up at some time in the past? Like if he was a patient in a mental institution? Otherwise, why would he say, 'Now *you're* locked up,' like he's getting back at me for something he's had to endure?"

Max rubbed the back of his neck. "It's a thought. Let's leave that one and go to the last. 'I'm striking back.'"

"Not a whole lot of new information there. We already have identified a revenge theme. That's just a reiteration of the theme."

"So it seems. There's got to be something we're overlooking. Maybe something to do with the 'Twelve Days of Christmas' song he's been following so closely."

"If he really was following it closely, he should have started it on Christmas. Christmas Day was the first day that the 'true love' of the original song sent the partridge in a pear tree."

"I wonder if the day he started them on has significance? Belle, did you do any of those first three reviews on December 13 of last year?"

"Let me see. Those of us in contention for the job arrived in L.A. on December 8. We went to the screening of *Major Change* the next morning, so that would count that out."

"Would it? You may have screened it on the ninth, but it might not have aired until the thirteenth."

"Yes, Max. I think you're right. I do think my review on *Major Change* aired around December 13. And what's more, I think that might also have been the day I previewed the other two films."

Belle finished her sentence over the ringing of the telephone. Max swung over to the kitchen wall phone and answered.

"Hi, it's Chris. It's been a bear running down, but I've got some info on that cast of *Major Change.*"

"Go ahead, Chris."

"Well, the male lead was a twenty-year-old called Terrence Tremont, a student at Pasadena City College. I called his number, but got a disconnect recording. His address must still be good. We sent out a membership renewal notice a couple of months ago. The post office would have returned it if he was no longer there."

Max recognized Terry Stut's stage name. He told Chris to go ahead and give him the guy's address and made a quick note of it.

"The female lead, Trina Cork, was a student at a private religious college. Apparently she was living in a dorm on campus there because she gave the school address and telephone number as hers. Her membership renewal came back 'not at this address.' I called the school. They wouldn't tell me anything except she was no longer a student. Sorry."

"Maybe I can get a line on her from one of the others. Locate anyone else?"

"Yeah. The rest of the cast—all eight of them—did renew their memberships this year. Seems they were picked up a couple of months ago by Russell Ramish for a production he's got going."

"Ramish?"

"Yeah, Max. And get this. One of the guys here remembers Ramish calling personally to ask for these people. And I mean personally."

Max thanked Chris and hung up the phone to share with Belle what he had learned.

"But we've already dismissed Ramish from the possibilities," she said. "He was at that football game when I was being locked in the storeroom. His movie made lots of money."

Max exhaled heavily. "Still, I don't like the way the man's name keeps turning up like the proverbial bad penny."

"So where do we start?" Belle asked.

"Let's go talk with Terry Stut, aka Terrence Tremont. Maybe he's got some answers."

TERRY STUT FINALLY answered his door after Max displayed his impatience by leaning on the bell. He was barechested, barefooted, and wearing just the pants to his security guard uniform, and a sulky look.

"I got nothing to say to either of you."

Max prevented the door from closing with a strategically placed foot. "If you're innocent, Stut, someone's gone to some trouble to implicate you in Ms. Breeze's affairs. Aren't you curious who it might be?"

Stut's fingers played with his beard for a moment before he motioned them into his studio apartment. It was small, marginally clean, littered with books and papers. A foothigh aluminum Christmas tree with a single strand of tinsel sat on top of a nine-inch TV. A notebook full of equations lay on the Formica-topped coffee table. Max and Belle took a seat on a worn plaid sofa that no doubt was made into Stut's bed at night.

Stut sat across from them on a straight-back wooden chair that wobbled. His sulkiness had disintegrated into something like worry. "You saying someone tried to set me up, Wilde?"

"I think it's possible. How'd you get your security guard's job?"

"Call came through over at the college. I've had my name down for a night job for months now along with half a dozen other people. My name was picked."

"You know why?"

Stut shrugged. "Figure my GPA. I'm holding down a 3.8. Stuff like that impresses some people."

"Tell us about last year and being in *Major Change*."

"It was the kind of stuff you read about happening thirty, forty years ago. I mean this guy walks up to me out of the blue one day while I'm studying under a tree and says, 'Hey, kid, how'd you like to be in a movie?' And damn if he wasn't serious.''

"Just like that?"

"Just like that. Next thing I know I'm dropping out of school and spouting lines in front of a camera.''

"You had to drop out?"

"We all had to. Rest of the cast were college students, too. We suddenly found ourselves on any one of various sets from early morning to late at night. Went on for months. No way to attend class, much less do homework. Not that any of us really cared to after we got bitten by the Tinsel Town bug.''

"Being actors went to your heads?"

"Man, it filled our heads. We got together nearly every night after shooting to talk about the big stars we were going to become. All the money we were going to make. All the fame. And then KALA ran their review, the first one on the film.'' Stut paused to poke a thumb in Belle's direction. "And Breeze here tore it to shreds.''

"How'd everyone react, Stut?"

"I'd say we were a fairly representative sample of everything from anger to tears. Trina went running from the room in hysterics.''

"She took it that hard?"

"Worse than anyone. Someone in her family had been really upset with her even doing the movie because the role conflicted with their religious teachings.''

"Because the character turns into a prostitute?" Belle asked for clarification.

"Yeah. But she'd gone ahead anyway on the sly. Kept pretending she was still in school so they wouldn't know. She thought after the film proved a success, no one would remember anything but the success. But everything you said in your review about the message in the movie highlighted those very areas that her family had objected to. She was blown away.''

"Where did she go?"

"Haven't a clue. She'd been a shy kid all the way through the shooting. Never smoked or drank or even talked much. But that night she grabbed a bottle of booze and went flying out the door. Haven't seen her since."

"And you and the others?"

"Our performances got a few nice comments in some of the written reviews done on the movie. Proved to be dangerous carrot sticks. Despite the dismal box office receipts, the others have been hanging around Hollywood ever since, trying to pick up bit parts and such. They'll be living on the edge of their dreams and the unemployment line probably for the rest of their lives."

"Had you heard Ramish picked them up to be in a movie a couple of months ago?"

"Oh, yeah. They called me just before they left to start shooting in Argentina. You know what Ramish has got them doing? Playing typical American college students on vacation. No close-ups. No lines. Just background camera fodder. That's all they'll ever be."

"But not you?"

"No way. I wised up. Reenrolled in college."

"So your relationship with Luana Halsey isn't so she'll help you back into the business?"

For the first time, Stut smiled. "The talents I got Luana likes to enjoy behind the cameras."

"She's not helping you financially through school?"

"Give me a break. Does this place look as if I'm living the life of some wealthy woman's pampered stud? Truth is, I like big, strong, vintage women with lots of power. Luana is that and then some."

Max read the man's smile as only a man could. He believed Stut. At least about Luana. "You ever have anything going with Trina?"

"Nothing serious. Oh, a little necking off camera. Helped our scenes in front of it."

"Nothing else?"

"I'm not saying I didn't try. But she was ... well, a little scared of sex. Her upbringing, probably. She had this naturally innocent look. Probably got picked for the part of the coed-prostitute because that damned look seemed so out of place with her bright titian hair and body by Venus. Maybe that's why a big agent like Luana was handling her. Saw the potential in that contrast."

Belle sat forward with a start. "Luana Halsey was handling an unknown talent like Trina Cork?"

Stut's blond eyebrows raised. "Of course. That's how Luana and I met. While she was out at one of the shoots watching Trina perform. You didn't know?"

"LUANA, WHY DID YOU AGREE to handle Trina Cork?" Belle demanded.

Luana shrugged, still looking a bit put out at Belle and Max's insistence on seeing her without an appointment. And a bit nervous about the topic they'd come to discuss. "I thought she had potential."

"A nobody? With no training or experience?"

"Look, Belle, I agree under normal circumstances I'd have given her a pass. But a friend suggested I take a look. So I crashed the gate at a shoot. Trina wasn't an actress by any stretch of the imagination. She was just a kid out of a cloistered school and restrictive family suddenly up in the clouds with Hollywood stars in her eyes."

"And still you took her on?"

"You saw the movie. She had this uncanny ability to look like an innocent in one scene and a prostitute in the next, without acting. I thought I might be able to do something with her."

"What happened to her after the movie flopped?"

Luana exhaled heavily and leaned back in her chair. "What does it matter? Why do you even care?"

"Luana, I'm still getting those presents from some maniac out there. Max and I believe the reason is connected with the people in one of three movies I reviewed last year. *Major Change* was one of those movies. That's why I care.''

"All right, Belle. But I very much doubt knowing is going to help. Trina called me several days after your review. She was drunk, crying hysterically, talking crazy, barely coherent. I thought it was because she'd been so devastated by what you said about the movie. I told her to call me when she sobered up. Hung up the phone. Put it out of my mind. Then the next thing I knew, she was dead.''

"*Dead?*"

Luana looked away from Belle's face. She ran a stubby, rickety hand through her short salt-and-pepper hair. "She'd been pushed off a building on a back set over at Paramount. The one that's a re-creation of a New York street. Murdered on Christmas Eve by some madman who'd been stalking her.''

Belle came right out of her seat. "She was murdered by a madman? Stalking her? Dear God, Luana, who?''

"I don't think the police ever found out. Only reason they even knew her death wasn't suicide was because they found some of his threatening letters in her apartment afterward.''

Belle licked dry lips. "What did the letters say?''

"I know what you're thinking, Belle. But they weren't song stanzas or anything like that. He was just some crazed fan who had seen her in the movie. Wrote something about her having the face of an angel and the soul of a devil. He told her he was going to kill her on Christmas Eve, have her die just like the character she played in the movie died, by falling off a high building. And damned if he didn't carry out his threat.''

"Didn't Trina go to the police when she started getting the letters?''

"Apparently not. They had no record of a report.''

"But I don't understand. Why didn't she seek their help?''

"Offhand I'd say because she viewed authority figures like an extension of a disapproving parent. Trina was very strictly brought up. Deep down I always had the feeling that no matter what she said, she felt guilty about playing the kind of part she'd been given. Maybe in some way she convinced herself she deserved to receive those letters."

"Luana, why didn't you tell me all this sooner?"

"For what purpose, Belle? You think I like admitting that some poor, scared kid calls me for help against some maniac stalking her and I tell her to call me back when she sobers up? Besides, how can what happened to Trina Cork have anything to do with what's happening to you?"

'CAN WHAT HAPPENED to Trina Cork have anything to do with what's happening to me?" Belle asked as they got back into Max's car.

Max's forehead was a mass of frowns. "I don't know, but there is a similarity in that both of you received threatening messages."

Belle sighed. "Just when we were thinking it might be someone from *Major Change,* they all get accounted for. Luana alibis Stut. Trina turns up dead. And the rest of the cast are out of the country on a shoot. Now what?"

"Well, now I'm wondering why Sergeant Morse didn't mention how Trina Cork died. You told him about the three movies. If he really did look into them as he promised, why didn't he learn about Trina? I think I'll give him a call right now and ask that question."

Max opened his car phone line and punched in the number for Morse. The sergeant wasn't on duty, but had left word for any calls from Max or Belle to be dispatched through to his home. He picked it up after a couple of rings.

"I didn't mention it because I didn't know," Morse answered in response to the question. "I was on vacation last Christmas, so obviously I didn't handle the case. But now that you've brought it to my attention, I'll look into the files and see what I can find. By the way, I tried to reach you two earlier today. Where are you?''

"We're on Santa Monica Boulevard going to pick up Belle's car from the body shop. Why? Something come up?''

"I suppose I can tell you over the phone. We got our first piece of luck. The lab finally analyzed the paper and envelopes used in these notes. There are several companies that order it specially.''

Max heard the small change of inflection in Morse's tone. "But one of them you feel is significant?''

"Yes. One of them is KALA. It's the second sheet of their executive stationery, Wilde, the sheet without the embossed name. I'd say this puts a little different complexion on things.''

Max thanked Morse then pushed the button to disengage the line. "You heard?''

"Yes. But, Max, someone at KALA? How can it be? No one at KALA was involved in any of those three movies last year.''

"Maybe we need to expand our definition of involved. What if whoever is doing this to you is someone who is not directly associated with one of the movies, but involved with one of the people associated with one of the movies?''

"Wait a minute. You mean a person at KALA might be so mad at a bad review I gave someone they care for that they've launched this vendetta against me?''

"Could be, Belle. Remember the personal message in the eighth stanza, '*I'm* striking back'?''

"You're emphasizing *I'm* because you think the writer of the stanza was trying to tell me that he was striking back at me for someone else?''

"It's a thought.''

"Then this maniac might see himself like the vulture in *Pound of Flesh*, an instrument of revenge for someone else who has suffered. But who at KALA might feel that way?''

"Maybe it's time to get this Santa Claus to step out of the wings. You ever do any acting, Belle?"

"No. Why?"

"Because you're about to." He smiled over at her. "But don't worry. I promise this is a part that will come naturally."

BELLE FELT EXCITED and expectant as she finished her scathing review that night in KALA's entertainment alcove. She even got in a personal verbal jab at Max. When her tally light went off, she looked over at him and he winked at her.

And that, Belle knew, was her cue. She got to her feet, raised her voice. "What an absolutely brainless review, Wilde. Don't you have any standards at all? You couldn't have spent more than five minutes on it."

He rose to tower over her, his hands planting themselves on his hips. "If I had spent only two minutes on it, it would still have more sense than that verbal dribble that comes spewing out of your mouth."

"Verbal dribble? Why...you...you...your head is so honeycombed with barbed-wire gore and garbage that no decent, coherent thought could possibly sneak through!"

"Yeah? Well, lady, your mind is so closed, the escalator up is wearing a perpetual Out of Order sign."

Belle's lips tightened. "I don't have to listen to any more of this and I don't intend to. Get out of my way, Wilde."

"You're the one in my way, Breeze. Go blow."

Belle stomped of the set and nearly ran into Neal and Paula, who had been observing the shouting match between Max and her. "Whoa, Belle," Neal said, grabbing her shoulders. "Save the fireworks for on camera."

"Oh, let go of me, Neal."

Belle tore herself out of Neal's restraint and stomped off. Max walked up to the startled program director and station manager. "Irritating, ungrateful woman. And after all I've done for her over this psycho Santa business, too."

Paula smirked at him. "This is Hollywood, chum. No good turn goes unpunished. The tally light might have been off, but the film was still rolling, Wilde. The camera caught that little impromptu spitting session. Should make a good promo for tomorrow."

"That's a low trick, Paula."

The woman's purple lips spread into a big smile. "Yeah. I know."

Max waved his hand in irritation. "Oh, do your worst. I don't care. I'm getting out of here."

"Without Breeze?" Neal asked.

"Not only without her but as far away from her as I can get."

JIM APPLE RESTED a hand on Belle's sleeve as she made to leave the building. "Ms. Breeze, it's early. Sergeant Morse isn't here yet. I really think you should wait for him."

"I appreciate your concern, Jim, but I'll be all right. It's not that far a drive to my apartment. And I—I just have to get out of the station tonight."

"Because of your fight with Mr. Wilde?"

"Yes."

"I'll follow you."

"No, thanks. Really. I'll be fine."

"But—"

"Really, Jim. It's okay. See you tomorrow."

Belle pushed through KALA's glass doors, the cool night air bathing her face as she dug into her shoulder bag for her car keys. Her high heels clicked on the pavement as she approached her Saturn, unlocked the door and slipped into the driver's seat. She immediately locked her door.

Within seconds she was shooting past the parking lot guard and out onto the Hollywood streets.

She glanced casually in her rearview mirror. She saw nothing. But she knew Max was back there. And Morse a street over. Staying out of sight. Watching. Waiting. While she provided bait for the trap.

Max hadn't liked this part. But Morse had agreed with her. A trap was no trap without the bait. Her.

Traffic had lightened somewhat. Was actually moving at the speed limit. Of course, there was no telling when this madman would strike. But KALA was being watched. When any of them left, they would be followed. She was safe no matter what he tried. She stopped for a red light.

She slid the driver's window down, let the cool night air surround her.

Her apartment was only a few blocks away now. There were policemen in the security garage. And the elevator. And waiting outside the hall to her apartment. She'd be watched all the way.

White, red, green and gold lights on the Christmas decorations adorning the street lamps flickered lazily in a slight breeze, the sounds of their tinkling bells drifting through her open window. In the car just ahead of her, a Santa Claus doll sat in the rear window, its head bobbing up and down as it grinned at her.

Belle felt a trembling in her hands as they clutched the steering wheel. Her heart beat hollowly against her ribs.

The traffic light turned green. The car in front of her sped away. Belle stepped on the gas. The Saturn accelerated across the intersection into the curving street ahead.

She couldn't wait for the day when she'd be able to look at a Santa Claus representation without cringing. Would this sadistic madman be caught tonight? Would she and Max be free to explore this relationship they'd begun? Was there a chance that Max might—

So far away had her thoughts taken her that when the car in the lane to her left suddenly plowed into the side of the Saturn, Belle froze in disbelief as it shoved her off the road, across the sidewalk, head-on into a brick building.

Belle's heart dove into her throat as she jammed on the brakes.

Too late. Much too late.

The building loomed in the windshield—coming closer and closer in absolute slow motion. Just as crystal clear as any picture, stopped frame by frame. She could even make out the texture of the old red bricks, see their chipped corners, count the cracks in the joining gray mortar.

Someone had sprayed white paint across the bricks. Repent! The End is Near!

It certainly was. The Saturn's front end hit the brick facing with an eerie, soundless force.

Belle felt herself shoot forward against the lap and shoulder belts, knowing they could not save her, knowing that by the time the sounds of the crash reached her ears, she'd be dead.

Blessedly, mercifully, a thick, diaphanous cloud swallowed her whole before the full impact.

Chapter Thirteen

Belle traveled through a tunnel with a blinding light. She'd read how people with near-death experiences always spoke of a blinding white light, and here it was. And she was moving toward it. And at its end would be all those loved ones who had gone before, waiting to greet her.

But all the people she loved were still alive. Max. Her family. Dear God, she didn't want to die! Stop. Please stop.

But the light kept getting brighter.

"Ms. Breeze? Can you hear me? Can you open your eyes?"

Belle tried and surprised herself when it worked. She blinked, surprising herself again when she identified the bright white light of her tunnel as a small flashlight balanced between two fingers of a man in a white coat who was trying to look in her eye.

She looked around to discover she was in a hospital bed in a small private room. Relief swelled in her chest and filled her heart. "Dear heavens, I'm alive. And everyone I love is alive."

The doctor's wrinkled face smiled. "I can attest to the first. I'll take your word for the second. You're a very lucky lady. You've come through without a scratch. Amazing, since as I understand it, your car was totaled. I'd say you owe your good fortune to an air bag."

"I'm not hurt?"

"A bit shaken, certainly. The force of the inflating air bag was probably what knocked you unconscious. But a full recovery is in your immediate future."

Belle felt a cold tremor of delayed fear sweep through her, leaving her stiff and achy. She'd come so close. When she thought again of that terrified instant in time when she'd come face-to-face with that brick wall—

"Doctor? What did you say?"

"I said that there are two very worried men waiting for you outside. I'd like to go relieve their minds. Shall I send them in?"

"Please."

Belle pushed herself into a sitting position. She wouldn't want to live through the seconds before the crash again for anything, but at least it was over. Everything was now over.

She hardly noticed Morse as Max shot into the room, immediately coming to her side to gather her in his arms. He held her close, so very close. Oh, how great it felt to be alive!

His voice sounded so wonderfully worried. "Belle, you're really all right?"

Reluctantly she leaned back. "Fine. Just a little air bag concussion. Who was it?"

Max's brow clouded immediately, and Belle's heart sank as she read the truth reflected there. She looked over at Morse, frustration weighing down her words. "But how could you not catch him? You were both following me. You had men watching everyone at KALA. What happened?"

Max exhaled heavily. "He shot out two tires on the Porsche. Then circled around the block and shot out two more on Morse's police unit. Once he got us out of the way, he went after you."

Belle slumped against the pillow, all her balled relief unraveling. She'd gone through this latest terror for nothing? Her car totaled for nothing? She almost died for nothing?

Tears stung her eyes. "How could he know you and Morse were following me?"

Morse squinted at Belle. "He's a cunning bastard. Obviously he's seen both of us with you, Ms. Breeze. He must have gotten suspicious over that fight you and Mr. Wilde faked. Smelled a setup. So he didn't go directly for you but looked for us first to take us out and clear the field to you."

"But your men were watching for anyone who left KALA to follow me. They have to know—"

"We ran into a snag there, too, I'm afraid. The two police units I had borrowed to help out in surveillance were deliberately drawn away to respond to a fake 'officer down and needs assistance' call at a fictitious address several blocks away. That kind of a call always takes precedence. This bastard has covered all his bases. This is the latest stanza. We found it in the door handle of your car after the crash."

Belle took it and read it silently.

On the ninth day of Christmas, Santa Claus gave to Breeze
Nine bones breaking.

> No one can protect you from me,
> Santa Claus

Belle exhaled in growing despair. "Who is this demon that he can always know where I am and can second-guess what we try to do?"

Max took hold of her hands. "Don't go imbuing him with supernatural powers, Belle. He or she is just as human as you or I. Smart, evil—but human. We'll get him."

"But how? Where do we go from here?"

"The idea of using Ms. Breeze as bait is still a good one," Morse said. "The next time, though—"

"No!" Max yelled. "There'll be no next time. I was a fool to have agreed to that part of the plan. I should have hidden in the back seat of the Saturn with a loaded shotgun like I suggested in the first place. Bastard would be dead now."

"Mr. Wilde, I told you I could not condone your riding around with a loaded weapon—"

"I heard you the first time, Morse. I don't give a damn what you condone. For God's sake, man, he almost killed her tonight!"

The doctor walked into the room then, throwing a frown at Max because of his raised voice. Then he turned to smile at Belle. "Ms. Breeze, all your tests have come back fine. But we'd like to keep you in the hospital for observation overnight. Just routine, you understand."

"She's not staying," Max said. "She's coming with me to pick up my car at the garage. And then home. I'm not letting her out of my sight again."

In spite of all the disappointment and danger she faced, a rather intriguing tingle wiggled up Belle's spine at the command and promise in Max's words.

But as soon as they picked up his mended car, Max didn't head for his town home in Pasadena.

"Max, this isn't the way to your place."

"I know. I changed my mind."

"Where are we going?"

"Your apartment."

"Why?"

"Because you're going to pack your things. You're leaving for Minnesota tonight. I'll call the airport and make your reservations."

Her eyes flashed to his face. "But isn't this what this madman has wanted all along? For me to be so frightened I can't continue with my reviews and I lose my career?"

"Belle, we haven't the faintest idea what this bastard wants. Your career won't mean a thing to you if you're dead."

Belle looked at his cold, determined expression, the pulsing vessel in his temple. "Would you run?"

"What does it matter? It's not happening to me."

"But if it were happening to you, I can't believe you'd leave town. Would you?"

Max suddenly pulled the Porsche over to the side of the road. He shoved the gearshift into Neutral, pulled on the hand brake and leaned over to grab hold of her arms. She felt the beat of his heart like the racing engine behind them. Hers began to race with it.

"Belle, that's all hypothetical. These threats against you aren't. Don't you understand? When I ran up to your car totally demolished after that crash. When I saw the driver's seat caved in. When I thought..."

He gathered her in his arms then and held her, tightly, possessively, as though he'd never let her go as he said her name over and over again, like a curse, like a prayer.

His breath was tortured with his fear for her. "Go home, Belle. Get away while you still can. Please."

He cared so much for her! His voice betrayed him. Belle never knew what the power of love meant until that moment when she felt its unbelievable strength fill her heart, telling her she could never willingly leave this man. Not now.

Happy tears stuck in her throat, gurgled through her words. "L.A. is my home, Max. Besides, I can't possibly go and leave all those poor viewers to your critical clutches."

Max released her to sit back and stare at her face in surprise. She looked so determined, so beautifully flushed with all that fight and cool passion smoldering behind her clear blue eyes.

He couldn't believe this was the same person who had gone through the hell she had over the last week. She had inner resources that even he had never imagined. He knew he should send her away, nonetheless. He knew he shouldn't listen to a word she'd just said.

He released the brake and jammed the gearshift into First. "Okay, Belle. You stay and we fight this bastard. But from now on, I'm controlling the show. Every part of it. You'll do exactly as I say. And Sergeant Morse be damned."

MAX WOKE LATE.

Belle was sprawled across his chest. Sunlight streamed through the window of his bedroom, stroked the peach of her skin, was captured in the golden strands of her hair.

He could feel her heart beating against his. Slow. Steady. Very different from its frantic pace of the night before when she'd ravaged his body. Counter-stroking to his every stroke.

He smiled in wonder at the memory. He smiled in wonder at her. And the feelings she'd brought out in him. And he was so damn glad she hadn't left on that plane the night before.

The clock on the dresser told him they had already missed a screening across town. He decided the night before they weren't going. They weren't going to do anything they were scheduled to anymore. Traps lay in activities known by others. So their activities wouldn't be known.

First thing this morning they'd be meeting with the friends he'd called the night before. In just about forty minutes, as a matter of fact. Time to wake her up.

He raised his hand to touch the exquisite silk of her hair. Then he let his fingers trace her spine from the enticing curve of her shoulder to the soft arc of her hip to the warm round globe of her bottom.

She stirred. Turned over on her back. Stretched. Blinked at him through sleepy, sexy blue eyes. Smiled. "Good morning."

Max kicked the clock off the table. What the hell. They'd be late. He reached for her. "Let me show you just how good a morning it is."

BELLE LIKED SAUL AND SAM Lane the moment Max introduced them. They were twins—short, skinny, bald, sixtyish bachelors who reminded her of two hummingbirds, flitting about on the wings of focused energy.

They both gave her quick, efficient hugs as they welcomed her into their home.

And what a home. It sat at the very top of the Hollywood Hills, a cantilevered wonder with miles of windows, anchored in about two feet of bedrock, with a view of the base that fell off at the other end of the earth. At least it would have on a smogless day. Unfortunately this wasn't one.

"Downstairs. Everything's downstairs," Saul or Sam called—Belle was already confused which was which. She obediently followed whomever down a narrow, deep staircase, fitted with deep green carpet. And stepped into a small theater with four rows of seats lined in front of a full wall-sized screen.

Max was just behind her. "This is where we do all our screenings for the next few days."

Belle's fingers ran over the plush gold velvet of a nearby seat. "How?"

"Saul and Sam know anybody who is anybody in this business. They'll get us copies of any films we need to review. Right at this minute, the one we were scheduled to review this morning is on its way here by special messenger. Come on. I have something else to show you."

Belle followed Max into the next room. There she found a large, professionally lit underground studio, containing several cameras sporting built-in encoders and sync generators, quality prism optics, automatic setups and self-diagnostic functions all hooked up to the latest in electronic control-room switchers.

"This is amazing," she said.

"This is where we shoot our spot from now on."

"Our reviews? For KALA?"

"That's right, Belle. We're screening the movies next door and then taping our reviews here to messenger over to KALA in time for their broadcast. Sam and Saul will be our crew."

Belle snuggled next to him, wrapping her arm around his waist. He'd gone to so much trouble for her. And it just might work. Damn, it just might work. "Paula and Neal agreed to this?"

"They'll find out when the tape is delivered to them this afternoon. They won't know where the tape is coming from or how to get in touch with us. That's the way it's going to be from now on."

A very sound plan. Worthy of the man beside her. But the concern intruded. "We won't catch him this way."

He kissed the top of her head. "No, but he can't get ▮ you this way to deliver any more presents or stanzas. An▮ right now, my sweet, that's a hell of a lot more important ▮ me."

His sweet. How nice that sounded. "What about clothe▮ And makeup?"

"You'll have to make do with what you've got on for t▮ night's spot. Afterward, we'll swing by your apartment ar▮ you can gather up what you'll need for the next couple ▮ days. You're staying with me at my place. I'll put you ▮ that plane to Minnesota Christmas morning. Until th▮ we're joined at the hip, Belle."

She smiled into those warm, possessive eyes, and raised▮ mocking, inquiring eyebrow. "Only at the hip?"

BELLE OPENED her apartment door that night to be greet▮ by the ringing telephone.

"Let it ring," Max said from behind her.

Belle swung her shoulder bag onto the couch. "I can▮ Max. It might be my family."

"All right. Go ahead. But don't tell anyone where you'▮ going to be for the next few days. And I mean anyone."

Belle nodded as she raised the receiver and said hello.

"Ms. Breeze?"

The voice sounded somewhat familiar, but Belle could▮ immediately place it. "Yes?"

"Ms. Breeze, it's Jim Apple. The security guard ▮ KALA?"

"Yes, of course, Jim. What is it?"

"Ms. Breeze, I'm sorry to bother you at home. I got yo▮ number from the emergency call list. I've been trying ▮ reach you all day."

"I've been out. What was it you wanted to talk to ▮ about?"

The security guard's voice lowered. "I followed you l▮ night when you left KALA, Ms. Breeze. I know you s▮ you'd be all right, but I just didn't feel right about letti▮ you go off all alone like that. I'm sorry to go against—"

"Jim, please. What is it?"

"I saw the car that forced you off the road. I think I know who's sending you those messages."

Belle's pulse began to race. She clutched the phone. "Who, Jim?"

"I need to check something out first. To be sure."

"But can't you tell me who you suspect?"

"Not over the phone. I'm calling from KALA. There are people all around. The line might even be bugged."

"Bugged? By whom?"

"Please, Ms. Breeze. I can't say anymore now. I have to talk to you in person. If what I think is true, no one would ever believe who... I can hardly believe it myself."

Belle tried to still her racing pulse. "Jim, when will you know? When can we meet?"

"I'll meet you tomorrow night at nine, Ms. Breeze. In front of the Griffith Park Planetarium. There's a special Christmas laser show. There'll be lots of people around. You must keep lots of other people around you until then. Understand?"

"Yes, I understand, Jim, but I don't—"

"I've got to go. Someone's coming. Tomorrow, Ms. Breeze. And until then, trust no one."

The line went dead in Belle's ear.

She replaced the receiver on the base with shaking hands, stared at it, replaying Jim Apple's words in his scared, breathless voice. *Trust no one.*

She actually jumped when Max's hands suddenly circled round her shoulders.

"Belle?"

She collected herself and turned to face him and related Apple's information.

"You're not going."

"But, Max—"

"I'll meet him there at nine."

"He may not tell you."

"He'll tell me. You can bet he'll tell me, Belle."

Belle was beginning to recognize when she could argu
with that bright black gleam in his eyes and when sh
couldn't. This was definitely one of the times when sh
couldn't.

"All right. I'll go get my things for the next few days
Give me a couple of minutes. I'd also like to take a quic
shower and change into slacks and a sweater and som
comfortable shoes."

"You're not coming back here before I put you on th
plane, so pack for your trip back East, too. I'll start gath
ering up these presents for your family. We'll take them wit
us."

Wonderful, dictatorial man. How much she wished sh
could ask him to come to Minneapolis with her. But he wa
nowhere near ready for that. Was she kidding herself b
thinking he ever would be ready? Belle sighed as she walke
down the hallway toward her bedroom.

Max went over to the Christmas tree and stooped dow
to pick up the presents. He read some of the tags. Mon
Dad. Charles. Kay. The physical evidence of parents and
family whom she loved.

The kind of world he'd never known. An alien world.

What he had with Belle was beyond anything he'd eve
imagined he could experience. But after it was over, the
would separate and resume their disparate lives.

Hers filled with family and Christmas trees and presen
and commitments. And his filled with what? Would it t
Hawaii again this year? Or Aspen?

He thought about the years of Christmases he'd spent i
the company of women whose faces and names he couldn
even remember. How empty and meaningless it all seeme
now.

He held the presents she had so lovingly wrapped. Wh
would it be like putting up a tree every year? Wrappir
presents like this for people you loved and who would sha
all those Christmases to come?

You're a crazy fool, a mocking voice said inside.

And then he heard her scream. A terrified, painful scream. And the blood in his veins turned to ice.

Max dropped the presents in his hands. He flew down the hallway, his heart a throbbing, scared thing in his chest. He found her lying on her side on the carpet just outside the bathroom, tears of pain streaming down her cheeks. And no wonder. The bottoms of her feet were bleeding profusely, pierced with dozens of razor-sharp glass shards.

He picked her up gently and sat her on the bed. The tears still flowing down her cheeks were brave, silent ones. Their cause made him so angry he could barely speak. "Where is your first aid kit?"

She swallowed before she answered. "In the bathroom. But you won't be able to see to find it in the cabinet. The light's burned out. That's why I didn't notice the glass on the floor."

"Flashlight?"

She pointed. "In that nightstand drawer."

Max retrieved it and headed for the bathroom. More glass crunched beneath his shoes. He was glad he'd brought the flashlight along when he got a look in the cabinet underneath the sink. Sharp pieces of glass were laid everywhere. He had no doubts that it had been done on purpose.

If Belle had reached in without a light... He didn't want to think about it. He found the first aid kit and brushed the sharp glass covering it out of the way with a hand towel. Then he brought the kit back into the bedroom and knelt down before Belle.

She winced when he used the tweezers to pull out the first sliver of glass. But then she seemed to steel herself. She didn't move a muscle as he extracted the rest.

The next unenviable task he set himself was cutting her hose away and unsticking it from her open wounds. She made not a sound. Even the tears had stopped. But as he glanced up at her face, he could see the pain in her eyes. And his heart twisted in his chest.

He could kill this person doing this to her. He *would* kill this person doing this to her if he ever got his hands on him.

Gently he washed off the blood. Dabbed the open wound with hydrogen peroxide. Bandaged them. He looked up to see her watching him with large, grave, anguished eyes.

He got up. Took the flashlight. Went back into the bathroom. Found the box of replacement bulbs. Put one into the empty socket above the sink. Switched on the light.

He'd expected it. Still he felt the jolt in his stomach when he came face-to-face with the long white envelope with Belle's name typed on it that was taped to the mirror above the sink. He tore it off and slit it open.

On the tenth day of Christmas, Santa Claus gave to Breeze
Ten balls cutting.

> I can get to you anywhere,
> Santa Claus

"THEY WERE MY Christmas tree balls. He came into my apartment. He took them off my tree. He deliberately smashed them on my bathroom floor. Scattered slivers under the sink. Unscrewed the light bulb. Removed it. Taped the message on my mirror. Left."

Belle knew she was repeating herself. She and Max had already gone over this with Sergeant Morse. But she couldn't seem to help herself.

Her voice shook. She shook. "Max, he *can* get to me anywhere."

Max set his cup of coffee down on the table in front of them as they sat side by side on his white living room couch, her bandaged feet resting on his lap. He draped an arm across her shoulders and brought her closer to him.

"He only wants you to think that to scare you, Belle. He must have gotten the keys out of your purse and copied them that night on the set when he doctored your glove with that rendered animal fat."

Belle drew in an insubstantial breath. "Which means he could have hidden another booby trap elsewhere in my apartment."

He cradled her in his arms, stroked her hair. "Morse is having a team go through it right now. If there's anything else, they'll find it."

Belle didn't want to cry, but the tears spilled over onto her cheeks and she couldn't seem to stop them. "They were my mother's antique balls, Max. They've been in the family for generations. I thought I could take this. Fight back. But no matter what we do, he still keeps coming. Max, when is it going to stop? How can we get it to stop?"

Rage welled up in Max, cold, deadly, leaving him too furious for words.

"APPLE DIDN'T SHOW UP to work today? And didn't call in?"

Paula's sharp voice shot through the telephone receiver into Max's ear. "I told you, no, Max. How many times do I have to say it? If and when he does show, I'm kicking him out on his ear. And stop trying to change the subject. You and Breeze are both in violation of your contracts. Having a tape of your reviews delivered less than thirty minutes to airtime hardly—"

"So take us to court. That's the way it's going to be from now on until we unmask this sadistic Santa Claus. Sergeant Morse has traced the stationery and envelopes to KALA, Paula. And Belle and I have figured out that someone associated with one of those three films I've told you about is to blame. And we both know who is dating a certain producer of one of those films, don't we?"

"Me? Do you have the gall to imply that—"

"I'm not implying anything. I'm stating a fact."

"Well, you'd best be careful of those stated *facts,* chum, because that *fact* might just land you in a slander suit in addition to a breach of contract!"

"Idle threats don't interest me, Paula. But I would be interested in knowing where you went after Belle's and my spot two nights ago. Neal tells me you left the station right after the broadcast."

"Why, that backstabbing little twit!"

"Were you out for a ride, Paula? Bumping into Belle, perhaps?"

"How dare you! I did no such thing! I drove to a late beauty parlor appointment. Why don't you ask Fort where he was going when he zipped past me. Why don't you just do that!"

"Why would Neal be interested in running Belle off the road?"

"You're such fools, all of you. And that goes double for Morse. If you're supposed to be investigating this thing, why haven't you found out about the relationship between Fort and Daark?"

"All right Paula. I'll bite. What is the relationship between Fort and Daark?"

"They're brothers, Sherlock. That's right, blood relations. Now, get off my back and go harass Fort. And tell the twit for me that if he really is responsible for screwing up my programming this way, he's fired."

Paula slammed the phone down in Max's ear. Belle hung up the extension telephone and stared over at Max. "Can what she said possibly be true? Are Neal and Daark really brothers?"

"Sort of boggles the mind, doesn't it?"

"Yes, and yet it sort of makes sense, too. Just the other day Neal was telling me that Daark was really insecure and shy inside, that like so many in Hollywood, he craves attention and adulation. How did he put it? Oh, yes. That Daark 'just dies inside' when he doesn't get that adulation."

Max nodded eagerly. "And maybe Neal just burns with revenge against someone who withholds that attention and adulation from his brother? Belle, this has opened up a new possibilities. Let's call Morse. I think it might be worth the sergeant's time, and ours, to have a little face-to-face chat with our program director."

NEAL'S HANDS FORAGED into his pockets as though they were hoping to find a cyanide pill. "Okay. So Justin and are half brothers."

"Why the difference in the last names?" Morse asked as he squinted at Neal like he was a bug at the end of a pin being readied for the formaldehyde.

Neal looked over nervously at Belle and Max, who sat on either side of him as he squirmed before the sergeant's desk.

"We had different fathers. Didn't grow up together. Justin's sensitive. Insecure. Shy. He had special problems."

"I'm over here, Mr. Fort," Sergeant Morse prodded.

Neal's mustache twitched as his eyes returned to the sergeant. "Look, we agreed not to broadcast our relationship. Then, if I recommend Justin for something like work on that new vampire series at KALA, I don't get hassled with accusations of nepotism."

"Paula knows about your relationship to Daark," Belle said.

"Yeah, but she normally doesn't get involved in selecting the talent for programs. Anyway, she's only interested in results."

"And what are you interested in, Mr. Fort?" Morse asked.

Neal's hands nervously picked at a loose thread in his slacks. "I don't know what you mean."

"Don't you? Ms. Breeze here has said some pretty caustic things about your sensitive, insecure, shy brother and his work. How did you like the things she said?"

Neal jumped up and quickly scurried around his chair as though positioning it between him and Morse might afford some protection. "Oh, no. You're not going to pin this stanza and present business on me."

"Where is KALA's security guard, Jim Apple, Mr. Fort?"

Neal's mustache didn't just twitch, it did a jig. "He didn't come in to work today. I don't know where he is."

"Did you know he called Ms. Breeze last night? Did you know he said he saw who ran her off the road?"

Neal's hands had begun to shake as he clutched and unclutched the back of the chair. "If he told you it was me, he was lying."

"So you're trying to tell us you didn't leave the station after Ms. Breeze two nights ago?"

"Okay, I did. But I drove straight over to Justin's place. There were some scheduling problems we had to discuss. I waited there until he got home. I didn't even see Belle. I swear it. And next time I come here will be with my lawyer."

And with that Neal turned and scurried out of the Hollywood police station.

"Think he's telling the truth?" Belle asked.

Morse shook his head. "Damn hard to tell, I'm afraid."

"Are you going to question Daark, too?"

"Most certainly, Mr. Wilde. But I think our most promising lead is Ms. Breeze's rendezvous with Jim Apple tonight."

"Belle's not meeting him. I am."

"Mr. Wilde, if Jim Apple did not show up for work today, that tells me that whatever he's found out has scared him. My men went to his apartment this morning. His bed wasn't slept in last night. His truck is missing. Do you really think the man will come forward tonight if he sees you and not Ms. Breeze waiting for him in front of the Griffith Park Observatory at nine?"

"You can't possibly be thinking of having her stand out in the open, alone and unprotected?"

"Not for a minute. My men and I will be behind every bush just in case. But since only Apple and us know about his assignation, Ms. Breeze should be safe."

"She's still not going to be standing out there alone. I'm going to be standing right next to her."

"I have no problem with that. And Apple probably won't, either. After all, he told you to surround yourself with people, Ms. Breeze. He might even be expecting Mr. Wilde to accompany you."

Belle took a deep breath. "Then it's settled. Tonight. Max and I together. At nine."

THE NIGHT WAS BLACK, cool and clear. An afternoon wind had swept away several layers of smog, leaving the air almost fresh.

Belle sat next to Max in his Porsche, watching the families leaving their cars in the parking lot to walk into the brightly lit planetarium on the top of Mount Hollywood in Griffith Park to attend the Christmas laser show.

They talked, joked—happy, carefree, unfettered, looking forward to a wonderful evening's entertainment. Belle wondered if she was ever going to feel that carefree again.

"It will be over soon," Max said beside her, as though he'd read her mind.

He rested a warm, strong hand on top of hers. "It's time. Ready?"

She nodded. But she waited until he'd circled around the car to help her out of the passenger seat. She was still wearing slippers on her cut feet, and she was grateful for a helping hand.

Max kept close to her as they slowly made their way to the entrance. They stood just outside the door, bathed in light, Max holding firmly onto Belle's arm as the steady stream of people passed heading for the back room and the show. Soon the crowd became a trickle. And finally ceased altogether.

After a brief, inquiring look in their direction, the ticket taker closed the front doors.

Max checked his watch. "Five after nine. Apple's late."

Tension quivered up Belle's spine in the ensuing quiet. A cool breeze sifted across her face. She laced her fingers into Max's and felt the strong, steady beat of his pulse.

The tension eased in Belle. Max was by her side. She had nothing to fear. A night bird called from the deep brush nearby. A mating call? Would his lady love hear him? Belle strained her ears, sure she could hear the beat of its wings as it took flight.

Suddenly a loud gun blast shattered the night. Belle felt the jerk of Max's body and knew instantly that he'd been hit. Her brain spun in horror as fear stabbed into her heart.

She whirled to grab him and the full weight of his collapsing body slammed them both to the ground.

Belle landed hard enough to knock the breath out of her, Max sprawled on top of her. Her arms circled his body as she called desperately to him. "Max! Max!"

But there was no answer.

Her heart hammered against her chest wall, as though pounding to get out. Immediately two more shots rang out, bullets tearing into the concrete next to where they lay.

Even now, shot, unconscious, his body was still protecting hers. She bit back the tears and the terror filling her heart. A new stream of bullets hit the pavement right next to her face, spitting fine dust into her eyes. Four. Five. Six.

She shut her eyes as her ears vibrated in pain, her heart raced in fear and her lungs clamored for air.

More shots rang out, the bullets pounding into the face of the building, less than a foot away, digging holes, knocking out chips of concrete, ricocheting in whizzing circles around them.

Seven. Eight. Nine. Ten. Eleven.

Then abruptly the shooting stopped just as suddenly as it had begun. Eleven bullets in all. Belle's mind instantly made the connection. This was the eleventh day of Christmas. Her anonymous Santa Claus had just delivered his latest present.

Only Max had been hit! Belle felt the warm sticky wetness against her chest and fought back the sobs collecting in her throat. She put her lips close to his ear. "Max? Can you hear me?"

But there still was no answer.

From somewhere in the distance more shots echoed into the night. Men shouted; what they shouted Belle could not tell and did not care. Her arms were around Max, and she was holding on tightly. "Oh, Max, darling. I love you so much! Please, please stay with me. Please don't die!"

And then she heard the new sounds. Footsteps pounding on the pavement. Coming closer.

"Ms. Breeze? Are you all right?"

Belle opened her eyes to see Sergeant Morse squinting down at her. She let out a sobbing breath. "Max has been hit. He needs an ambulance."

"One's been called," Morse assured her as he gently rolled Max off Belle and onto his back. A uniformed officer with a first aid kit immediately began to put pressure on an ugly chest wound.

Belle knelt beside Max, cradled his head in her lap, knowing she was soaked in his blood. She barely paid attention to Morse's continuing explanation, her eyes riveted on the officer's attempt to keep the bleeding from the wound controlled.

"I'm sorry, Ms. Breeze. He surprised us when he opened fire like that."

She swallowed, trying to keep a swirling, fright-filled nausea at bay. Belle stroked Max's hair away from his forehead. His color was chalk beneath his tan, his skin too cool. Her heart stumbled and fell.

Morse sounded apologetic. "We'll get him, Ms. Breeze. Now that we know it's Apple—"

Belle's eyes flew to Morse's face. "What?"

"Yes, Ms. Breeze. This meeting was just a ruse to get you in his sights. He stuck this on Wilde's car just before he ran away."

Belle took the familiar-looking sheet of paper from Morse's hand, in a wooden daze. She read the stanza, her fingers, mind and heart numb.

On the eleventh day of Christmas, Santa Claus gave to Breeze
Eleven bullets sniping.

> See you Christmas Eve,
> Santa Claus

Belle followed the paramedics into the ambulance, kneeling beside Max's supine body on the stretcher, her heart beating desperately inside her chest.

She took his hand, laced her fingers around it, willed her strength into him. "I'm here, Max. Right here."

The paramedic crowded Belle aside. "I'm sorry, miss, but you can't ride in here. Our liability coverage doesn't extend to passengers."

Morse reached inside the ambulance to take Belle's arm. "Don't delay them getting Mr. Wilde to the hospital."

Very reluctantly, Belle let Morse help her down from the ambulance. She watched as it sped off into the dark night, feeling an immense and aching hollowness expanding inside her chest.

She resisted Sergeant Morse's pull on her arm, tears streaming unchecked down her face, barely aware of the crowd of planetarium attendees gawking on the sidelines. "I have to get to him."

"I'll find someone to drive you to the hospital as soon as I can. Now, come on and step over here out of the way. Come on, Ms. Breeze. We've got a nightmare of a crowd control problem as it is."

"Why did Jim Apple do it?"

"I don't know yet, Ms. Breeze. Apple is the last guy I would have picked. But we'll find out. Now, stay here, right here, out of the way at the side of the building. Okay?"

Belle barely nodded. She turned to face the building, resting her head against its cool stone and tried not to think of Max and his desperate fight for life. And her here, useless.

Apple? Her sadistic Santa Claus?

God, this was like a Russell Ramish production of a Justin Daark script! Horror and terror. Friends turned into enemies. Vividly she remembered Jim Apple's quiet smile of pride when he talked to her about being brought up in a small town. And just days before his jaw had locked in determination when he told her he'd keep an eye out for her and rested his hand on the butt of his revolver. The gun he had used to shoot at her tonight?

His revolver. A six-shooter. But there had been eleven shots.

The inconsistencies swirled through Belle's brain, torturing her, tormenting her.

She opened her eyes, stared at her pink slippered feet. She remembered how gently Max had washed them, bandaged them with strong tender hands.

Tears stung her eyes.

She gulped them down, put her head in her hands. *Max! Please, God. Don't let Max die. Take me.*

She had just finished her prayer when the dark shape came up behind her and shoved a towel across her face. Even as she instinctively sucked in her breath, she knew she'd done the wrong thing. After one white blazing flash of false light, the fumes from the chloroform she'd inhaled rendered her instantly unconscious.

Chapter Fourteen

Belle awoke to the worst headache in her life. She opened her eyes against the pounding in her skull and remained motionless, waiting for things to focus.

It was still night. Far away beneath her a faint, diffused light raised to reflect off the falling snow.

Snow?

She was outside, lying on a cold wooden surface. But it didn't feel anywhere near cold enough for snow. The flakes stuck to her face. Didn't melt. She tried to move her hands to help herself up and found she was lying very uncomfortably on top of them. Disoriented and confused, it took another moment for her to realize that her wrists were tied with a coarse, scratchy rope. As were her ankles.

Memory flooded into her numbed brain in a rush. She had been slumped against the outside of the planetarium wall when someone had shoved a cloth soaked with chloroform over her face. The scent still permeated her skin— sweet and noxious.

Belle struggled with all her might to sit up. How she made it she wasn't sure, but she immediately regretted the erect position as dizziness and nausea spun cold and sick inside her. She fell back onto her shoulder. Landed hard.

She was so damn weak. So awfully damn weak. Slowly the dizziness subsided, the throbbing in her head eased. She opened her eyes again.

There before her stood her tormentor, holding a lantern, all decked out in a Santa Claus costume, the curly white beard obscuring the face. She blinked, sure it must be a figment of her dulled, sick brain. But then it grinned—a horrible, sinister grin that sent an icy chill through her bones. "I told you I'd see you Christmas Eve, Breeze. I always keep my word."

There was no mistaking that voice. Yet, still her mind couldn't accept what her senses were telling it. "Sergeant Morse?"

"Santa Claus to you, Breeze."

Belle gulped, the terror striking through her fuzzy thoughts like razor-sharp knives as his words sank cold and deadly into her heart. "It was you? All along it was you?"

He grinned, a large, ugly grin. "From the very start. I knew your case would be sent to my desk when you finally sought police help. And I was ready to manipulate you. As each day passed I watched you quake and quiver."

"Then Jim Apple had nothing to do with it."

"Not until he followed you from the station and saw me run you into the brick wall. I was in a patrol unit, so he couldn't be sure, but old resourceful Apple called to the station the next day to see who'd checked it out. Good thing I had bugged your phone and overheard his call to you."

"You bugged my phone? You were the one who shot at me?"

"Of course. I've got Apple chloroformed and tied up in the back of his truck. When I'm ready, I'll shoot him and he'll take the blame for everything. Posthumously. I had Jerry Stut ready for the fall, but this worked out even better."

"But you missed me tonight. You hit Max."

"I intended to. He was getting to be too much of a pest, interfering with my plans for you. Had to get him out of the way. The rest of the shots were just to make you nervous. But you're mistaken, Breeze. That wasn't tonight. All that happened last night. You've been unconscious nearly twenty-four hours."

Belle swallowed as a new wave of nausea grabbed at her stomach and buzzed through her head like a swarm of angry bees. "Max? Is he...is he all right?"

Morse gave her foot a kick, his boot connecting with the bottom of one of her sore soles. She cried out uncontrollably. He smiled. "He'll survive. I didn't shoot to kill. I'm not mad at Wilde."

Max was going to be all right! The knowledge gave Belle her first ray of hope. She tried to clear her mind of the terror and the pain. "Why are you mad at me?"

A sneer drew Morse's lip. "My daughter was Trina Cork."

Belle felt her breathing stall. "Trina Cork? The young woman who starred in *Major Change*."

"Yes. Your review killed my gentle child and made her mother the dead-eyed woman who now looks at me over the breakfast table."

Belle fought for understanding. "You were the family member who didn't want Trina to take the part?"

"No, that was her mother. But Trina wanted it so bad I couldn't refuse. So I kept it from her mother. Told Trina to use Cork as her stage name. I got Luana Halsey to go see her so she'd be properly represented. I never could deny my child anything that would make her happy. And she was happy. Until your damn review."

Morse kicked at Belle's sore feet again.

Belle bit back the pain, trying to cling to some reason in this living nightmare. "But my review was a full twelve days before her death."

"And she had suffered through every one of those last days and nights! Why do you think I picked the 'Twelve Days of Christmas' song? Why do you think your presents started on December 13—exactly a year to the date you broke her spirit!"

Morse's voice cracked and split like a freshly opened wound on his last words. Belle knew he was crazed with grief. He needed to blame someone for his daughter's death. He had latched on to her.

With a vengeance.

"My Trina disappeared. For twelve days she drank whatever she could find. Took any drug offered her. One bad trip even landed her in a padded cell. For two days she screamed until the poison worked its way out of her system. That's where I found my little girl. Locked up. Screaming. Because of you. That's why I locked you in that storeroom. I wanted you to feel her terror."

Belle listened, fascinated, horrified.

"I was determined to make you suffer like you made my daughter suffer. I took months planning it. Getting Stut selected for that security guard's job. I even flew to Minnesota and pretended to be a newspaper reporter to find out things about you. That's when I learned how allergic you were to hornets. So I had those hornets flown in especially from South America. Every step of the way, I wanted to be on hand to see your fear—to hear it, to smell it. And I was. I am."

His eyes gleamed brightly. Triumphantly.

Belle could feel his hatred, like a palpable force being shoved at her, a force she was powerless to deflect.

His voice continued on, in a quiet, eerie tone now. "It was here on this very roof in this back lot at Paramount studios where it happened, you know. They used this set for the outside shots of New York in the movie. This was where her big scene took place in *Major Change*. Do you see the snow, Breeze? I created it for you just like the special effects people created it for her."

Morse drew a long white envelope out of the pocket of his Santa Claus suit. "The final stanza, Breeze. Since you're tied up, I'll read it for you.

"On the twelfth day of Christmas, Santa Claus gave to Breeze
Twelve stories a-plummeting.

Christmas Eve you die,
Santa Claus."

He folded the paper. Returned it to the envelope. Threw it over the edge. "Now you, Breeze."

Belle choked out her protest. "But I didn't kill your daughter. A crazed fan stalked her. A crazed fan threw her off the building."

Morse's laugh was more like an ugly oath. "No crazed fan ever existed. I wrote those letters afterward. Planted them in her room. To protect her memory. Her mother would never have been able to bury her in consecrated ground otherwise."

The awful truth finally dawned on Belle. "You mean .. Trina committed suicide?"

His eyes burned down at her. "No! You pushed her. Just like I'm going to push you."

Desperately Belle looked around through the falling lace of the funny, fake snow. She was alone against him. Alone with a madman. And she was bound. Her fear raged with fever as her body turned to ice.

He stared at her with a frenzied hatred in his eyes, grabbed at her feet. But the fake snow was making everything sticky and slippery at the same time. Her feet fell through his grasp. He wrapped his hands around the rope that tied her ankles together and dragged her toward the edge.

Belle cried out in terror and pain as her hands scraped beneath her on the rough wooden slats. In mere seconds he'd have her at that edge. In mere seconds he'd be shoving her off it.

She closed her eyes and reached for every ounce of her remaining strength as she had never reached for anything so hard in her life. Then opened her eyes again and struck out at him with the only weapon at her disposal.

"Killing me won't bring Trina back. And it won't absolve you of your guilt, either. You know your wife was right. Trina was a sweet child. She never should have played that terrible role."

Her words stopped him dead still. For a moment, Belle thought it might work. A look as clear as any guilt she'd

ver seen flashed into Morse's eyes. But the guilt faded and
vith it her last hope. His eyes flashed hard with the bright
litter of fury. "Damn you, no! You'll not blame another
or your crime. It was you who killed her! As I'm going to
ill you!"

Morse grabbed at her feet again, yanking them toward
im, toward the slippery edge in a final burst of his anger-
ed strength. But his hands missed the rope this time and slid
n the fake snow coating her slippers.

His arms swung back from the force of the unrestrained
iomentum, flailing in the air, as he desperately struggled
or his lost balance.

And then just stopped struggling when he realized it was
utile. For one horrifyingly magnified moment, Belle
vatched him floating at the edge—wearing a look of in-
omprehensible disbelief.

He made no sound as he fell to his death. No sound at all.
It was Belle's scream that shattered the night.

MAX SAT UP in his hospital bed and smiled as Belle set a
mall decorated Christmas tree on his nightstand. Then she
tepped forward, took his extended hand and kissed him on
he cheek.

"Merry Christmas, Max."

He smiled, bringing her to his uninjured side, feeling her
varmth as she laid gently against him. Thanks to the mira-
le of painkillers, he felt amazingly good considering the
xtent of the surgery to remove the bullet lodged near his
eart. Just a matter of time now before he was as good as
iew.

He knew what had happened of course. He'd heard all
bout how the technicians at the Paramount studios had
ound her on that rooftop Christmas Eve when they came
investigate who had broken into the lot and turned on the
ake snow. And how they'd found the remains of Sergeant
Aorse on the street below and a chloroformed but other-
vise unhurt Jim Apple in his truck nearby.

Max was almost glad he'd been unconscious yesterday. If he had been awake, chained to this bed because of his injury, wondering where she was, finding out she'd disappeared without a trace—

He shoved the disturbing thoughts aside. She was safe. She was here. She was with him. He was never more grateful for anything in his life.

"How do you feel, Max?"

He rested his head against her golden hair. "At the moment, wonderful. You didn't worry?"

She nestled into his shoulder. "About *my* Rambo? Of course not. I knew a little bullet couldn't get you down."

The false bravado in her voice struck all the right chords in his heart. She was tough about the right things. And not so tough about the right things, too. He kissed the silk of her hair.

"How are *you?*"

She sighed, didn't pretend to misunderstand. "Still numb, I think. You said that many people in Hollywood craved that unconditional love that only a parent could give. I think I've just seen how dangerous that kind of unconditional love can be."

Belle's head rose from his shoulder. She shivered. From the troubled glaze that had just come over her eyes, Max knew she was seeing Morse fall again.

He covered her hand with his. "In time the memory will fade."

She nodded. "I know."

"You think he fell purposely?"

She took a deep breath. Let it out slowly. "No. But I think when he realized he was going to fall—he couldn't stop himself from falling—I think suddenly it didn't matter to him. Maybe he thought it was a way to atone for his guilt about his daughter. Maybe that's why he didn't...scream."

She shivered again, and Max clasped her hand more tightly. He knew then that it would be a long time before Belle would stop hearing that deadly silence. He brought her back to his side.

He held her there for several minutes until he could feel her heart slowing and matching beats to his own. He felt so good now that the terror was finally over. That she was safe by his side.

But as good as it was and as much as he wanted to keep her with him, he knew the right thing was to send her away. He steeled himself and took a deep breath.

"I have something for you, Belle. It's under the pillow. Take it out."

She leaned forward, looked at him in surprise, and reached beneath the pillow. The envelope she extracted was green. It had a red bow tied around it. She undid the bow and removed the airline ticket from inside it.

"The police lieutenant who questioned me this morning told me you missed the flight back to Minnesota. I called a friend at one of the airlines. He arranged to get you a seat on a flight out late this afternoon. He sent the ticket to me by special messenger. I've cleared it with the police. You can leave. You'll be late, but you'll still be able to spend Christmas with your family. Merry Christmas, Belle."

Belle stared at the ticket in her hand. "Max, I called my folks. Told them I wouldn't be coming."

He traced a heart across her open palm with his index finger. "Now you can call them back and tell them you'll be there."

She looked up at him then and he saw the tears, swimming in the deep blue of her eyes. "Max, do you want me to go?"

He pulled in a jerky breath. "Belle, of course I want you to go. Didn't you tell me Christmas wouldn't be Christmas unless you spent it with the people you love?"

"But, Max, you're the one I love most in the world. That's why I'm here. That's why I want to spend Christmas with you."

Warmth expanded into Max's chest, trickled out into his shoulders and arms, rushed down through his legs. It made him feel strong, weak, invincible, vulnerable, full and empty all at the same time. And very happy. He exhaled a lifetime

of loneliness in his next words and he knew it. "Belle, I lov
you very much."

Her tears sparkled with the warmth of the sunshine tha
reflected through them. "Oh, Max!"

She leaned over and kissed him exuberantly, passion
ately. Definitely too passionately considering his curren
condition. Or was it? Deep within, further than even th
pain pills could reach, he felt his body responding. Damn
this woman could raise him even if he were dead. H
chuckled at the image and drew her closer to his uninjure
side.

She smiled and snuggled back against him and sighed
deep and audible and happy.

He had just one concern still bothering him. He raised hi
finger to feather the softness of her hair. "Belle, would yo
tell me something?"

"Anything."

"Who are those four guys you lived with whom I'm sup
posed to be like?"

She leaned away from him, looked at him with taunting
tantalizing, mischievous eyes. "Are you jealous, Max?"

He scowled with only partial annoyance. "Vehemently
As soon as I know who they are I'm going to kill them wit
my bare hands."

She laughed and gently leaned back against him. "You'
have your hands full, then. They all made defensive line
men on the college football team. They're my older brotl
ers—two, four, six and eight years older, to be precise. The
also were consummate ladies' men, until they, too, met thei
match."

Max chuckled, surprised and—he admitted to himself—
relieved. "Too?" he echoed.

She cuddled closer as she ran a proprietary finger dow
his cheekbone. "Your wild-man days are history, Wilde.
intend to keep you thoroughly tamed."

"And your Arctic Breeze days are also gone, my love.
intend to keep you thoroughly defrosted."

He kissed her warmly and she kissed him back, seals to both their pledges. Then, as casually as he dared, his heart beating just a bit too fast, he said, "You want to get married here or back in Minnesota?"

She surprised and delighted him completely when she didn't even blink. "Oh, back there, of course. A lot less hassle for my family to attend. But you don't have to worry. It won't be too big a wedding. Close family only. Two-, three-hundred guests at the most."

Max would never have believed a woman could make him so happy by just being who and what she was. One day maybe he could find the words to tell her. Right now, all he could say was "Not a big wedding? Close family only? Two-, three-hundred guests. What am I letting myself in for? Are you related to the whole damn population of Minnesota?"

"Nearly," she said with far too much nonchalance. "Scared?"

"Quaking in my bed slippers. I suppose you've already picked out the date for my introduction into the tribe?"

"Only vaguely. Spring. Early April. The eighth maybe. We have a two-week break in our spots then. I checked with Paula and Neal this morning. Not that I told them why I wanted to know, of course. I mean, I thought I should discuss it with you first."

He smirked. Thoroughly entranced, entertained, enchanted with all her assumptions. With all of her. "Considerate of you."

"Yes, well, we might not even want to let them know at all. It could ruin the image of our controversy if people knew we were married."

"Oh? Why?"

"Well, because all married people fight. Our viewers might not be inclined to take us seriously anymore. Although I'd probably risk even that to see the look on Paula's face when she finds out the critics she so gleefully set at each others' throats really like each other."

Max couldn't keep his amusement in anymore. He laughed so hard that he thought he might burst his bandages. She laughed right along with him.

He drew her back to him, kissed her cheek, drank in her scent, drowned in it until he felt dizzy. "I can't wait for this April honeymoon. Let's make it sooner."

"You're going to have to wait. I want you fully recovered."

He cupped her ear with his mouth and blew enticingly into it. "Belle, my love, you have no idea how ready I'm already getting for this honeymoon."

"Max, my love, you have no idea how strenuous a honeymoon I have planned."

He smiled at the gleam in her eyes and she smiled back. Definitely his match. His mate.

"Now, Max, I figure I can do the two scheduled spots alone the week after New Year's while you're recuperating. Then the following week we can get back into the point-counterpoint. *Desert Stormin'* is the first scheduled movie we'll review together. It's a war story based on the action in the Persian Gulf. Like we needed another war movie."

Max straightened. "*Desert Stormin'?* I've heard about that one. Can't wait to see it. Lots of action and good raw realism."

She leaned away and fixed her eyes on him. "Good raw realism? Come on, Wilde. It's about time Hollywood stopped fixating on war. Maybe if kids stopped seeing so many military movies, they'd grow up thinking more like peacemakers instead of warmongers."

There it was, that wonderful combative gleam in her eye. All ice and fire and passion and challenge. And all his.

Just looking at her made his blood race and his heart pound with all the juices that made it feel so good to be alive. This woman would always be the spark and spice of his life.

"Belle, my love, promise me we'll always fight."

She laughed, a deep, happy sound that rumbled through his heart as she rested against it. "Max, my love, you can count on it. It's written into our contracts."

HARLEQUIN®
INTRIGUE®

'Tis the season...

for a special Christmas "43 Light Street" book from Rebecca York!

All wrapped up, especially for you, is Rebecca York's gift this Christmas—a heartwarming tale of suspense and holiday emotion.

What Child is This?

Two people, drawn together by circumstance and bound together by love, put their hearts and lives on the line to uncover the secret of the *real* meaning of Christmas....

In December, don't miss # 253 WHAT CHILD IS THIS?—coming to you just in time for Christmas, only from Harlequin Intrigue.

My Valentine 1994

Celebrate the most romantic day of the year with
MY VALENTINE 1994
a collection of original stories, written by
four of Harlequin's most popular authors...

MARGOT DALTON
MURIEL JENSEN
MARISA CARROLL
KAREN YOUNG

Available in February, wherever
Harlequin Books are sold.

HARLEQUIN ®

VAL94

Are you looking for more titles by

M.J. RODGERS

Don't miss these additional stories by one of
Harlequin's favorite authors:

Harlequin Intrigue®

#22140	BLOODSTONE	$2.50	❏
#22157	DEAD RINGER	$2.75	❏
#22176	BONES OF CONTENTION	$2.79	❏
#22185	RISKY BUSINESS	$2.89	❏
#22214	TO DIE FOR	$2.89	❏

Harlequin American Romance®

#16492	FIRE MAGIC	$3.50	❏
	(limited quantities available on certain titles)		

TOTAL AMOUNT	$	
POSTAGE & HANDLING	$	
($1.00 for one book, 50¢ for each additional)		
APPLICABLE TAXES*	$ _____	
<u>**TOTAL PAYABLE**</u>	$ _____	
(check or money order—please do not send cash)		

To order, complete this form and send it, along with a check or money order for the
total above, payable to Harlequin Books, to: *In the U.S.*: 3010 Walden Avenue,
P.O. Box 9047, Buffalo, NY 14269-9047; *In Canada*: P.O. Box 613, Fort Erie, Ontario,
L2A 5X3.

Name: _____

Address: _____ City: _____

State/Prov.: _____ Zip/Postal Code: _____

*New York residents remit applicable sales taxes.
 Canadian residents remit applicable GST and provincial taxes.

HMJRBACK1

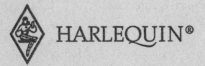

HARLEQUIN®